Blood & Skin

Steve Malley

Special Thanks to: Jesika Rabid, my cover model and to FK Irons, whose tattoo machines both feature on the cover and perform so wonderfully in my own tattooing. And to all of you who read and enjoy my work, especially when you say so in online reviews!

http://SteveMalley.com

ISBN: 978-0-9876599-5-8

To Holly,
who had no idea
what she inspired

One

The woman's breath came in a sharp hiss as the icy metal bit down on her nipple. The ghost of Lisa Torres seemed to approve.

"Deep breath in, and... out." Like a tiny razor, the surgical needle slid effortlessly through flesh to embed itself in the cork on the far side of the forceps.

"Okay, hard part's all done. Now all you have to do is sit back while I do all the work." I hardly paid any attention at all to my words. They were just a steady stream of patter to help the client feel more at ease. I was focused on the most dangerous part of the piercing, where an accidental stick was a real risk. I pulled the cork off the needle, slid the forceps over the naked and potentially infectious point and refastened the cork.

The woman with the needle through her nipple was practically a suburban mother, the type who drives the kids to soccer practice in a minivan or SUV. For her, this was a big adventure, a sexy present for a husband or lover. For me, it was a job.

I fit the end of the steel ring up against back of the shaft of the needle, gently pushed until ring came all the way through and the corked needle fell into my left palm. The used needle went directly into the heavy plastic SHARPS container with its bright biohazard stickers. The steel ball closure clicked into place and the piercing was finished. The ghost beside me had a hungry fascination with the bead of blood on the soccer mom's breast.

She appeared now as she had on the day she died. Limp white hair showing greasy brown roots. Dark bruised eye sockets hooding eyes as haunted as my own.

Between her polyester tube top and denim low-riders lay three dark spots like drops of wax from a great crimson candle.

Entry wounds.

She had shown me many times how the hollowpoints had torn great ragged chunks of meat and viscera away from her spine.

Lisa Torres was born in East Texas, a skinny little white girl all corners and angles, bone-bleached hair gone brown at the roots and that hard pinched look poor people learn early down there. I met her in New Orleans right before she died. Since then, she followed me all the way north across the frozen prairie to Minneapolis, Minnesota.

I suspect she may follow me everywhere. Forever.

I wiped off the blood and ignored the sharp look from the ghost at my elbow, cleaned up the piercing station and chucked my gloves in the waste bin.

The soccer mom was all over her new toy, preening in the mirror. I felt happy for her-- this was all fresh and new. I started tattooing at seventeen, piercing a couple years later. Somehow twenty-eight seemed too young to feel so jaded. Today I felt tired and old, ready to lie down in the snow this winter.

Once the soccer mom got herself tucked away again, I opened the curtain, walked with her over to the reception desk, accepted her credit card and dug out a green sheet with her aftercare instructions on it. The green sheets were for regular body piercing care, the white for tattoos. Client releases were filled out on a blue form, and special issues relating to genital piercing were addressed on that yellow the copy places like to call 'goldenrod'.

Usually, there would be a receptionist to go over the white and green sheets, see that the blue ones were filled out and wait for the credit card machine to ratchet its approval. My latest receptionist lasted less than a month, the third one this year. It was to the point where young men and women came in, all excited and full of talk about how keen they were to tattoo, pierce or both, and I didn't believe a word.

It was no big deal, though. I ran Astounding Tattoo single-handed before bringing Hamish in, and it was only the last couple of years we'd been able to afford a staff member. Another few weeks on our own wouldn't kill us.

Hamish was my best friend, the brother I never had. He was one of the first people I met off the bus in Minneapolis, a Southern transplant just like me even if he was more charming and better-looking. He was also part owner of Astounding. Four years ago, when the strain of sixty-hour weeks was getting to me, he agreed to help out at the shop. By his own admission, he's no artist - I still do all the tattooing around here - but he did learn how to pierce. At first he was on a straight commission, helping me until I could find a 'real' piercer. Inside of a year, it was obvious he really enjoyed it, and we went partners.

Astounding was the second tattoo studio I had owned, the first success. I built it from nothing to a comfortable living, less than a banker might make but more money than I ever thought I'd see in my life.

Then again, if anyone had asked me ten years ago to imagine my life now, I would have admitted that my main chances were prison or the grave.

I was fortunate, and I knew it. Not everyone has both financial security *and* a job they love. I also had a career that probably saved my life.

The soccer mom was gone, and I stood there at the edge of my desk after she left, watching the afternoon through my window. The sun was down near the horizon now, and the sky around it was a riot of gold and orange. A muffled drumbeat to a song I didn't recognize drifted up from the bar downstairs, and the clock on the wall above me moved that little bit closer to time for me to go home. From around the corner, the flash rack clicked as someone flipped through its panels.

A customer must have come in while I was busy piercing. I hadn't noticed, so I stuck my head around the corner.

"Sorry, I--"

There was a jolt, a physical impact like a sharp blow behind the eyes.

Her eyes were gray. Not blue, not green, not hazel. Dark as thunderclouds at the edges, clear as Christmas morning in the middle. A ring of gold ran around the edge of the pupil. They put me in mind of the timberwolves at the Wildlife Center up north. They caught and held the light.

The effect was devastating.

She knelt on the carpet to get a good look at the bottom rack of designs, graceful as anything I had ever seen in the Louvre. I was vaguely aware of a fall of dark shining hair, but it was impossible to say while her eyes pinned me where I stood.

"Um, hi. Hope I didn't keep you waiting too long," I finally managed. I felt about fourteen years old.

"No worries." She had a smile every bit as sweet and sunny as the rest of her. "I could see you had your hands full."

She was a small girl, hardly bigger standing up than when she knelt on the floor, and she stood in that incredibly straight way that small girls have. Gleaming dark hair did in fact fall across bare shoulders, and her mouth was soft and full and kissably perfect.

"I was just after a piercing." There was something about her voice, a music I was too tone-deaf to place. I got her a blue sheet and a clipboard. I didn't want to stare, but I did try to steal a glance when I didn't think she was looking.

"Seems to be the night for it. I haven't done a single tattoo. What would you like?"

"Not sure." Her vowels were singing and musical, the consonants light and clipped. The effect was vaguely British, but that wasn't it either.

"I was thinking either my eyebrow, or this one." Her finger touched her lower lip right in the center.

"Go for the labret. It's a great look, and you've really got the lips for it." She blushed prettily, a lovely seashell pink from her neck to her hairline. I couldn't believe I said that.

"Tell you what, you can finish up your form while I set up the station. Just go on in and make yourself comfortable."

She shot me another smile, this one more shy and nervous, still delightful. She had a dimple on the right hand corner of her mouth.

The look Lisa Torres shot me was pure venom.

***

I scrubbed my hands with Purell from a pump bottle while she sat on the piercing table and filled out the form. Her name was Rebecca Temple, age twenty-two. I saw the address and did a double take.

"Christchurch, New Zealand?"

"Yes, New Zealand. You know, *Lord of the Rings, Once Were Warriors, Flight of the Conchords*..."

"Y'all had that earthquake down there."

"Don't remind me." Another smile, again different from any that had gone before it. The young lady had a truly impressive range. The dimple at the side of her mouth winked at me just often enough to keep me thoroughly charmed.

Her eyes dropped again to my forearms: easy to understand why. From my wrists to my shoulders, battling samurai from 19th century woodcuts fought with demons from Tibetan sacred art. The tattoos were a well-planned and perfectly executed riot of color and movement.

"Did you do those yourself?" It was most people's first question.

"No," I said, "it takes two hands to tattoo. One's gotta hold the machine while the other stretches the skin. These," I rolled my forearms over to show the insides off, "were done by a friend of mine. John, over at Inky's."

One fingertip traced the folds of a kimono, patterned in autumn leaves. Her touch raised goosebumps on my skin. Our eyes met, and we both looked away.

"They're beautiful."

"Thanks."

"You're welcome," she said. There was a richness to her vowels that I could listen to all day.

"You've got a great accent."

"Thank you. I like yours too." She said it with such prim and quiet dignity that I burst out laughing. It was so much like my little sister Tabitha, back when she was still young enough to be adorable, before she turned spooky.

Who was I kidding? Tabitha was always spooky.

10

The young New Zealander laughed along with me, and fortunately that broke the tension well enough to remind me why we were there.

"All right, Rebecca, you want a ring or a flatback?"

"It's Bex. No one calls me 'Rebecca' except my mum, and then only when she's mad at me."

"Bex then. So do you want this one or this one?"

She went with the flatback, a stainless steel post with a flat disk on one end and a gleaming steel ball on the other. I had one just like it in my own lip, my only facial jewelry.

I swabbed her skin with an alcohol pad, marked the spot where I thought it should go and got her to check it in the mirror.

After that came the usual business with clamp, needle and cork, the delicate transfer of jewelry following behind the needle. I had never been so careful in my life, or so sure it would all go as perfectly as it did.

Maybe thirty seconds or so after I started, I gave the steel ball one final turn to tighten it and said, "There you go, one labret. Perfect."

"That wasn't too bad at all," she said. Again I got a smile full of sunshine. I wondered if it was something in New Zealand's water supply; I had never met a woman so charming.

As I stripped my gloves, I realized we were finished and she would leave at any moment now.

"So," I said, "Minnesota's kind of out the way for most people. You doing classes at the U or something?"

"No, my best friend married one of you lot. This is the first time I've seen her in three years."

"How you like it here so far?"

"This is only my second day. It's hard to get used to policemen carrying guns everywhere, and it feels strange being so warm this time of year. Back home, it's winter right now."

"How long are you here?"

"I'm just finishing my Big OE. I've got a month with Kate, then back home."

"Your big what?"

"My OE - Overseas Experience? It's a bit of a tradition in Australia and NZ." She said it 'En Zed'. "You take a few months or a year off and travel around as much as you can while you're still young enough to enjoy it."

It turned out Bex was a reader, harder and harder to find these days. Our taste in books overlapped, though she ran more to the classics and shook her head sadly at the soft spot I had in my heart for anything with a title like *Nazi Robots From Planet X*. She had a way of crinkling her eyes at me when I spoke, and her laugh was like flowing water on a mountainside.

When she mentioned she was crawling the walls for something to read this late in her trip, I saw my chance.

"One great thing about Minnesota, we've got some fantastic used bookstores here. I'll take you around to a few, let you stock up."

"I don't know, the people I'm staying with have quite a lot planned for me."

"I won't twist your arm or anything, but you *would* have fun."

She sat on the edge of decision, maybe weighing up how much like a serial killer I looked, maybe wondering how to get out of this situation without embarrassing both of us any more than she had to.

The wind chimes hanging in front of the door to the waiting room chimed and tinkled and took me off the hook for the moment.

I left the piercing bay to greet the two young men who just walked in. They were dressed in the baggy logo-covered gangsta fashions, probably a couple of U students planning how to spend their Christmas money.

Except that up close these two were older than they looked. Dirtier, too.

The tall one up front had oily skin broken out in patches of rash, black dirt in the seams of his neck and hands, and the worst teeth I had ever seen on a human being in my life. His bare arms were covered in mottled gray tattoos, the sort of homemade crap you see come out of prisons, or that junkies use to try to hide their track marks. Catching the swastikas worked into the indistinct gray mass and the White Power lightning bolts on his emaciated chest, I was certain his work had largely been paid for with cigarettes.

His shaved head showed the bones in his skull with disturbing clarity, like there was a flashlight inside it.

His partner was a small, hunched little toad of a man: pasty greenish complexion, bad acne scratched to scarring, and a chinless bug-eyed face clearly wanting to be anywhere else right then.

Both of them had a hinky, jerky, twitching dance to their posture. A scratching craving that all but shouted *JUNKIE*.

I came around the desk, said, "Sorry guys, we closed a little early tonight."

They stood hesitating, scratching and shuffling, looking from each other to me to the room around them and back again. The big one was taller than I thought, at least six and a half feet, all of it bone and tendon.

I took another step, to within an arm's reach of both of them, silently wished I had never stopped carrying my gun.

"You want an appointment for tomorrow?"

The lead one's eyes kept skittering around the room. Up close, the whites were yellow, and a greenish light swam beneath their surface. He scratched at the rash on the side of his neck, up under his chin.

13

There was a moment. The tension in the room twisted tighter. My eyes focused on nothing, waited for that wrong flicker of sudden movement.

Then the skeletal one's eyes faded in their sockets and he nodded to himself.

"Nah, that's okay. We'll come back."

"I'm open twelve to eight. Now if you'll excuse me." I kept moving toward them while I spoke, gently but firmly herding them back out the door. Once I heard them thumping down the steps to the street, I locked the knob and turned back to Bex, found her standing in the center of the studio floor.

"What was that about?"

"Probably nothing. Those two just rubbed me the wrong way. Did you drive here?"

"No, but it's not far to my friend's apartment."

"I'll see you home. I'll drive you, walk with you, call a cab, whatever. I just don't like the idea of you going home alone right now."

"If you want to walk me home, that would be fine." Her smile was rich and sweet and densely layered with meaning. I gave up trying to read it.

"Be happy to. Just let me close up, okay?"

I killed the shop lights and hustled through my closing, trying not to be too obvious about sneaking glances at Bex waiting with one hip propped on the corner of the reception desk. Much of what I would normally do at closing could wait until morning, but there were counters to wipe down, trash to change out and forceps to take care of.

I'm no neat freak in the rest of my life, a bit of a slob if anything, but my job was another matter. I don't like leaving at night without at least getting my equipment in the ultrasonic cleaner, even if I leave the rest of the sterilization for the next morning.

"Bex, I just have to give these clamps a good scrub and throw them in the bath before we go. I won't be a minute."

"No worries, I'll wait." I really *was* concerned about those two catching up with her outside, but the way she dimpled at me didn't hurt, either.

My back room was an L-shaped space on the far side of the reception desk, more a bent corridor than a proper room. The long end was lined with high shelves full of cleaning products and tongue depressors, crates of rubber gloves and paper towels. At the shorter end of the L were sinks, ultrasonic cleaners and autoclave sterilizers.

All gloved up again, I took the used clamps out of the stainless steel receptacles in each piercing bay, carried them back to the cleaning sink and dumped them in with a jangling clatter. I elbowed the water on and let it run over them, giving them a preliminary rinse before they went into the ultrasonic where any clinging particles of blood or other biomass would be shaken loose from them. I saw and felt gooseflesh creep up my arms and pebble the colors tattooed there, wasn't surprised to find a polyester tube top a hair's breadth from my elbow. Lisa had decided I was having too much fun.

I forced my attention on the steel clamps in the sink and the patterns the water made tumbling over them and down the drain.

Cruel fingers, nail-bitten with cracked black polish, dug into the flesh of her hips and her mouth twisted into a nasty sneer. Her voice in my head was the rasp of fingernails down a granite headstone.

You think you're so big, but you're not. You're nothing. Just wait, you'll see.

"Lisa..."

Asshole.

Her mouth opened, but all that came out was the blood-bubble she had on her lips when she died.

"You recreate every detail so perfect, why is it you always forget the gun in your hand, or what you were doing with it?"

Six years of this.

You like her, don't you? I can tell.

In the years of her death, Lisa showed a single-minded determination to keep me from being happy. With only one exception, she prevented me from getting close to a woman, and that one time I suspected it was because she knew how poisonous the woman was for me.

I tried to ignore her. She was determined not to be ignored. Finally, I realized that if I stood there staring down the bottom of the sink long enough, the dead girl would get her way and Bex would eventually leave. I could feel her hot breath, summer in a butcher shop, on the back of my neck.

I turned to face her.

She stood before me, not as she had in life, but horrific in her death. Her skin was waxy and blue, her lips a cracked and bruised purple. The fabric of her top clung obscenely to her nipples, and there was a smell in the air like a closed and sweltering room where a bowl of fruit had been left to rot.

The three bullet wounds were back again. Now the blood fell thick and dark from them, tracing clotted streams down the front of her body. Her hair hung matted and limp in her face. With her head held down like that all I could see were the deep bruises under her eyes, making them look like empty sockets.

The fingertips of her right hand traced a slow caress down her bare shoulder, over her left breast, down to the uppermost of her wounds. With an obscene squelch, the dead girl thrust her middle finger deep into the wound.

Languid and slow, she drew the bloody finger to her lips, took it in her mouth. Sucked it and moaned.

She looked up at me from under her hair and a slow grin spread across her face. Blood poured from her mouth, ran down her neck to her shoulders.

A single drop fell from her chin, landed at my feet in a thick red splat.

I felt cold shoot through me.

I *knew.*

***

I spun hard on one heel, slipped trying to find traction on the smooth lino, launched myself off a stack of crates, sensed more than saw or heard the boxes falling behind me as I sprinted around the corner and into the front room.

What I saw there pulled me up short.

A leathery skeleton covered in homemade tattoos. Bald head, hard-boned skull and bad teeth. And at the end of one long jerking agitated arm, a fat black pistol pressed flush against Bex's forehead.

Two

It was one of those moments when time stops. Adrenalin jacked into my bloodstream, froze everything to a crystal-clear tableau. All of us stood at a threshold, all the time in the world.

The feeling was an old friend to me.

The tall one with the bad teeth stood still as a statue maybe eight feet away. Too far for an easy lunge, close enough if I got desperate. He held the oily black pistol sideways in his fist, just like he'd seen in the movies and on TV. The tendons in his hand and wrist stood out like high-tension cables.

The orange dot above the grip was a predator's eye gleaming in the darkness. The safety was off.

Bex's face was a study in anger and outrage. Safe to say no one had ever pointed a gun at her in her life. No way to guess how she'd move.

I could even see the wicked black automatic reflected in her eyes.

The chinless toad with the acne scars stood hovering near the entrance to the studio. I was aware of the door I had locked earlier standing open, of the deserted hall beyond it. The chinless one had a yellow cup with red letters in his hand. A soft drink from Wendy's.

In one single moment of clarity, perfect and cold, I took all these details in, formed a relationship with the bodies and furniture in the room as intimate as my teeth and tongue. In that one single moment, we were all frozen in place.

Then with an inaudible sound like the crack of rotten ice on a frozen pond, time broke free and crept forward again.

The toad saw me first. His eyes went big and round and showed the whites on all four sides of them. He opened his hand and dropped his drink.

The tall, gaunt one's neck was shot through with puffy veins and oozing rash. A jailhouse swastika was tattooed on the front of his throat, beads of sweat coming up through the ink. Tendon after tendon stood out against the skin, muscle bunched along the side of his throat, and his skin-covered skull turned in my direction.

Then he did the most natural thing in the world under the circumstances.

He turned the gun on me.

It was like all those childhood nightmares all over again, the ones that stayed with me right up until I left home. Everything was slow. Painfully slow. Danger coming and every movement I made a struggle. In my dreams, I would strike as hard as I could, and the blows would land softly, without force. A fighting equivalent of running in place.

But this was the real world, not the trap of my dreams. We were all of us caught in the same glue-stuck world, and to an outside observer I had an impressive real-world momentum.

I watched with a calm and distant interest as the barrel of the pistol, the only truly dangerous part, gradually sailed away from Bex's perfect forehead and travelled a long, slow, useless arc to the place where I had just been, then continue in its circle, trying to find me.

By then I was alongside the arm, one hand on the greasy wrist and my elbow sinking deep into the tall man's armpit.

The yellow Wendy's cup hovered inches from the little toad's fingertips.

In my childhood nightmares, my struggles came to nothing, but I was an adult now in a more mundane nightmare, where the laws of physics still applied. There was a terrible crunching and popping from the body in front of me. It meant nothing to me in that moment.

My right hand came away with the gun by the barrel. The tall one left his feet in a boneless way. My attention turned from him to his partner. I spun, shifted, and the side of my fist hammered his mouth. The butt of the gun would have made a good club, but the empty left hand was closer.

Watching my fist crash through tooth and flesh and bone, there was a strange, surreal moment as I noticed I still had my dirty gloves on. I had a flash of worry about infecting him with bloodborne pathogens.

Time began to crawl faster, then found its legs and moved normally again.

The tall man crashed into the wall behind him at the same time as the Wendy's cup hit the floor. He crumpled in three stages, the way a nervous piercing customer once did when I opened the packaging on the needle. His knees went straight into the ground with a round hollow THOK, his butt bounced off his heels, then chest and forehead smacked at once. It sounded like someone dropping a steak onto a countertop.

There was a muffled boom as his fleeing partner ran into the side of the doorway in his headlong flight down the front stairs.

I stood straight again, turned and looked to Bex. Time flowed normally again-- the drink cup rolled from side to side and the orange soda splashed on my jeans began to seep in and wet my legs. But the lovely woman with the gleaming dark hair stood motionless, her left fist cradled in her other hand, frozen in shock.

When I was nineteen, I took a girl from my painting class to an evening exhibit at the Art Institute. I had an enormous crush on her, and we were having a great time together. Waiting for the bus back home, we were mugged by a drunk with a knife. It never even occurred to me to give up my wallet, or her purse. I kicked him in the crotch hard enough to curl him up on the sidewalk, shivering and spitting blood. It was late, and not the sort of neighbourhood much patrolled by police or watched by dutiful citizens, so we escaped any more trouble by fast-hustling down the street, my hand guiding her elbow maybe a little harder than I knew. At one point, she began walking under her own volition, and I let go. A few steps later, she bent over double and vomited in the street. When she finally retched herself empty, the girl looked up at me with the most horrified expression I had ever seen.

She was silent and self-contained while we made our way back to our own neighbourhood. And she never spoke to me again.

I was once an eager student who learned from some very rough and competent professionals, and I handled that situation, and my situation now, just as I was taught. If anything, I was gentler.

Unlike my Avi and Uri, I wasn't able to strike and vanish like I never existed. I was tied to my business, to the life I had built here. It was precious to me. I'd worked too damn hard building this up to lose it in some bullshit lawsuit or have to sell it off paying some lawyer to keep me out of jail.

First, I secured the area by going downstairs and turning the big deadbolts on the outer, street level door. Now that nothing would be sneaking up on us, Bex was my next concern.

I realized I still wore my dirty latex gloves and stripped them off. I got Bex sitting-- she seemed pretty calm. She hadn't been visibly harmed, and she assured me neither of them had even touched her.

My last concern was the man I downed. Until that point, I honestly hadn't heard him moaning. He lay on the linoleum tile writhing in agony, clutching himself around a shoulder that sloped away from his neck at an awful, unnatural angle. Dislocated, probably broken.

I knew that burnt-styrofoam smell rising off his skin, had known it from the time I was in diapers. It was a junkie smell. Boozers and potheads, they use enough, often enough, it gets so their pores are constantly oozing the residues of their drugs. Both smells are distinctive, but they're nothing compared to the effluvium of the ones who go for the hard stuff. I've seen it with heroin, cocaine, methamphetamine, all the shootable/smokables. That stench like someone filled a plastic cup with bugspray and set it on fire.

I shivered in revulsion. There was no way I was touching him again without protection.

The fresh gloves were cool and smooth against my skin. His voice was high and whiny as he cried out for Jesus and his momma: a dislocated shoulder is pretty bad pain. His noise hardly mattered.

My studio shared the upper floor with two other businesses, a Korean family of hairdressers and a tax consultant. Both were closed by five every night, and there was no way anybody in the bar downstairs would hear him over the thumping bass of their Top40 jukebox.

I grabbed his feet and flipped him over on his back with an eye toward seeing what I could learn from his pockets. He let out his loudest yell yet and spit at me, so I reached out and gave his shoulder a hard squeeze. The bones underneath felt all wrong. I ground them together in my fist until he passed out.

Some people think I must be sadistic to poke people with needles for a living. I don't actually take any pleasure in anyone's suffering, it's more like the pain is a side affect of what they want. But I wouldn't be wholly honest with myself if I didn't admit to a coarse and brutal side of my nature that I was not entirely comfortable with.

In the case of the junkie lying in front of me, his pain was a natural product of his decision to pull a pistol in my shop. Certainly not the outcome he wanted, but that's the way it goes. I knew I put him in a lot of pain-- I just didn't *care*. Putting him out that way was less dangerous to me than having him continue to struggle, and it was less dangerous to him than using a chokehold.

I was very careful going through his pockets, more than a little afraid of an accidental stick from a pocketed needle. It takes a fair amount of biomass, roughly one full drop of blood or saliva or whatever, to transmit HIV. But Hepatitis would put me in an early grave just as surely and was capable of transmitting in much smaller quantities. This guy was a major risk for both.

He didn't have a wallet, did have what the plastic heads on the TV news like to call 'drug paraphernalia'. No surprise, either one. He had a Minnesota driver's license and twenty-four bucks in wadded up bills in one pocket, a thin smooth packet of folded fifties in the other. I counted eight hundred in the packet, with a few pieces of paper folded on the inside. I took the ID and paper, put the money back. I didn't want Bex thinking I was robbing the junkie bastard.

He was still out and starting to snore. Even unconscious, his breath was a foul presence coiled around him, rotten meat in an uncleaned bathroom.

I bunched one fist in the front of his shirt, the other in the slick nylon fabric at the crotch of his pants, picked him up like a bale of hay. That was something about him. He was lighter than a tall man like him should have been, just a bundle of rags and sticks.

I carried him like that down the common hallway I shared with the hairdressers and the accountant, down to the back stairs. He wasn't too heavy, but too many years sitting on my ass for a living made me take a couple seconds to rest at the top of the stairs anyway.

I got him down to the back alley without too much bumping and jarring, slung him like a sack of potatoes onto the pile of trash bags beside the dumpster. The three of us on the second floor share the dumpster with Murphy's, the bar on the ground floor, but it generates a lot more waste every week than one dumpster can hold. I left the junkie sprawled on a pile of garbage, turned my back and headed back upstairs.

Bex was still in the chair where I left her. Her small white hands cupped around the can of Sprite from the fridge.

"Bex? Just one more minute, then I'll take you home, okay?" She nodded, a good sign.

The last thing I did before leaving the studio that night was to grab a spray bottle of ammonia from the back room and use it to destroy any DNA left behind.

I didn't think I drew any blood from the tall one, but the chinless toad left a couple of teeth on the carpet and a trail of red spatters all the way to the street. I soaked them all thoroughly, even though those two were unlikely to go to the cops, and the cops were unlikely to get the crime lab out if they did. It might seem paranoid, but despite a violent and eventful life, I was nearly thirty years old and had never been charged with a major crime. Like I said, I had expert teachers.

I was on my knees cleaning a small splatter off the front of the desk when I noticed Bex standing behind me.

"Need any help?"

"Just about done, thanks." I was surprised to hear so much relief in my own voice.

"Is that it? The gun?"

I stood up. I had completely forgotten about the gun. Smooth. Make sure there's no incriminating DNA to tie me to the assault, leave the damn pistol with the asshole's fingerprints all over it sitting out in plain sight.

It squatted on the desktop, fat and black and oily and lethal. As pregnant with menace as a sleeping adder. The oiled metal snared wicked blue highlights out of the air and trapped them in its mocking depths.

I picked it up again carefully, once again saw the orange dots. Safety off. Keeping the barrel pointed away from either of us, I thumbed the safety back on.

"Is that real?"

"Yeah."

"I've never seen one up close before."

She seemed to regard it with a terrible fascination. A shudder ran through her.

"It's revolting. Get rid of it. Please, Sam."

I found a paper bag in the back and popped the magazine into it. The clip hit the bottom of the sack with a heavy authoritative sound.

When I racked the slide, the noise was like an axe blow. A live round arced through the air with a coppery twinkle.

Bex's eyes went very large and very dark.

"One in the pipe and the safety off. He's lucky he didn't shoot his own foot off."

I tried to keep my tone light and make a joke of it, but I couldn't stop my hands from shaking when I dropped the pistol in the bag with the clip and scooped the loose shell into the sack as well.

"Come on," I said. "Let's get you home."

Three

I locked up the shop and set the alarm. Out in the hallway, Bex was full of concern for the man who might have shot her in the forehead. When I assured her he wouldn't be going anywhere but he wasn't in danger of dying either, she favored me with a fine shy smile that made me feel nine feet tall. She put her hand in mine as we headed down the stairs and through the front door.

It was still just barely light out when we reached the sidewalk. The rose light of late afternoon had deepened and shaded, on its way to a graceful purple twilight. I was surprised. It felt like hours since the young woman beside me had walked into my studio.

It was June in Minnesota, as close to heaven as it gets anywhere in the world. It was hard to believe that just six weeks ago, snow still clung in the shade under trees and along the highways and black ice was a driving hazard on the underpasses where the sun never quite reached during the day. Now it was light until after nine o'clock and too warm for any but the lightest clothing.

Cafes and coffeehouses, bars and bistros put their seating outdoors, and every one of us enjoyed it. It was a time for laughter and parties, young brides and new romance. The air smelled of flowers and happiness. In June, it was easy to see Minnesota as it would have been in the Jazz Age. Flappers and garden parties, gin and tonics and daring women with bobbed hair, cigarettes and bared knees. It was easy to imagine the ghosts of F. Scott and Zelda Fitzgerald presiding.

Murphy's had its doors open to the evening air, a heavy bass beat thumping out from inside. On the patio facing the parking lot, the crowd noise was loud and raucous and inviting, but there was no way we were going to linger for drinks around a potential crime scene. Soon enough, someone would go out back to throw another black plastic trash bag on the pile or smoke weed or mess around in the alley, and Bex's assailant would be on his way to the hospital. If the officer who answered the call found the junkie's works and the deceptively small amount of white powder tightly rolled in plastic, his time in the hospital would likely be spent handcuffed to the bed.

Bex pointed our steps across the U of M campus, and the voices and music barely made it across Washington Avenue. The U was in its summer quarter-- ninety percent of its students were out of school, busy drinking and flirting and generally being young all the way from here to Mexico, none of them in sight at this hour. Bex's warm little fingers squeezed mine tight in the silence.

Our footsteps were loud in the quiet. Something about the air in that lavender twilight made them ring off the University buildings as we cut through the campus. The old Gothic hulks were mostly dark and silent. Here and there a light burned, but somehow that just made it seem all the more isolated. It was indescribably beautiful, except for the panic buttons under the lights every few yards.

There's a magic to twilight. As the light shaded from lavender to violet, all over the city friends and couples responded, felt closer to each other, understood and connected. The courtship dances would go on for hours yet, but this was the time when eyes met and bonds were forged, whether the people forging them knew it or not.

Bex and I walked together in a private little world, no more immune to that forgotten ancient call in our blood than any other.

"Once, when I was sixteen," she finally said, "I saw a guy get stabbed, right in front of me."

"I'm sorry."

She shook her head as though brushing away a gnat.

"This was worse than that, I think."

"I'm sorry you had to be there for this, too."

"What you did back there was that karate?"

I shrugged. "Some Israeli stuff I guess. All I know is it works when I need it."

In the deepening light, I saw her reach out to touch her forehead, catch the gesture and turn it into a brushing of her hair out of her eyes. I remembered how it was for me, the first couple times someone pointed a gun at me. Afterward, I couldn't stop thinking about the spot where the barrel had pointed: it burned like a red-hot dime for hours afterward.

"That man... if he'd shot me, I'd be dead now."

"It's probably best not to think too much about it. You're okay, and that's the important thing."

She bit the edge of her thumb a moment. Our hollow ringing footsteps carried us out of the University campus and into the student neighborhood known as Dinkytown. Misogynist rap blared from nearly every house along Fraternity Row: the frat boys in full swing.

What you did to those men," she said, "I'm glad."

***

We stopped in the Purple Onion for coffee. The adrenalin burn had long since sizzled its way out of my system, and my body reacted as it usually does. I was chilled and shaking, thoughts jumping across the front of my brain like water drops on a hot skillet. I saw the same signs in Bex's trembling lips and darting eyes, and despite the warm summer evening, her hand in mine was icy. She asked for a 'flat white', changed her order to a latte when neither the counter staff nor I knew what she meant. We took our drinks to a table near the window. Her eyes were large and gray and dark as she cupped the warm mug in her hands. The ring of gold around the inner edge of her iris was nowhere to be seen.

"Does this sort of thing happen to you often?"

"Not in years. My life is usually a pretty peaceful place. Almost boring, really."

"But it's happened before."

"Yeah. I was a screwed-up kid, got into a lot of fights and stuff back when, but like I said, it was all a long time ago."

"You say that like you're an old man or something."

"It's not the years, it's the mileage. And the number of times you make the trip dragged behind the car."

She laughed politely, with that brittle edge the adrenalin leaves behind. She tilted her head to one side, eyed me speculatively.

"It's not fair, you know. You know my age, but I don't know yours."

"I'm twenty-eight. Too old for you?"

"You're very forward, aren't you?"

I didn't know what to say to that, and the moment passed.

Right then and not for the first time, I wished I had some of Hamish's gift for always knowing the right thing to say. The conversation moved on.

***

An hour later, calmer now, we walked together to her friend's home. We chatted as we went, comfortable, getting to know each other a little better. I wasn't sure what she got out of it, but getting to know Miss Bex Temple sounded like a great idea to me. Everything about her fascinated me, and I wasn't ready for it when she looked up and made a surprised sound.

"That's my flat!" she said. "I mean, that's the flat I'm staying in." We had walked past it without noticing.

I looked up at the building. It was that type put up all around the Midwest in the 30's and 40's. Three stories, two apartments per floor, a stone facade. This one was capped with an elaborate, fluted seashell carved with the date this building was born, 1947. I could almost see gorgeous natural woodwork inside and the deep-ground smell of other people's cooking.

"Well, this is me."

Bex stood close to me, our bodies nearly touching. In the light of the street lamp, I clearly saw the gold ring in her clear gray eyes.

It was the most important thing in the world to kiss her, but I just couldn't figure out a way to do it. Figured: I can charge straight into an armed gunman, can't figure out how to kiss a pretty girl. Her hair framed her face in a dark halo, the contrast making her skin glow like it was lit from within. She looked like an angel, pure and innocent.

Finally, she shrugged and took my hand.

"Samuel Matthew Roark, thank you for piercing me, and for... an eventful night."

She gave my hand a final little shake, took a couple of steps backwards and threw me a little finger wave from the entrance door to her building.

I waited until she was safely inside her building and the front door closed behind her. Bex sped up the stairs and never looked back once.

Four

Bex's friend Kate lived just a half-mile or so from my own house, and the temptation to leave my car at work until morning and keep walking until I got home was strong. But it wasn't even full-dark yet, and I didn't feel ready to call it a night. I turned back the way I came and went to get my car. I didn't realize it, but I already knew where I was going.

The Terminal Bar is my kind of place: stubborn, dark and quiet. The working class neighborhood around it fell victim to a creeping tide of boutique stores selling gourmet cheeses and hand-painted pottery, the homes now belonging to the sort of people who buy such things. Even though the industrial mill whose workers were once its clientele is now a bondage club, the Terminal has kept its own sense of itself. The world around it may change, but as long as Matt is still able to stand behind the bar The Terminal will remain a place of dark and dusty pine, prize walleye stuffed and mounted on the walls, two dollar draft beer for his regulars and the perfect place for a quiet drink or three.

Matt answered my hello with a curt nod. "See the new store opened up across the street?" He tossed his chin in that general direction.

"No, what about it?"

"Cat and dog furniture." He shook his head in disbelief. "Don't that just get all? I went over there to say how do, maybe see if they got something old Bo can't do without."

While he spoke, Matt's hands took up a frosty mug from the cooler and drew a perfect draft of Lienenkugel from the tap. In Matt's place you drink Lienie's, Miller or Bud, and he knows I go for the local brew.

"Know what I saw in there? A doggy bed. Know how much that lady wanted for it? Five hundred dollars. Five. Hundred. Dollars! I figure old Bo's just going to have to keep on sharing mine."

"Next thing you know, you're going to have to get some ferns in here, start serving drinks with little paper umbrellas in them."

"Over my dead body. Let me tell you something," His fingertip drummed the top of the bar for emphasis. "I saved near about every penny they paid me while I was in Korea, had enough when I came back to open this place up. Saved near about every damn penny I made out of it, too. Back when the rest of this whole damn country was in the crapper, back in '74, I had me enough saved to buy this here building. Lock, stock and barrel." He stood back, his point made, fixed me with a tough stony eye.

"You saving?" he said. I told him truthfully that I was. Matt nodded. I think he was disappointed at my virtue, but he didn't let it stop his lecture.

"You kids, you don't know how to save, most of you. I saved all my life, and now the rest of the world can go to hell for all I care. I got no landlord tryin' to boot me out like they did old Chuck Simms cross the street. Used to be I could get my oil filters and antifreeze there, just walk across when I got a slow afternoon. Now Chuck's gotta go live with his girl and her idjit husband, and it's five hundred dollar dog beds. God's way of taking care of folks got more money than sense. Two bucks."

I gave him a five, left a dollar on the bar from my change. I tried to tip him more than that once and insulted him so badly I was worried he'd throw me out. I'm pretty sure he doesn't know my name, but neither does he notice my tattooed arms, where a lot of people over forty act like I might've escaped from a circus. About a year ago he decided I was a two dollar customer, and for me, it just doesn't get any better than that.

I took my beer over to one of the two red vinyl booths, sat down and spread the contents of the junkie's pockets out in front of me.

His driver's license said my attacker's name was Jack Rose, no middle initial. It seemed too normal a name for the man who attacked me. Made me think how he'd probably been like every other smiling baby and played like any other kid. I wondered how he went from pulling himself up on the bars of his crib to pointing a .45 in the face of an unarmed woman.

I wondered how any of us got where we were.

Jack's license also told me he was thirty-two years old and listed an address in South Minneapolis. The rest of the papers, the ones rubber-banded in with the folded cash, told a different story. There was a torn scrap with a phone number on it and my name written on it in clumsy block letters. Folded into tiny squares, there was a page torn out of the phone book, the Tattoos to Tax Services section of the Yellow Pages. My ad was circled with a thick, red marker.

Across from me, Lisa Torres leaned with both elbows on the edge of the table and eyed my beer with a lean and hungry look.

"You're not even old enough to drink," I whispered.

And thanks to you, I never will be.

"You dealt the play that night, no use bitching about the cards you turned over."

Asshole.

She reached across the table, pulled Jack Rose's driver's license around to face her.

Can you believe the haircut on him in this? I'd shave my head too.

I said nothing, sipped my beer.

What you think? Would I look good with my head shaved? I remember that one girl you liked, with the bald head and the earrings.

She affected a look of childish slyness, looking up at me out of the corners of her eyes and letting a grin spread across her face.

Or maybe I should dye my hair dark, huh?

"What is it you want, Lisa?"

You know, sugar. She blew me a kiss.

I didn't know what she wanted, never had in six haunted years. But I was determined not to let her get to me. I took another sip of beer and looked away from her at the rows of prepackaged peanuts and other bar snacks at the far end of the bar.Her taunting smile transformed into a furious glare, and she flipped the junkie's license into my face.

Next time I hope they fucking kill you.

Lisa stood up hard enough to bang the table against me and stormed off in an icy wind that rattled the pictures on the walls and riffled the stacks of napkins on top of the bar. Two men in another booth stopped their conversation, looked at each other and went back to discussing the Twins and the Vikings and their chances this year.

The night she died, Lisa Torres was three months past her sixteenth birthday. She was also in her fifth year as a runaway, with multiple arrests for soliciting, sixty days in a juvenile facility and ninety days of court-ordered rehab.

Her only known attempt to move from prostitution and petty theft into armed robbery ended up a complete disaster.

Had she lived, Lisa would be twenty-two now, with a birthday coming up. The same age as Bex. She loved telling me how had she lived she would have turned her life around, married some rich guy or become a secretary or dental hygienist, something like that. The odds were against it. Every year, too many street kids like Lisa end up on the icy steel tables with drains running down the sides. They overdose, or they owe the wrong people money, or they get in the wrong argument, or they climb into the wrong car with the wrong man.

The odds were against Lisa, but stranger things have happened. People *do* turn their lives around. After all, I went from being a teen runaway to local businessman, with my own accountant, lawyer, health insurance, bank accounts and everything.

"Earth to Sam," said a familiar voice from the other side of the booth.

"John. How long you been sitting there?"

"Long enough to wonder how that autism's treating you."
"Sorry. Lot on my mind, I guess."

"No kidding," he said. "Tell you what, I'll get us a couple beers, and you can tell me all about it."

John was an enormous bear of a man, with a hand like a T-bone steak and a thick cigar perpetually clamped in his jaws. He had spiked hair, pierced earlobes stretched wide enough to comfortably fit a magic marker through, and the latest fashionable chin-beard. Also, at twenty-six his face still carried traces of the overweight sensitive child he had once been.

He was also probably the best friend I had these days. Tattooing is such an insular little world, usually full of petty feuds and ridiculous professional jealousies, but from the first day he came to town, John had never treated me with anything but respect and friendship.

He set a fresh beer in front of me and sat down opposite. He was short and stocky, with a broad face and a grin like the Devil's Own Mischief.

"Come on, spill-- what's on your mind?"

I opened my mouth to tell him about the two junkies, to talk about the idea it wasn't a random robbery, to bring up my first fight in years. I was surprised at the words that came out of my mouth.

"I met a girl today."

"No shit!" He reached across the oak table and chucked me on the shoulder.

"So what's this girl like?"

"Her name's Bex, and she's from New Zealand She's nice."

"I sure hope so, cause I gotta tell you Sam, when it comes to women, you ain't got the sense God gave monkeys."

"I'm not that bad."

"You always go for the broken ones. Sometimes, it's like a chick's gotta start fires or icepick an ex-boyfriend just to get your attention."

"Come on," I said, "you ever going to quit giving me shit about Debbie? It's not like I knew that about her when I met her."

"Shit, buddy, for you, it's past knowing. It's some kind of scary voodoo shit."

John finished his beer, saw that mine was still half full and went up to the bar for his next round. He was right. I generally had pretty terrible taste in women. I managed to steer clear of the buy-me-presents crowd: too much like hooking. I could smell the ones want to get two men all worked up and aim them at each other. Their kind always knew without being told about the violence in me and took a greasy pleasure in asking about it.

But I did attract a lot of women with broken glass in their heads. The twisted, bent and broken ones. Girls with barbed wire wrapped tight around their souls who couldn't imagine intimacy without pain threaded through it.

When I did go out with someone normal, it was always some sweet and smiling woman being 'adventurous'. As though being with me was some sort of walk on the dark side of the street, or an overgrown adolescent urge to piss off her parents. Either way, they didn't even try to see past the tattoos and piercings, and it gets tiring feeling like something in a carnival.

Bex Temple seemed genuine, and I could see no trace of the familiar, brittle, glittering madness. Of course it wasn't surprising that she was just passing through. What did shock me was the small pang I felt when I thought about her next trip to the airport.

John came back, this time with a shot and a beer. He took gentle sips at the one and generous pulls at the other. He made a point of noticing the scraps of paper on the table in front of me for the first time. I told him about the rest of my night.

When I finished, he looked out at me over his hands and let out a long breath.

"You do realize these guys were hired help, right?"

"I don't know," I said. "Addicts get desperate. They lie and steal and do all sorts of insane dumb shit, some of them crazy and dumb enough to do it with a gun in their hands. Just because I'm not an all-night gas station doesn't make these two Mafia hitmen or anything."

"'Just look at it. This guy, this Jack Rose," He picked up the folded-over Yellow Pages ad in two fingers, "you got this off the inside of his roll, all tied up in there where it won't fall out. He have a wallet with him?"

No, his ID and phone and shit were just loose in another pocket."

"Other money *besides* the roll?"

"It wasn't a roll. Sixteen fifties, bank-crisp and folded in half. The paper and shit on the inside."

"So did he have any other money?"

"Twenty-four bucks in wadded-up singles and fives." I didn't like where this was going.

"So here you got this desperate, armed-robber junkie, half-crazy for a fix even though he's got solid cash money in his pocket, decides he's going to rob a *tattoo studio* of all things. This guy goes looking through the phone book for a good one? Tears the ad out in case he gets lost or something? Come on, buddy. You know better than that."

I stared at the scrap of paper with my name written on it. I also remembered the white powder rolled in plastic. You're not desperate for a fix when you're still holding.

"So they were hired." It was my turn for a deep breath. I could feel a cold spot on the back of my neck, centered just below the base of my skull. It wasn't a pleasant sensation. "It was the first fight I've been in in six years. Bad enough thinking about it as a robbery."

"Better think about it how it *is*, you'll stay alive longer. And what do you mean six years? You forget about Abby's Christmas party last year?"

"That wasn't a fight. Poor guy had a few too many, and when Abby asked him to leave I walked him outside."

"I do seem to remember that old boy running into the doorway a fair few times on the way."

"What can I say? He didn't want to go." What I can't deny, I make a joke. Healthy. I wanted another beer.

"Seriously though," John's eyebrows raised a series of deep forked lines in his forehead, "something you got to remember about tonight. You got somebody out there didn't get what they paid this guy for. Chances are, this ain't over for us."

"That's what-- the thought had occurred to me." I almost said, that's what Lisa Torres said, but something stopped me. Ghosts and hauntings and all that shit were for my sisters and grandmother, not me. John was a friend, there were limits.

I stood up out of the booth.

"Want another beer?"

***

I hit the bathroom before ordering. Waiting at the bar while Matt drew our beers, I saw his eyes flick behind me and his eyebrows drift up high on his forehead. I turned, and there was Tasha, standing behind me as though she'd always been there. It was a trick worthy of Lisa.

Tasha was like a cat that way. One minute I was alone, the next there she was, staring up at me from under thick, black lashes. Her witch green eyes were full of mischief and light.

"I might have *known* I'd find you here, Sam." Her voice was always a rich purr. "You know, if you'd join the *rest* of the world and get a cell, we wouldn't have to keep randomly bumping into each other like this."

"Have we ever *randomly* bumped into each other? Besides, being hard to get hold of is why I don't have one-- you know how I like my privacy. You wanted to find me, all you had to do was call me at work."

"I didn't say I wanted to *see* you, Sam. Only that I might have known I'd *find* you here." The words were cruel, but the tone was soft, even affectionate. Pure Tasha.

"Sorry Tash. I didn't mean to be rude. It's just been a fucked-up day is all."

Tasha was a tall girl: her forehead came to the level of my lips. Standing there wrapped in some kind of clinging cape that ate all the light around it. Her hair was the color of ice, her face and throat pale as ivory. The effect made her seem both fragile and dangerous at the same time.

Her lipstick was the color of blood, half-dried and sticky, but her mouth softened into a tender smile and she brought the eyes up from under the lashes again.

"In that case, you're forgiven." A perfectly manicured hand touched my cheek, and her eyes warmed up a couple of degrees. "As it happens, I *did* want to see you tonight."

I noticed the mugs of beer standing on top of the bar, Matt leaning against the rail and waiting for his money.

"What can I get you?" I asked. Of course she had to ask for some unpronounceable stuff Matt never heard of, make a show out of settling for Jack Daniels. I figured that was the way it had always been with us. I got John another shot, too. If Tasha noticed that the shot I ordered cost half what hers did, she gave no indication.

Coming back to the booth, I avoided John's attempts at eye contact, sat down and put his drinks in front of him. Tasha walked over and made a show out of it, one of those women who move from pose to pose without appearing to think about it.

We saw she had come from the bondage club around the corner. She shrugged out of the black cape-thing and stood there in something considerably smaller and more complicated. It was soft dark leather, mostly buckles and straps. Her pale creamy skin set off her full-sleeve tattoos beautifully. One arm was swirling fire, the other jagged teeth of ice, probably the finest work I'd ever done.

She pulled in beside me. One leather-cupped breast brushed the side of my arm, and John downed his shot, drank off half his beer to chase it.

"Do know what day this is, Sam?" Her hair smelled like jasmine when she moved, and her skin gave off a scent like burnt cinnamon.

"Thursday?"

"It's two years *tonight* from the first time we met." That was the first time she ever remembered anything like that. Names and dates and times and anniversaries were things that happened to other people, not to Tasha. I was surprised to find out she was even capable of such a thing.

John drained his remaining beer and started to get up out of the booth. Tasha waved him back down with a rhythmic flicker of blood-dark nails.

"Please, *don't* go on my account. I can't stay myself, and it wouldn't be *fair* to leave dear Sam here all alone by himself." John's mouth screwed up at one corner but he kept his silence, just gathered up our empties and headed back to the bar.

Tasha moved in closer beside me until her hip was touching mine. I picked at a callus on my palm and ignored what she kept trying to display. I noticed that none of the stuff I had taken out of my attacker's pockets was on the table. I knew it had to be John, looking out for me: Tasha had no pockets.

The cold conditioned air skirled through the Terminal as the front door opened. Tasha looked up and her expression transformed into childish glee.

"Arthur!" She clapped when she said it. Tasha's latest man wore a black turtleneck, steel-rimmed glasses and a long curly ponytail. Like all her men, he was agitated.

"Where did you go? I was with you in the club, and I just looked away for a second, and…" He had a soft voice that traveled up toward shrill even as it trailed off. Tasha sat at the table, watching him with a flat-eyed stare. Nothing in her face moved as she held out her hand, palm up.

He wiped one hand on his slacks, tentatively reached for her, saw the most fractional shift in one eyebrow and pulled back.

"Oh, oh right." He unzipped a leather folio and produced a magazine, placed it in her palm. Tasha handed it to me.

"Two years ago tonight, and I got you a *present*!" Her smile was as bright as Christmas morning, completely oblivious to the way she was treating her date.

"Would you like to join us for a drink?" I asked him.

Tasha answered. "We have to be leaving. Arthur's been a *very* good boy tonight, so *he* gets a present, too." Arthur turned a very embarrassed pink except for his mouth, which became a tight, white line. Tasha didn't see any of it, as she was leaning into me to show me the magazine in her hand. She flicked the hair out of her eyes, and said, "But first I had to make sure I gave you *yours.*"

Tasha stared out at me from the cover of the magazine. She held her arms in front of her in a pose as old as Lilith, making her tattooed sleeves look spectacular and quietly drawing attention to the fact she was nude behind them.

"Congratulations," was all I could find to say.

"It hits the stands next week. That's the contributor's copy they sent me. *Your* work got a damn fine write up."

"I'll be sure to buy one. Thanks, Tash."

"You keep that one. Like I said, my gift to you." With that strange flowing grace of hers she stood up out of the booth without ever bending her spine. "Good night, Sam. John, *always* a pleasure."

And just like that, she was gone. Turned away and melted out the door, a small silence left behind her like sitting in traffic and accidentally witnessing a funeral procession.

For a long moment no one spoke. Finally, it was John who broke the ice.

"Old Tash always did like to be noticed, didn't she?"

I chucked my friend on the shoulder and bought us another round.

Five

I stepped out of The Terminal and into a cool summer rain. Weather in this part of the country is a strange, strange thing. At sunset just a few hours ago, there wasn't a cloud in the sky, but now a gentle rain looked to have been coming down for some time. People here like to say, if you don't like the weather, just wait a minute.

I drove home on slick streets without paying it too much attention. After winter's heavy snows and spring's ice, treacherous and lingering, a little shower wasn't going to bother anybody. I liked the way the traffic lights reflected bright snaking worms of color in the rain-slick streets.

I only live a mile and half from The Terminal: a five minute drive, ten at most. In that time the air temperature fell off so sharply I was tempted to use the car's heater, lightning forked the night sky and a silver curtain of roaring rainwater came marching down the street like an advancing army. This time of year, farmers were as likely to suffer from drought as hail damage, and everyone kept a nervous eye on the dark clouds, looking for the telltale funnel-shapes to begin reaching toward the earth. I turned the corner from Hennepin onto my street thinking that even the best seasons here had their dangers.

I parked in the street and ran through the pelting rain for the shelter of my front porch. I got my key in the lock and my front door open, stepped across the threshold and froze.

There was someone in my house.

I couldn't explain it any better than that. A house feels one way when its empty, another when a person is inside it, no matter how quiet or how still they may be. I thought of my home phone number in Jack Rose's pocket.

I stool at the threshold between the mudroom and the house itself. The smells of old umbrellas and galoshes behind me mingled with dust and wood and all the subtle scents of the inside of my home. Under them all lay a faint foul thread, acrid like smoke and sweet like rot.

My living room lay in deep shadow. The stairs to my left rose into forbidding blackness. The only light came from the porch light shining through the front window, too weak to do more than make the darkness that much darker.

I had already shut the front door behind me on my way in. Good, in that it didn't leave me standing there as a silhouetted target, not so good in that the loss of precious seconds working a doorknob ruled out running as an option. It was impossible to hear anything over the drumming rain but that didn't stop me from imagining I did. I knew if I listened long enough, I would freak myself out with the pops and clicks and creaks and groans of an eighty year old house taking the abuse of the storm overhead.

When it came right down to it, I didn't like thinking of myself as a man who waited for anything. I could *feel* someone else in the house with me, close by. Three steps to the light switch were all I needed to prove that I was just jumpy after the earlier attack. Or give me a fighting chance, either way.

I took the first two steps before I saw him. A man sat in my overstuffed armchair in the corner, where he'd been hidden by the nearest bookcase. In the deepest pool of shadow.

Bald head, long beard, some sort of dark garment that came up high on his neck and made him look hunchbacked. I couldn't imagine how it was that I hadn't felt him more strongly. He radiated such intense and brutal animosity. It was a burning desire to hurt, to kill. Anyone who ever stepped down the wrong dark alley knows that feeling of focused malevolence.

He turned his head toward me, his face pooled in black. There was no rustle of cloth when he did it. I reached out, flipped on the light switch, intending to blind or startle my intruder.

What confronted me was an empty chair.

"I don't need this," I said out loud and headed for the kitchen for a glass of water. Way I figured, what can't touch you can't hurt you. My childhood had been full of people who weren't really there, and the last six years with Lisa had only made me more weary of it all.

I didn't think to check the chair for a body's resting warmth. I'm not sure it would have made any difference.

***

I dragged my ass upstairs and stripped for bed. Cool night air came through the open bedroom window, took some of the sting out of the day-long heat trapped in the room with me. Rain must have blown in as well. Beads of moisture clung to the windowsill and the tops of the sheets.

Think I'd look good with dark hair? a familiar voice said in the darkness.

The dead girl stalked the shadows of my bedroom, prancing and turning and playing with her hair. Her face was a ghastly parody of Bex's sunshine smile.

"You ever going to let me be happy?"

It's not me, sugar, remember?

She did one of her worst tricks then. I wondered if she had been a gifted mimic in life, or if it was something that came to her in the grave.

Lisa swept her hands back over her face, pulled the stringy bleached hair out of her eyes and there was an instant and unnatural resemblance to my little sister Tabitha. Lisa's own features were small, sharp and pinched, but the face before me had Tabitha's doll-big blue eyes, heart-shaped face and smooth rounded forehead. It was even easy to believe that the dead girl's hair was Tabby's long, straight black.

Pouty baby lips smiled at me with a shadow of Lisa's old mischief and began singing Happy Birthday to me in a soft, familiar little lisp.

Then, as I knew they would, those huge eyes went dark and blank and rolled up in their sockets. Her head rolled loose on the column of her neck and thick white froth poured from her mouth.

> *It was my eighth birthday. We were all in Grandma Roark's parlor, cranky old Irish woman so ancient she didn't have a living room or den or anything, like normal people. No, she had to have a parlor. It was dark and creepy and lit by candles, like someone doing set dressing for a haunted house in a movie. It was like every other room in Grandma Roark's home.*
>
> *I didn't know it then, but by the time my next birthday came again, it would be my home too. That night, we children were just visiting. My mother was still alive.*

All of us acted like it was supposed to be a happy occasion, as much as any of them ever troubled themselves to act about anything. Grandma Roark rarely smiled. It was like she could already see all the bad things waiting up ahead for you in your life and didn't see the point.

Which for Grandma Roark, was very probably the truth.

My oldest sister, Agatha, was very much like Grandma Roark in her ways, and for much the same reasons. Tabitha was only just turned four and happy about anything with candles in it. She was still little enough that year that she had to touch them with one outstretched finger to light them.

I remember my mother that night, beautiful and dark and smelling like exotic spices and moonlight. It seemed especially important to her that the birthday I shared with my twin sister be a happy, happy time. She said so, over and over.

But the combination of whatever pills she would grind to paste in her back teeth and whatever she packed into that ornate brass pipe of hers that night had turned her into something made of colored glass: pretty, brittle, and in danger of shattering into thousands of deadly sharp pieces. Her constant smile looked like it had been carved into her skin with fish hooks, and the heavy crystal wineglass she raised to her lip as regular as breathing shook in her hand and rattled on the tabletop when she tried to set it down.

I tried my best to act happy, but I was no better at false fronts than the rest of them. I had wanted pizza and video games at Chuck E. Cheese, not a brown birthday cake full of prunes and raisins in a haunted house. But I did my best to act happy and thrilled. I wanted my mother to have that happy day she wanted, and I feared what might happen if she didn't get it.

And then we were all singing Happy Birthday, and Tabby's eyes rolled back in her head like that, and the white foam started rolling out of her mouth and down her chin.

Except instead of dripping onto the bib of her dress, it curled into the air, rising and massing like a cup of cream poured into a tank of water.

Thick ropy streams of it poured up out of her mouth, until enough of it hovered above her to form the head and shoulders of an old woman, her features hidden behind a thin veil.

The veil clung to forehead, nose and chin, stuck wetly to thick rubbery lips. She leaned in to stare directly at me.

The old woman spoke then, words which the rest of my family believed doomed me forever. 'A chain of sorrows, forbidden to live,' she said and everyone else took it to heart. The woman was Old Rosie, spiritual guide and protector of the women in my family. Or at least, that's what they claimed.

It didn't matter much to me. Except for spoiling everyone's mood that night, she never showed any other sign of interest in me. Which suited me fine.

Lisa shook her hair back into her eyes and was once again the teenaged street hooker I killed six years ago. She wiped the white foam from her chin with the back of one wrist. Her smile was wicked.

There was no Tabitha, dazed and confused, sad that she missed out on all the excitement. No mother, weeping into her hands and running upstairs. No pitying looks from Agatha, no Grandma Roark looking even tougher than usual, if that was even possible. She always looked like you couldn't knock her down with a hammer, like throwing her into a furnace might do nothing more than make her angry.

There was just my bedroom, such as it was. Queen-size futon unfolded on its frame, dresser in a corner, last night's laundry on the floor. Ghost in the shadows in front of me, hands on her bony bare hips, fishbelly white skin glowing in the moonlight. Her eyes glittered like a night sky reflected on deep still water.

See Sam, it isn't me. You were cursed from birth.

She licked her lips.

Just like me.

"I'm nothing like you, Lisa. You know better than that."

I *know picking up a gun didn't do either of us much good.*

Six

The shop felt different that morning. Standing at the door with the keys in my hand, I knew how soldiers felt in enemy territory. Astounding was more my home than any place I lived, and that home had been violated. It was like I could feel the psychic stain of last night's attack.

But that was my sisters. Not me.

My world was the concrete, the here and now. Agatha always said I had the talent, same as our mother, that I refused to use it. The way she said it made it sound like an accusation. Like she remembered a different mother.

I set my key to the lock and turned. The steel bolt slid out of the doorjamb.

An envelope waited for me on the waiting room carpet just inside the door. Inside was a blurry xerox of a letter. It looked like someone had copied a copy too many times. The letterhead was something called The Brethren: the text filled both sides of the page with a rambling single-spaced tirade in a nearly unreadable small font.

It was typical apocalyptic frothing. The Final Days were Upon us, the Hour of Judgement was At Hand, my Soul would be Judged. The writer had a thing for capital letters.

The envelope had no address on it, no postmark either. Someone had come here and put it under the door personally. I went across the hall to the hairdresser's and asked but neither Mr. Kim or his wife noticed noticed anyone this morning. They were usually busy in the hours before lunch, but it hadn't hurt to ask.

I chucked the letter and its envelope in a drawer and put it out of my mind. I had more important things to do to get ready for the new day.

I had just got the last load of forceps cleaned and sterilizing in the autoclave when I came out from the back room and found Hamish on his hands and knees looking up under the reception desk. He unfolded when he saw me.

"I thought I'd check and see if I spotted anything you missed." He seemed a bit sheepish about it.

We both gave the place a quick once over. It wasn't long before Hamish found the cellphone behind the potted plant by the door. Slid there in the fight, maybe. He handled it with gloves, opened the clamshell and showed me the four-digit PIN screen. Snapped it closed, wiped it down with germicide and dropped it in the same drawer where I'd put the letter from The Brethren.

I didn't feel I had done anything wrong, but I didn't necessarily trust the cops or the courts to agree with me. Nobody had that kind of faith anymore.

The night I shot Lisa Torres, I was locked up immediately. It took the attorney I had on retainer down there over two hours to find out which station house I had been taken to, but she did manage to reach me before the cops broke any bones.

Twenty-four hours later, when they had to either charge me or let me go, the DA cut me loose. Not a word of apology, just turned back onto the sidewalk holding a plastic bag with the contents of my pockets in it, followed by a six month ordeal to recover my firearm. Not that I ever wanted to see the thing again, but damned if I was going to *donate* it to the New Orleans Police Department.

Officially, I was never even arrested. I was 'held for questioning' and released, all in good order.

I didn't believe the cops in Minneapolis would be quite as savage as those in New Orleans, but I was in no hurry to test the matter. For me and everyone I knew, police were people best left out of every aspect of your life. The cops were also those most eager to get in.

Besides the phone, our search turned up nothing new. The floor was still drying in places and the vacuum had just been put away when the chimes over the door rang.

I came out and saw Bex framed in the doorway.

If anything, she looked even better than she had last night. She had done something I couldn't quite figure out with her makeup. Her eyes were even more large and luminous, her lips sparkling and delicious. When our eyes met, her smile had a flavor of slightly embarrassed boldness in it. She brushed a strand of hair back behind her ear.

"Um, I forgot to pay for my piercing last night." She held up two folded twenties. When she put them into my hand, the touch turned the world sideways for a second.

I became conscious of the two of us standing in front of the desk, staring at each other.

"Um, Hamish, this is Bex I was telling you about. Bex Temple, Hamish Lockwood."

Hamish reached across the desk, shook her hand with a grave politeness. We stood there together a moment more, feeling the silence start to stretch out to awkward.

"Well," she said, "I guess I should be going..."

My hand actually shot out, stopped short of touching her.

"Don't forget, I promised to take you book shopping, if you want."

"I did see some little bookstores on the way over here."

"There are some pretty good places in Dinkytown," I said, "but what I've got in mind is even better."

"Sounds great. When do you want to go?"

Hamish surprised me by speaking up. "Why not now?" he said. "Go on, Sam. I can cover the store for a couple hours. Any tattoos, I'll book em in for later."

I looked down at the girl beside me. I loved the way her gray eyes danced with light when she looked up at me. I was pretty sure I wasn't imagining it.

***

The first part of what I had in mind was easy. I drove us to my house and pulled up at the curb out front, asked Bex to give me two minutes while I ran inside.

She had a book open in her lap when I came back out. Her hair fell across the blade of her cheek and hid everything but her eyes from view. She didn't see me cross in front of the car, looked up with a start when I fell into the seat beside her.

"What's this?"

"A traveler's best friend," I said. "It's called an e-reader."

"It's so thin..."

"Yeah, I was thinking last night, last thing you need is twenty more pounds of books in your luggage. This thing, you can read in full daylight with no eyestrain, the batteries last for weeks and you can buy more books anyplace you can plug into a computer."

"It's lovely."

"Best part, I've already got over two hundred books loaded on it. A few of them I even know you like."

"How much do I--"

"Forget it. This one's yours and I don't want to hear another word."

She protested a couple more times, but her attention was already on navigating through my booklist.

"You've got Wilkie Collins in here!"

"Guy writes a damn good novel."

Bex held up the book in her hands. It was The Woman in White, one of my favorites.

"Are you serious? I can really have this?"

"Put it this way, now we've got time to kill. You hungry?"

***

We went for lunch at a little Italian place I knew. Bex told me stories of her childhood. She had been a rough and tumble kid, and had the scars to prove it.

"You can really just take off like that?" Bex asked. "Aren't you worried about missing business?"

"It's not like this is something I do every day. And this is more important."

Her eyes crinkled at the corners and my face grew warm.

"Ask you something?"

"Sure."

"Let me take you to dinner tonight?"

"I'd love to, but my friend and her husband have something planned for me tonight." She fiddled with the crumbs on the tablecloth. "Tomorrow?"

"Sounds like a plan."

We were quiet a little while then, Bex sipping at her glass of white wine, me trying to figure out where I'd take her tomorrow night.

I felt about fifteen again, without the knife wounds.

Seven

When I finally did roll back in to the studio, Hamish had just finished putting a couple rings in a skinny emo guy's lip. From the paper towel he was holding to his face, the guy had been a bleeder. Hamish saw me and glowered.

"Well, well, I was starting to think I'd seen the last of you. Nice of you to join me."

"It's not that late, is it?"

"Well now, that depends. Four o'clock might me just considered early by some. Me, I say--" He shook his head and flashed me a bright smile. "Hell Sam, I can't keep it up. You look like you had fun, and about time you did, too."

"It's no big deal, really. I mean, I like her, she's great--"

"Best damn woman you been out with in forever."

"Yes, best damn woman I've been out with in forever, and she leaves town in less than a month."

"Ouch." Hamish took the kid's cash and reached for an aftercare sheet. "Course, that'd figure. You start up with someone doesn't have major mental problems, you gotta have a built-in time bomb, keep you from having any real kind of a relationship."

"This, coming from you?"

"Only saying it cause I love you, bud. Single life agrees with me - I love playing the field. You, you're a one-woman man. No sin, just the way you are."

The emo kid shifted his eyes at me and said nothing

.

***

Most of what I know about fighting and violence, and also about honor, decency and how to be a man, I learned from two Israeli men who lived near my grandmother's house. I owed them an enormous debt, from the time I was nine through my runaway years and right up to last night, when I knew what to do with an armed intruder.

After the death of my mother, my sisters and I were sent to live with my grandmother. Avi and Uri were distant neighbors and outcasts like myself. No one lived that far out in the sticks because they wanted attention, and they seemed comfortable with the isolation my Grandma Roark's proximity brought.

People were afraid of my grandmother, and they were afraid of my sisters, even Tabby. Maybe especially Tabby.

As a nine year old boy, I suffered for it. It was a small community, and I was new there: thin, frail and living in the local haunted house with the town witch. At least, that's how the kids in town saw it, and I was too wrapped up in my grief to try making them see me as a normal kid. More than a few days, I walked or ran home with a crowd of children taunting and throwing rocks at me from a safe distance. Even then I had a rotten temper and fought in a deadly serious, black rage when I could get my hands on one of them, not that it did much good without size, mass or skill to make it count. I was just a small angry child.

I'll always remember the day Uri found me. Something had changed in the other children that day, an ugly ripple running through them and a hot-blooded need for larger and sharper stones.

They had me surrounded out in the middle of the street and I couldn't see for the blood in my eyes. I was struggling to keep my feet, because I instinctively knew that if I went down they would be on me with rocks and bricks and feet and I would never get up again. It was my first experience of mob violence and very nearly my last.

Then Uri was among them. Just over five feet, he wasn't that much taller than they were, but he had a solid blocky body, a gleaming cannonball head and the largest, thickest hands I've ever seen on another human being, before or since. The kids scattered and he stood in front of me, watching me sway on my feet, trying to look at him with the eye that wasn't swollen shut. Without a word, he led me back to his car, where Avi waited behind the wheel, and they took me to their home.

Even while they cleaned me up, bandaged my cuts and stitched up a flap of scalp over my left ear, I remember Avi and Uri arguing about me walking to the car. Avi seemed to think Uri should have carried me, but Uri wouldn't hear about it.

"A man can walk, he walks. No other way." His English was thick, guttural and heavily accented. "Anything else, an insult." It was the first time anyone had ever called me a man.

Over juice and homemade cookies, Uri and Avi took turns showing me how I might have handled the situation better. Some other adults might have given me well-meant but lame advice about making friends or solving problems together or something. These two strange quiet men talked strategy, tactics, and pragmatic advice from a moral viewpoint cold and sharp. After the ugly animal frenzy I had just been subject to, it was a comfort.

The next day, I took their advice, and a fair-sized stick, and caught the worst of the children alone. That afternoon, I didn't go straight home after school. I went to Avi and Uri's house instead.

The walk was peaceful.

*   *   *

I hate cellphones. For some reason my sisters found them a lot easier to manipulate than landlines: the couple of months I'd carried one to feel like a normal member of society had been hell. Even being around one for very long was an invitation for my sisters to pry into my life.

Tabitha called them digital crystal balls.

But Jack Rose's phone sat in my desk drawer. Turned off and the battery removed, I was safe from my sisters and Jack's secrets were safe from me. There weren't many tattoos that day, and Hamish was there to handle the piercing. I had a lot of downtime, Uri's voice a constant presence inside my head. It was almost sundown before I gave in to my curiosity.

The phone lay on top of the Brethren letter. I opened the envelope, read the contents again and put it back. I was stalling.

An opening animation played on the screen as the phone powered up. Of course he had a four-digit PIN for security. It turned out to be his birthday, month and year. I navigated around until his directory of stored numbers came up. The only one I recognized was Pizza Hut.

His list of recent calls, one number was mentioned more than the others. There was one incoming call seventeen minutes long, an outgoing one twice that, and two more outgoing calls to that number last night. Both were brief, under thirty seconds each, but it was the times they were made that made them interesting.

Five minutes apart, Jack Rose called this number immediately before each time he came into my studio.

The number highlighted when I thumbed the cursor over it, leapt to graphic life when I pushed the button to call it. It picked up on the first ring, but there was only silence at the other end. After a couple of seconds, it disconnected.

I called back immediately, and again. The voicemail was two seconds of silence and a beep.

I sat looking at the phone, trying to shake the image of a narrow trail deep in the emerald jungle, the tree branch above me slowly uncurling.

Eight

Once we finished closing up shop for the night, Hamish and I headed downstairs to Murphy's. It catered to the sports and college crowd. Not quite my scene but the drinks were fine, the food better and the location right downstairs more than made up for the jukebox.

It was only eight on a Wednesday night, but Murphy's drew a good crowd all week long. Tall thick boys and men with wide necks and baseball caps drank, laughed and flirted with women who wore lots of hairspray and held serious thoughts on the lives and work and relative merits of Kei$ha and Lady Gaga.

Hamish headed into the throng to find us a table. It wasn't quite standing room only, but I didn't see any free tables, either. Still, I knew better than to second-guess the charm and resourcefulness of my friend, or to waste time trying to figure out how he does it. I elbowed up to the bar for our drinks.

The bartender was a new guy, one I didn't know. I waited for his attention, got my round and left a good tip. Sure enough, Hamish was already sitting at a small table in the corner studying a menu. I set his bottle of beer down in front of him.

"What, not drinking tonight?" He pointed at the ginger ale in my hand.

"I'm taking Bex out tomorrow, so I figured tonight I'd see what I can turn up about last night's bullshit."

"Want company?"

"Thanks man, but I'll be all right. I'm just going to do some visiting, ask a few questions, that's all."

"You got a bad habit of trying to handle all your problems yourself, like you don't have any friends." He took a pull from his beer and leveled his eyes at me. "This thing gets *any* kind of hairy, I don't want to find out afterward I could've had your back and you didn't tell me."

"Deal," I said. I hoped he believed me.

We stopped talking when the barmaid cruised up to us, order book and pen in hand. Hamish looked up at her and said "Hey Kirsty," without losing a beat. He has a perfect encyclopedic memory for names. It's probably a part of what makes him so likable. Kirsty showed him a smile full of dimples.

"Hi guys! Did you hear? Last night this guy got mugged right out in the alley behind the kitchen."

Hamish sounded like this was the first he heard about it, innocent and interested.

"Yeah! One of the cooks called the cops. They took the guy off to the hospital and everything."

We made the appropriate sounds and gave her our orders. She started heading toward the kitchen with it, spun on one heel and came bouncing back to our table.

"Oh Sam, I almost forgot." She reached up under her shirt and pulled down skirt and panties to reveal a thin slice of bare flesh. Just at the mound of her pubis was a small blue butterfly. Its colors shone like a jewel.

"See? It healed perfectly. I never got a chance to show you." She dimpled at me and headed back to the kitchen again.

I noticed Hamish grinning at me.

"What?"

"Mighty friendly little girl, that's all."

"I did that tattoo for her last spring. Healed pretty well, don't you think?"

He gestured at my glass and stood up from the table. "I think it's my round and about time you had another ginger ale."

I left Murphy's warm and pleasantly full from my burger. Hamish stayed behind, talking and laughing with a mixed group of swimmers and divers from the U.

Out in the lot, it was noticeably cooler and a licking breeze had picked up.

I had been racking my brain trying to think of anyone who might have something personal against me, with no luck. I had hurt a few people's feeling over the years, but as far as I knew, any old grudges were settled or those who held them were gone. Certainly, nobody came to mind mad enough at me to hire an armed gunman to take me off.

I just couldn't quite buy the idea either that some random group of religious loony tunes would hate tattooing enough to be responsible for last night. Terrible-toothed Jack Rose and his chinless little friend had a lot of answers I needed. I'd try the address on Jack's driver's license first.

As I pulled out onto Washington Avenue, I saw the advancing storm front, black towers of cloud dragging their misty blue skirts across the landscape and blocking out the sunset.

***

For the best part of an hour, I drove in big lazy loops through the city, radio off, alone with my thoughts. The address on Jack's license turned out to be a dead end: a burned out shell with weeds growing up through the foundation, and I was out of ideas. So I drove, lost in some private place deep inside. The storm front was directly overhead by now, threads of lightning pulsing in its upper reaches.

As the first fat drops clattered against my windshield, Lisa Torres sat beside me in the passenger's seat. The dashboard light hitting her skin evoked images of cold tile rooms and rolling steel drawers.

The dead girl saw me look over at her. She licked her lips and arched her back, made a lewd little face at me.

"Don't you ever get tired of that shit?"

Tired of what, sugar?

Now she made a show of wide-eyed innocence, batting her lashes and sucking one of her fingers. I shook my head and turned back to the road, working my way over to the freeway.

Just as I had for the last six years, I tried to ignore her. With about as much success.

You really don't know what's happening, do you?

I glanced over at her. She had changed. The cadaverous look was gone. Instead of the chalk-white skin and clotted bruising of post-mortem lividity, Lisa once again looked as she had in life. It was easy in that moment to see her as a good kid who just made a few wrong turns in life.

"I know that attack wasn't random, but I still don't know who or why." I missed my turn for the freeway on-ramp, kept going straight instead. "You're the only person I know with a grudge against me, and you're dead."

You do know you're not the only one can see me, right?

"First I've heard about it."

Think about it. There's your family, and they ain't the only ones. Some of them don't even know it.

"So you say."

You ask that girlfriend of yours, See what she says.

I took a turn at random. The poor residential neighborhoods around me eventually gave way to rail flats and grain elevators. In the darkness and rain, the enormous hulking silos and empty barren space around them looked like desolate remnants of an alien civilization.

It was a place that made me vaguely uncomfortable at the best of times. All that heavy infrastructure was built to handle the volumes of much busier times. They were almost like ghost towns now. I got onto Hiawatha, knew that it would eventually carry me back where I wanted to go.

Out in that lunar landscape, there was nothing to check the wind. It moaned across the flats and rocked the car on its springs, sent the icy rain pelting and skutting at the roof. It felt as though God had grown tired of being so sadly disappointed in His Creation but was too lazy to make a proper effort to wipe us from the earth.

Warm and protected in the glass and steel and plastic bubble around us, Lisa and I watched the silvery drops skirl and dance in the headlights as the car carried us through that No Man's Land.

Them two, you think they were just going to fuck y'all up, or would they have killed you? She never looked away from the window when she said it, and I wondered what a ghost would see in the rain.

"I don't know. That's the thing about people waving guns around. By the time you know what they're gonna do, it's too late. I didn't wait to find out the hard way."

Lisa just stared through the windshield. Her head bobbed and lips moved subtly, in time with the thump of the windshield wipers or perhaps just her own thoughts. The landscape around us gradually became more industrial, a part of town built up for the war effort in the 40's, great stone buildings with broken glass in the windows and the names of their original owners in tall steel Art Deco-style letters. Not a light burned in even one of the buildings around me.

"Lisa?"

She turned to me. She could look at me like that sometimes, all big soft eyes and little girl innocence, none of the hardened cynicism of life on the streets and childhood stolen. When she looked at me like that, she looked sixteen years old.

"I'm sorry."

She reached over and touched my knee and looked very, very sad.

I know.

She curled up in her seat then, something in her awkward posture reminding me of a newborn colt. She stared off into the distance and absently bit at the flesh on the side of her thumb.

Eventually the lights of the city rose around us again. When I looked back beside me, the ghost was gone.

Nine

Tattooists of the generation before mine were as lone and dangerous as any of the big cats. They staked out their territory and often fought when another of their kind strayed into it. They were social outcasts, beyond the pale. All of that was different now. Formal art training was commonplace. Tips and techniques, from basic to advanced, were easily found in books, DVDs and the internet. We even had our own television shows.

For the new generation, tattooing was a chance to be *cool*.

The bars change from night to night and month to month, but on any given night of the week, somewhere in Minneapolis just as in any other city in the U.S., the scene was in session. A roomful of tattooists and piercers, collectors, boyfriends and girlfriends and so on all gathered together to drink, flash their jewelry and rolls of cash, lie about how much they were making, swap stories, all the usual stuff.

Mostly, they made the scene just to be part of the scene, to look at each other and tell themselves how cool they were. For almost six months now, the Wednesday night place to be was Resurrection Joe's.

For a wonder I found a parking space right around the corner. Rain hit my car and the sidewalk and street around me with sounds like gunfire. I reached into the back seat for a flannel shirt I keep there. I'd lived here for years, but I was still a Southern boy in my blood and I'd learned that even in summer, you might still need an extra layer or two.

Even with the flannel pulled up around my ears I got thoroughly soaked going thirty feet from my car to the bar. I stepped inside and stood dripping at the entrance before making my way through the room. I let the smoke and the laughter and the sights and the noise of a room full of my peers wash over me. No one stopped their conversation or openly stared at the newcomer. At most, a few eyes here and there tilted briefly in my direction and dismissed me.

Up at the bar, Angeline had another of her outfits on. Tonight it was a black bustier, blue tutu and knee-high combat boots. Her hair was black with vivid blue streaks and her makeup continued the theme.

"Well hello, stranger. Long time no see." Her open and sunny smile was strangely at odds with the Living Dead Girl look. I knew her lipstick would be alternating coats of blue and black. It would have taken forever to put on and would come off sticky and tasting of the cinnamon gum she always chewed.

"Surprised to see you here tonight. Don't you always call these guys, what was it, self-important wank artists?"

"Yeah, but they're *my* self-important wank artists. How you been, Ange?"

She lifted one shoulder in a good-natured shrug, leaned forward at the bar to show me how she'd been. The chrome spikes on her black leather dog collar winked in the light from the cooler beneath her.

"What's your pleasure?" There was no double-entendre intended, at least I didn't think so. But I also remembered how innocent everything seemed right up until the night she came walking out of my bathroom wearing nothing but that collar and those boots. I ordered a ginger ale and left a generous tip.

One thing about my profession. We might flout every anti-smoking law on the books, but as a class we drink like fish and tip like sailors on shore leave. Giving Angeline the change out of a ten for a glass of ginger ale wasn't special treatment.

Ange wasn't a friend in the 'come over and watch the game' sense-- she was a friend in that we'd had a few nights together three years ago and neither of us much regretted it or wanted to go back either. By contrast, her three month affair with Hamish last year would seem downright serious.

As she scooted down the length of the bar to take care of the next group of people waiting for her, I turned and scanned the room for familiar faces. When I saw John, I brought my drink over to his table.

He looked up at me, momentarily pissed at something off behind my shoulder. Then his eyes focused on me and the sunshine broke out across his big soft features.

"Sam!" he yelled, warm and cordial as ever. "I thought you were dead, man!"

It took a second for the penny to drop.

"Oh shit, sorry." I was supposed to have a shading session on my chest after work that night. "I totally forgot, you know it's been a pretty crazy couple days."

"Ah, no harm done. We weren't going to drag the river for your body til at least midnight. Good to see ya anyway! Pull up a pew, church is in session."

At the table with him were another tattooist I vaguely knew named Aaron, an ascetically thin Goth boy with long, curly hair, and two strippers. Like some kind of uniform, the strippers had those strangely waxed eyebrows they all wear, carefully applied lipstick brown at the edges fading to pink inside, and facial expressions as blank and impenetrable as a concrete wall. All three ignored my presence among them, smoked with similar effeminate gestures and kept watching the room over their shoulders.

I pulled up a chair and threw my wet flannel shirt across the back before I sat down. John held his big meaty hand out for a complicated soul-handshake. I only made it halfway through. A ripple of involuntary interest surged around the table.

Seen in a tee shirt, it was obvious I wasn't just some random schlub who knew someone in the profession. I was a member of The Tribe. Both arms, from the wrists up into the cloth above my biceps, were carefully planned contrasts on swirling darks and blazing swathes of color. Since they featured in a profile Skin Art did on John last year, my arms have become more famous than me.

The two women at the table reached out and grabbed my forearm to get a better look at the samurai locked in mortal combat with a Tibetan demon. People take liberties with tattooed flesh they'd never take otherwise. I couldn't imagine reaching out and grabbing *them* to take a closer look, but that's exactly what they did. White-tipped fingernails traced out the interesting bits, and I made sure John got the credit he was due for a fantastic job. Even the sallow Goth leaned in briefly, raised his eyebrows in a way that made his nose seem twice as long and thin as it was, then sat back in his seat to resume scanning the room at large.

"Hey man," John said when I had my arm back, "we oughta finish that Bettie Page piece for my thigh soon. Sometime this weekend?"

"Sure. That'd be great. Have to be after hours, though."

"Yeah, we're in the middle of our busy season too. Way of the world. Cold weather, all the normies cover up and forget all about how much they always wanted that little butterfly. Sun comes out, clothes come off, half the world seems to be tattooed and they come pouring into the shop, desperate for that same damn butterfly. I tell ya, my first couple winters here, I just about starved."

"You got your regulars now though, right?"

John sat back, pleased. He let out a short puff on his cigar and unconsciously patted his belly.

"Thank God for the regulars. After that photo spread in Skin Art, it's been great. Get your picture in the magazines and all of a sudden, you get folks coming in with wild ideas. They want big work, crazy work, and they pay BIG money."

I didn't see the satchel of drawing pads and art books until he lifted it into his lap. He pulled out the new Tattoo Society.

"Which reminds me..." He put on his best satanic grin. "Can I have your autograph, now you're a Big Star and all?"

"Am I the only one waits for the damn thing to come out at Shinder's?"

"Tash always said you oughta put yourself forward more. Looks like she finally went and did it for you"

"Blindsided me with it, to tell you the truth."

We sat awhile, gossiping, talking shop and hanging out. At some point the two strippers got up together to go to the bathroom and never returned. When next I noticed them, they sat at another table. Aaron stayed where he was, quiet and still, removed from the world around him. When I finally worked my way around to the original purpose of my visit, John confirmed he did in fact get a letter from The Brethren as well, but no nocturnal visitors.

"Sorry man, I've been asking around for ya, but no luck. You heard anything, Aaron?" Aaron shook his head. John smiled that Devil's smile. "Looks like you were just born lucky, I guess."

"Story of my life." I let it go, sat back. "Lot of new faces here tonight."

"And more every week. New Yellow Pages comes out, I heard it's supposed to have something like two dozen shops in there."

I whistled. "Lot of new talent."

"If you want to call it that." John made a face. "Lot of shitty work out there right now. That Skin Art piece made me look like God's Gift to the Cover-up, so now I got every fucked-up tattoo in town knocking on my door."

He waved an arm around the room. "Hell, you just *know* half these guys aren't going to be around this time next year."

He was right. We saw it all the time. A tattoo studio is a cheap business to set up and profitable to run. They opened and shut like the life cycle of some sort of colorful insect. In the past eleven years, I had opened one shop, closed it down, spent a couple more years gypsying around and working for other people before I was ready to run my own place again. And I would be considered one of the more stable ones.

"What can you tell me?" I said. John and I weren't that far apart in age, but we were in very different places. He knew his fellow artists as friends, cranky and cantankerous maybe, but friends. I remembered the days when they might break your hands if they thought you were trying to horn in on their territory.

Also, John was basically a likable social guy for whom the tattooing world was a second family. He leaned in conspirational-close and pointed out a table of headbangers who apparently hadn't heard that even Metallica had gone with short hair.

"See those guys over there? Dragon Wizard Ink. They're tracers, fine if you want flash off the wall but don't ask for more. Unfortunately, one of them thinks he's got talent. Aaron spent two hours last week fixing a tiger came outta there."

Next he turned his attention to a group of rockabilly types doing shots and thumping the table. Guys and girls alike sported lots of small, eye-catching tattoos of dice and cats, wrenches and spark plugs. It wasn't a crowd I understood, but I enjoyed their music, fashion and especially their imagery.

"That's both Stray Cat Studios and Boxy's Tattoo. They're two different places, but I don't know why. The artists move from one shop to another, work on each other all the time, hang out together. Date the same girls mostly too, but that's kinda the way of it for all of us if you think about it. One big incestuous family."

One of the artists saw us looking over and raised a shot glass in our direction. John raised his beer in chuckling salute, and continued.

"Anyway, they do good work. If they can keep their brains from running out their ears, at least some of them ought to do alright."

"You ever notice an awful lot of us have some pretty major drug problems?"

"Pretty major problems all around, but what do you want? We get paid cash at the end of every night, and not just a little, either. I know what you mean, though. There's even rumors some of the new places are *selling* out of the shop. That kind of shit we don't need."

"No shit. Any idea who?"

"Why? You looking for a new bad habit? You want, you can just give *me* all your money and I'll hit you in the head with a hammer."

"You know I need that money to buy your mom a little something pretty."

"Asshole. Lemme getcha another round." He held his empty up, caught Angeline's eye and circled his finger to indicate all of us.

The fresh drinks came by way of one of the rockabilly crowd, a young guy with a tall pompadour and a gorgeously colored tattoo of a horseshoe and dice on the inside of his left forearm. We shook hands, and he stopped a while to chat with John. It seemed both Stray Cats and Boxy's had received Brethren letters and didn't think much of it. He admired John's work on my sleeves, made happy sounds at the vampire pinup I did on John's calf and went back to his friends' table with the rest of his drinks.

"What's with Mr. Dark Side over there?" I gestured with my chin to a table in the corner near the bar. The guy sitting at it had his head shaved right down to gleaming skin, no eyebrows and a full-chin goatee that fell all the way past the tabletop. He looked familiar, but I'm terrible at remembering faces.

"Marcus I thought you'd know. You two being neighbors and all." He saw the blank look on my face. "Dark Rites, it's in Dinkytown somewhere, very *'ooooh, scary'*." He wiggled his fingers for emphasis. "So far, everything I've seen come out of there has been wobbly lines, false starts and fucked-up shading. I had a girl come in with a rose looked more like a wineglass, another one had a goddamned *five-legged* horse on her. Worse, Aaron fixed one up where Marcus actually *misspelled* the woman's kid's *name*! I mean, how the fuck do you spell Anne with three n's?"

"I didn't even know they were there."

"Won't be for long. Has that look, you know?" The four year veteran, already used to seeing newcomers sink beneath the waves. I looked back over to the table. A couple of guys in black tee shirts sat with Marcus, and as I watched, a hard-faced woman with blonde pigtails and a naughty schoolgirl outfit came back with her drink and sat on his lap.

"Seems popular, anyway."

"What can I tell ya? No accounting for taste."

"I'm not used to seeing this side of you, John."

"The man misspelled a damn *name*. I know the cream always rises and the sludge always settles and all that, but fuck! How hard can it be to *trace* a fucking name?"

The bald man at the dark table had a trick of lowering his head to stare straight at us. It made his eyes seem to glow from black and empty sockets.

"I'm going to go over and introduce myself. Be polite and all that." He really did look familiar, and the feeling was nagging at me. Also, his stare sent a low-voltage prickle crawling along my neck and arms. It reminded me of pissing off my sister Agatha when I was a kid.

Marcus kept his eyes on me the whole time I was walking over. It was insult bordering on direct challenge, but I figured it was at least partly my fault for so obviously discussing him as we had. After my own experiences starting out all those years ago, I was generally polite to even the least talented new artists. Like John said, the good ones always rose to make a place for themselves and the others faded away without my help.

As I neared the table, the two younger guys broke off their conversation and turned to look at me. The one on the left was frankly fat, with an oily black ponytail, soul patch and Rammstein tee shirt. The one on the right had a lean pinched look about him that put me in mind of Lisa Torres. He had an overgrown mop of dark hair hanging in his eyes, and his shirt had a picture of a naked clown with an erection.

Up close, I could see a thin film of blond stubble on top of Marcus's scalp and blond roots at the base of his beard. His right hand was around the waist of the woman on his lap, his left resting on the tabletop and drumming a small twitchy rhythm. Every finger was covered with silver rings, large and cheap and clunky, and the nails were cut to sharp points. His mouth was a small red bud, delicate and feminine. The girl regarded me with a level stare that said nothing I could do would possibly be of any interest to her, but she had to watch just the same.

"Hi, you must be Marcus. I just heard you've got a new studio. Dark Rites, right? I'm-"

"I know who you are, Samuel Roark." He had a thin soft voice and a way of sniggering through his nose as he spoke. "I know exactly who you are."

"Um, yeah. Anyway, I just heard you've got a place near the U of M too. Dark Rites, right?"

His smile was a black slice in his skull, full of sharp little teeth. His eyes had an unnatural glitter. I thought I saw something red swim up out of them, something ancient and scaled surfacing before it rolled back under the black water.

I knew where I had seen him before. It was an impact like being dropped into that same icy water. His was the apparition I had seen in my home the night before. I felt the cold rise on the back of my neck.

In that sudden way she had, Lisa Torres stood behind his left shoulder, opposite the blonde sitting on his knee. Both women's mouths twisted up in identical predatory smiles.

The woman in the schoolgirl outfit sought and held my eye. Her own eyes sparkled dark, cruel and full of mirth. I could see dirt in the creases of her neck and an angry skin rash on the inside of one wrist. She blew me a kiss.

"Dead man." There was something wrong with her voice, like a Raggedy Ann doll gargling broken glass. When she spoke again, Lisa's lips moved in perfect time with her own.

"The restless dead are always around you, waiting and hungry," they said together. Whether mimicry or something darker, I couldn't tell. The effect was chilling.

Off to the side, Angeline stood at this end of the bar, alert and ready for trouble. Behind the living, Lisa's eyes went wide and her mouth dropped into a round, frightened *O* and she was gone again. It was like she'd never been.

"Nice meeting you too," I said, "see you around."

I turned and damn near fell over Tasha. She was the only person capable of sneaking up behind me, and I have no idea how she always did it. I didn't even know how long she might have been standing there. Running into her everywhere was one of the reasons I didn't do this scene so much anymore.

In the time I had known her, I came to believe Tasha had an almost pathological need to be the center of attention, and she usually dressed for success. Tonight she had on a black velvet sheath that rose from the floor to tie off behind her neck, leaving yards of bare flesh from the sides of her hips to the tips of her fingers. The sleeves of fire and ice were the only color about her. Something about her witchy-green eyes wasn't tracking quite right and her mouth when she smiled had an intoxicated looseness.

"Why Sam." She patted my chest and leaned into me. "We've got to stop meeting like this. People will talk." A stray fingernail brushed my nipple. Probably an accident, but with Tasha nothing was ever exactly what it seemed.

"I doubt they'll say much. I was just leaving."

She had both hands flat on my chest and her weight listed forward. Her boozy breath tickled inside the shell of my ear, and Marcus's stone chip eyes were a physical presence between my shoulder blades. I cupped both her elbows in my hands and moved her back onto her own feet. Her skin was soft and sticky in my palms, so warm it felt like the flesh beneath was packed with hot coals.

"Don't go away mad, Sam." Her voice was a parody of what she intended, husky and slurred.

"No, dead man," came a hissing little voice from behind me. When I looked over, the sharp teeth once again showed in the wet girlish mouth. "By all means, don't go away mad. Join us, for a drink."

"Some other time, maybe. Tasha." I turned her to one side of me, moved past her. She bristled and tossed her head in anger. Icy blue lights flickered in the ends of her hair when she did it, and the green fires burning in her eyes were cold and wild. She wasn't quite finished with me yet.

"Tell me Sam, do you like it?"

I turned back to look, knowing full well I shouldn't. Her back was turned to me, silky hair falling forward over one shoulder. The black velvet dress she wore was open all the way down the length of her back, past the dimples at the base of her spine to the full swell of her buttocks.

Across her shoulders, I'd brought the two sleeves of fire and ice to very nearly meet at the pentagram she'd long ago had inked at the base of her neck. Now, flaring out from beneath the sleeves and trailing down her spine to her tailbone was the most elaborate cutting I had ever seen.

Even in a world of bodysuit tattoos and earlobes stretched to accommodate beer bottles, aesthetic cutting is something of a radical body mod. The artist incises the skin with a surgical scalpel, leaving a design for as long as it takes the cut to heal. Scarring depends on the desire of the collector and the skill of the one with with the scalpel. The deeper the cut, the more vivid the scar. Also the greater chance of severing nerves and causing serious damage.

Because there's no way to effectively shade with a knife,the designs are always linear. Tasha's flowed over her back in loops and whorls and patterns I knew just enough to recognize as occult symbols.

"Well, Sam, what do you think?"

Not for the first time, I wondered if I'd ever really known her at all.

***

About the time I was leaving Resurrection Joe's, in a six-unit apartment building over in Dinkytown a certain New Zealander was still awake. Her lower lip was throbbing where it had been pierced last night, and Kate and Paul, had gone to sleep hours ago. The last time Bex saw her friend, the two women were out raging til dawn every night, but the baby had put a stop to all that. The big night out she'd been promised turned out to be a trip to a steakhouse and home before nine or the babysitter became terribly expensive.

Bex sat in the armchair in the lounge with a single floor lamp on and her new e-reader in her lap. She flicked through the books on the contents screen, opening one and then another, unable to find anything she wanted to read. She knew she was just stalling because she wasn't ready to go to sleep yet.

Despite the rain, Kate and Paul's flat had stayed quite warm, enough so that she had kept the windows opened. After it stopped, the temperature inside steadily rose until it was felt like being clutched in a hot wet fist. Also, the fold-out sofa was horribly uncomfortable, and when she did manage to fall asleep she had the most dreadful dreams of a horrid little slut, skinny and cheap-looking. She wore a tacky yellow boob tube and was covered in blood. Bex dreamed the nasty thing kept whispering to her and calling her utterly vile names. In one dream, she saw the girl's back and it looked like it had been torn apart.

Bex looked down to see gooseflesh crawl up her arms from the wrists up past the elbow. She felt the room go chill, enough to tempt her to dig in her bag for a warm jersey to put on. She had an unmistakable feeling she was being watched, a creeping of the flesh at the back of her neck.

Possibly it was having the curtains open on the large window behind her. Anyone at all outside the apartment could see in. When she stood to draw them shut her eye fixed on a car parked on the street outside, very pale with an extraordinary amount of rust, right up to the door handles. She was sure it was parked there earlier too, when they walked out to Paul's car on the way to dinner.

Of course, residents here parked in the street. Paul's car was only three cars down from the rusty one. As she stood looking at the street below, her face close to the glass and the light from the lamp silhouetting her from behind, Bex saw something through the windshield of the pale rusted car. Something moved in the shadows inside.

As she watched, the cherry dot of a lit cigarette floated up through the blackness behind the steering wheel, flared briefly, and descended into darkness again.

Bex jumped with a start and made a small sudden sound that embarrassed her, even though no one was awake to hear it. She stood up straighter than ever, stepped resolutely to the heavy curtains and pulled them shut with considerable force. She spun on one heel and stomped into the kitchen to boil the kettle for tea.

It was going to be a long time before she would be able to sleep again.

Ten

The man whose missing driver's license said he was Jack Rose felt no pain. Like rancid grease dropped onto a hot grill, his thoughts and memories swirled and burned just out of reach, hidden in a medicated fog.

It had hurt like hell, and he'd thrown up on himself doing it, but Jack had managed to dig the drugs out of his pocket and throw the baggie over his head and into the dumpster with his good arm before the cops got to him. He hadn't gone down on an assault, drugs or weapons beef, any one of them a third offense that would have tagged him a habitual offender and earned him a mandatory twenty year sentence. He claimed to be a mugging victim, wide-eyed and innocent and willing to swear out a complaint against the three black men he said jumped him.

Jack still spent the night in the Emergency Room at Ramsey County and ended up with his arm in a cast. At least the other hand wasn't cuffed to the bedrail in the security wing, a situation he had been in twice before. Instead of an orange jumpsuit and paper slippers, Jack was in his own clothes, sitting in his own chair in front of his own TV.

On the Salvation Army table beside him were two brown plastic bottles, a thirty day supply of painkillers and muscle relaxants, already more than half empty. From time to time, he would pop one or the other, or both, into his mouth and wash them down with tequila from the bottle beside them.

He must have known he had reason to fear. Along his left thigh a .44 Magnum just like Dirty Harry's lay concealed under a newspaper. His right hand was useless and bound up in a cast, but even with that much gun in his weaker hand, the chance of him hitting anyone coming through the door from his chair were good.

There was the sound of a key in the lock on the front door, the sight of a familiar face or the sound of a familiar voice. Jack didn't reach for the cannon in his lap. His friend pulled a kitchen chair around to sit facing him. They probably spoke for a short time.

When his friend walked out the door at or near 6:30 that morning, Jack Rose lay slumped in his own chair in front of his own TV, sightless and still. Four soft-nosed nine-millimeter hollowpoints had flattened to the diameter of nickels on impact and torn bloody high-velocity paths through his chest and abdomen. In that moment of light and thunder and the smell of a thousand burnt matches, Jack learned some awful truths about the life he led and the people he trusted.

A neighbor heard the shots and remembered the time, but did nothing.

Eleven

Ever since I can remember, I was troubled by nightmares. As a child, the bad dreams all had a common theme: in some normal, safe situation, all the adults around me suddenly turned into monsters. They chased me night after night, intent on devouring me. Not too surprising for someone being raised by an addict, my mother with her sudden scary mood swings.

By the end of that single eventful year of my mother's death, being sent to live with my grandmother and beginning my tutelage under Avi and Uri, the character of my dreams changed, as did the waking person I had become. I stopped running away in my dreams, began to stand my ground and fight. The terror after that was that nothing I could do to defend myself would work.

Again, probably not surprising. The bad dreams had tapered away for the most part as I grew older, but that night I once again found myself thrown bolt upright in bed and bathed in sheets of icy sweat. My mind still rang with the bark of a cannon, gunpowder stinging my nostrils and an impact like a great hammer in my hand. A sixteen year old girl had once again died in a sheet of flame.

A lifetime of troubled sleep taught me better than to try to go back to bed after that. The floorboards were smooth and cool under my feet when I swung out of bed and stood in the bedroom window looking out at the night. A pleasant breeze stirred the drapes, last legacy of that night's summer storm. Not for the first time, I thought about that night in New Orleans, wondered if there was any way it might have played out differently.

The clock in the corner read 4:12AM. Too early to be up, too late to go back to bed. I told myself to pretend I was a dairy farmer and reached for my pants.

***

Mickey's Diner was the natural choice to wait out the dawn. Truth to tell, it's one of my favorite places any time of day. It's one of the last remaining Pullman diners in America, built out of an old railroad car and painted its trademark red and yellow. Since it opened in 1934, Mickey's has been a twenty-four hour host to an amazing cross-section of St. Paul and Minneapolis. When I ran away from home, it was the first place I stopped for a meal after the Greyhound dropped me off and I got tired of wandering around.

Not too much had changed since then: sharing a booth in a corner and a couple glasses of water were a young couple who couldn't be out of their teens yet. They had backpacks and dirt, and that desperate look that said they might not have too clear an idea of where they'd be sleeping tomorrow. They also looked heartbreakingly in love and determined to make it work against all odds. I wished them luck. The world can be cruel when you're hungry.

The rest of the diners were the usual mix of white- and blue-collar workers and one old guy whose tweed jacket and leather elbow patches gave him an academic air, all united by nothing more than being awake at this hour. I took a stool at the counter alongside them.

A hundred year old waitress stood across the counter from me, order book in hand. She greeted me with a Norski accent thick as North Woods ice-fishing. Behind her, the wiry guy working the grill looked like a refugee from America's Most Wanted, but that was fry cooks everywhere. I gave the waitress my order, got a 'ya sure, you bet' in reply.

Over the years, I've eaten here once or twice a month on average and at every hour of the day and night. A couple hours earlier, the place would have filled with diners emptying out of the clubs, slightly lit and talking too loud. Before that, the evening crowd would be kids out on dates, a few older couples and the odd shift worker coming on or going off work. Days, Mickey's got everything from students and tourists to recovering addicts and others from the Dorothy Day Center across the street. Much as I hated the odd bout of insomnia, this was my favorite hour here. The food tasted better, somehow.

Waiting for my breakfast to come up and watching the cook effortlessly handle the mix of burgers, eggs and pancakes on the grill, I couldn't help overhearing the kids in the booth counting change and holding a whispered debate. I made no particular effort, but it's a small diner: the corner booth was less than six feet from my end of the counter. Before too long, the waitress came out from around the counter to stand at their table. She held her order pad significantly in her hand. They ordered coffee and soup and held hands across the white formica. There was something touching in the way they looked at each other.

Back around the other side of the counter, she put my plate in front of me and gathered up two cups and a coffeepot for the teens. I looked down at my breakfast-- sausage, eggs and pancakes, glass of juice-- and gestured her over.

"Ya?" Her look implied she'd seen it all in the last century or so and the sooner I quit using the time she had left, the happier she would be. I gestured at my food.

"Give 'em both one of these, on my check."

She shrugged, utterly indifferent, and moved off to bring the teens their coffee.

"You didn't have to do that, man," said the boy in the booth. "I mean, thanks, but you didn't have to."

It was my turn to shrug. "Bout a million years ago I got off a bus here, seventeen years old and less than thirty bucks in my pocket. I guess I remember what it was like."

"What'd you do?"

"Got a room, got a job, busted my ass and saved every penny. Worked out okay, but not without a lot of rough going, too."

When I had decided to see the new day in from the front counter at Mickey's, the natural thing to do was to grab a book. It was an old favorite, *Tales of the Jazz Age* by F. Scott Fitzgerald. I sat with my hot tasty breakfast and bottomless cup of coffee while Bernice once again bobbed her hair. I never could decide which of Bernice's weaknesses was more irritating to me: that the character let her pride push her into the dare, or that once she showed she had the stones to go through with the haircut, she was devastated at the fallout. I was surprised not to find Lisa Torres at my elbow to point out the parallels.

I looked through the long front window at the street outside. There's nothing quite like St. Paul at six o'clock on a Thursday morning. Even though its officially the state capitol, the city has been all but a suburb of Minneapolis for almost a hundred years. Six AM on a weekday in June, it was like finding yourself in one of those movies where all the people on earth mysteriously vanish overnight. Except for the quiet menace of the occasional slow-cruising police car, the streets were deserted. The teenagers in the booth had long since vanished.

As I paid my check, the waitress shook her leathery head and tapped the bill with one long fingernail.

"You shouldn'ta paid for them, ya know. It don't do no good."

"Can't do any harm either, can it?"

"Can if they start thinking they only gotta put on them puppy eyes and good folks'll pay their way for them." She made change for my hundred, completely ignored the ten I dropped in her tip jar.

"Do them some harm too, they go out there thinking people're all nice. They're not. Lot of bad folks out there hiding behind a smile and nice talk. One of them kids trusts the wrong one, and it's no good, don'cha know."

"You might have a point there," I said, "but there's a lot of good people in the world too, and I wouldn't be here today if some of them hadn't lent me a hand."

"I just hope those two don't wind up in a ditch somewhere just because they got in the habit of accepting handouts from strange men." She crossed her arms and turned away from me.

Twelve

One good thing about a sleepless night: all that extra time. Even after a long breakfast and a morning walk down by the Saint Anthony Falls, I still got into work an hour early. The food and the walk both helped, but I still felt grainy and washed out, like a TV channel that won't quite come in right. Waiting at my feet was another plain white envelope. I left it on the desk while I did my morning cleaning.

Once the shop was ready to go, I got a bottle of water out of the mini-fridge, brought it over to the desk and sat down to read envelope's contents. It was more or less what I expected.

*HELLFIRE will be yours for Eternity. Cease your
Wickedness and Look to your Immortal Soul.*

I dropped it in the bottom drawer of the desk with its companion and opened up *Tales of the Jazz Age* again. I had time to read two more stories before my first customer of the day.

My booking that day was an Oriental dragon. It was a big piece, basically a half sleeve, and I took the whole day doing it. The outline, solid blacks and graywashes I did in the first pass, a couple of hours. The cool tones came next: blues and purples in the background mostly. Lack of sleep was a weight behind my eyes, pressing me into the ground, but after a break in the afternoon we were ready to start working the reds and oranges and yellows into the dragon's scales. The lightest colors, pinks in the cherry blossoms, shots of white for highlights, would come at the end.

Finally I finished the last highlights in the dragon's eyes and teeth, wrapped the client's arm in Saran Wrap and accepted the thick sheaf of ATM-crisp twenties for the work. I went in back to was the glove powder off my hands, came out to find my ghost lying back on one of the waiting room couches. She stretched her arms over her head and smiled at me.

"What do you want, Lisa? Come to tell me I'm in danger, make more dark threats? Talk more shit about Bex? I'll pass."

Is that any way to talk? Anyone'd think you hadn't missed me.

I turned away, only to find her standing behind the desk, between me and the back room.

They're still coming for you, you know.

"I think I can handle those two."

They were just the tip of the iceberg, baby. Just the tip of the iceberg.

"What do you know about it?"

More than you think, smart guy.

"Liar." I walked straight at her to the sink. Just before I would have walked through her, she vanished. I flicked on the taps, heard her voice behind me.

Your little girlfriend's part of it too. Originally it was just going to be you, but now they'll kill her if they get the chance.

I concentrated on washing my hands. The cool water felt good, and I knew from past experience that the worst thing I could do with Lisa was to let her know she got to me. She leaned in whisper-close, gave me her granite headstone purr.

You think she's safe now? Do you?

I reached for the paper towels, dried my hands, left her standing by the sink as I headed back to the reception desk.

The waiting area was still empty, so I took a seat at the desk, opened up my book to the last short story. One thing about a slow time in a tattoo shop, it's dead slow. You have to have something to do, or you'll go insane in less than month.

Might even start talking to dead teenagers.

As if on cue, Lisa walked past me again, as though she just happened to be strolling from some indeterminate space off to my left into the waiting area on my right. She trailed her fingertips along the desktop as she went, paused at the corner of the desk to look back over her shoulder.

That little foreign girl of yours is a good kisser. You tell her i said so.

"What?"

"Um, I'm not interrupting anything, am I?" I looked up and saw Bex framed in the doorway, more beautiful than ever.

"I know I'm a bit early, but I got tired of sitting around the house and wound up in the neighborhood. Is that okay?"

"Better than okay. Let me get you something from the fridge. Coke or Sprite okay?"

"Sprite's fine, but I'd love a water if you have it."

"One water it is, then."

I headed into the back room for the little mini-fridge Hamish and I keep there. It sat on the floor, cartons of folding paper towels stacked on top of it. I bent down to get a couple bottle of water, found my nose inches from Lisa's denim legs.

The ghost bent down to my level. Her skin looked warm and alive, but her eyes still told the cold dead truth.

She shot me a smile I could no way interpret, blew me a kiss and vanished.

***

When I brought her water back out, I found Bex already sitting on one of the waiting room couches, clicking pages on the e-reader I had given her. I looked over her shoulder. It was *The Woman in White*, and she was already more than halfway through.

"Fast reader."

"Just heaps of time, I'm afraid. I didn't sleep very well last night, little else to do."

"Hey," I said. "I only had the one tattoo to do today. Why don't we get out of here a little early tonight?"

"You sure?"

"Let me check with the owner." I smiled and reached for my keys.

Thirteen

I took her to the river. Mark Twain's mighty Mississippi begins somewhere in northern Minnesota. When I lived in New Orleans, the river was a great constant presence, too wide to see all the way across in places. Up here, it's a little more than a stone's throw wide, narrow enough that I swam across it a couple times in my skinny-dipping youth. It's also polluted enough to make my swimming in it a pretty stupid thing to do.

It's lovely down here, especially in the summer. The land on either side of the river has been left as parkland, a popular spot for joggers, roller-bladers and cyclists to get their exercise. And plenty of people like Bex and me, just out for a walk. We strolled along, talking about nothing in particular, enjoying the beautiful day and each other's company.

At one point, we stopped at a good spot to look out over the limestone cliffs around us, the sun dancing on the river's surface, the cool green trees. We were on the Minneapolis side, looking over at St. Paul. Without being too obvious about it, I stole a quiet glance over at the young woman at my side. Maybe it was just that straight tall way small people have of standing, but there was quality to the lines of her, something free and proud that had more in common with trees and rocks and sun and water than concrete or glass. She truly was beautiful.

She stretched her arms high over her head and let out a little kitten yawn. "I could really go for a good cup of coffee."

"You said you didn't get much sleep last night."

"Too right. I was up real late, then bad dreams when I *did* get to sleep."

"About the same for me," I said. "I've been up since 4:30 this morning."

"Ouch. That does explain those bags under your eyes, though."

"I could have said the same, but I was being too polite to mention it." That earned me a great smile, but then something clouded over behind her eyes and she bit her lower lip.

Some subtle quality had gone out of the moment right then, and without thinking about it, we turned our steps back in the direction of the car.

For some reason, Bex being lost in her own private places seemed to make it that much easier for me to get caught up in mine. In a way, Lisa's comment about Bex came as a relief. The dead girl was far too bitter and angry to stand the prospect of me in a happy relationship. I knew she'd try something, and now I thought I knew what. I supposed it was better than a lot of other things she'd done in the past. Who knows? Maybe she was jealous.

It was great being out of doors that afternoon. Warm without being too hot, cool in the shade, with a soft breeze moving through the leaves overhead. I put the dead girl from Texas out of my thoughts, gave my attention back to the young woman from the South Pacific at my side.

"Penny for your thoughts?"

She made that batting at cobwebs gesture again. "Oh, nothing really. I was just thinking about my nightmares last night. They all had the most dreadful girl in them. Cheap little thing, perfectly horrid." She put her arms around herself as though that beautiful summer day were suddenly cold.

"She was all bloody, with the most terrible wounds. When she turned around, I could see white bits of bone around her spine."

She had to repeat her next words before I heard them. I felt as though my blood had turned to ice.

"Sam, I said can I ask you a question?"

"Huh? Yeah, sure. What?"

"Who is Lisa Torres?"

Fourteen

"Sam? Is something wrong? Are you okay?"

"How did you hear that name?"

"I don't know. It just popped into my head. Are you sure you're okay? You don't look well."

I should have known something like this would happen. Not this exactly, but something like it. There was no way a guy like me could be with someone so sweet and good and real, even for a couple of weeks, without some element of my shameful past rising up to spoil it. It wasn't that I wanted to hide those details, just that I was afraid it was way too soon to bring them up.

I made the silent decision to face up to the situation, the way I'd faced up to everything else. When I began to speak, my voice sounded flat in my ears. It was the voice of a stranger.

"Six years ago, I was living down in New Orleans at the time, tattooing out of a little shop called Poppabilly's. One night, this street kid came in. She was a runaway out of East Texas, one of thousands just like her there. She wanted-"

"She wanted a love heart tattoo, with no name, just an empty space in the banner," Bex whispered. A chill ran up past my shoulder blades and into my scalp. Outdoor sounds were the only ones around us for some time before I continued.

"She got her tattoo. Talking to her, she wasn't such a bad kid. Screwed up, trashy and nervous, but all right."

"Did you fancy her?"

"No, nothing like that. It's just, I'd see all these people down there who were abused as kids, damn near everyone in town it seemed, all just throwing their lives away. It was like, God handed them a pretty bad deal at the start of things, and they were just determined to wallow in it."

"What were you doing there, Sam?"

I wanted to give any of the standard excuses I gave whenever anybody asked. I was surprised to hear the words that actually came out of my mouth.

"Trying to find bottom myself, I guess..."

Bex bit her bottom lip but said nothing.

"Anyway, five minutes to midnight August the third, she comes back into the shop, only this time she's lit up on black speed and cheap wine and she's got a big old .357 Magnum tucked in the front of her jeans."

"It was a silver color, with black tape on the handle," came Bex's creepy whisper. "She also had on a yellow polyester boob tube, real trashy. She knew it and just didn't care."

Bex snapped out of whatever private space she had been in, shook herself all over and turned her attention back to me.

"What happened then, Sam?"

"She went for her gun, I went for mine. She got there first, but her shot missed. Mine didn't."

"Lisa Torres is the name of the girl I shot to death that night."

Bex was quiet for a long time then. We got to the car, and she sat curled up in her seat, chewing the flesh at the pad of her thumb in a gesture eerily like that of Lisa Torres the night before.

"I'll take you home if you want."

"Where were we going to go?"

"I figured Da Vinci's, over in St. Paul."

"Do they have a children's menu and high chairs?"

"I don't think so."

"Then by all means, let's go." She broke out in the most delightful impish smile, but I could see the strain around her eyes.

I put the car in gear and headed down toward the Lake Street bridge and across the river to St. Paul. I didn't think to look for anyone following us.

Fifteen

Leaving the restaurant after dinner, I put one hand around her waist and saw her smile up at me. It was as beautiful an evening as anyone could ever ask for, clear and warm and still. The afternoon heat still drifted up gently off the sidewalks, and the air around us was full of fragrance and promise.

I pulled her close and we stopped there a minute, sharing a kiss soft as the skin of a ripe dark cherry.

The one-way street we parked on was deserted: the only company in sight were the colorful fiberglass sculptures of Peanuts characters on the sidewalks. Our smallest whispers still echoed faintly off the sides of the tall buildings all around us. As I held the car door open for Bex, the sound of a grinding starter turning over a powerful engine with a bad muffler was startlingly loud.

We both snapped our heads up the street in the direction of the dark cloud of exhaust rising from the parked car up the street. I felt Bex stiffen against me.

"That's the car. The same car I've seen parked outside my window." - parked outside my window last night.

"Wait here."

I pressed the car keys into her hand and started walking up the center of the street to the idling car. It was a pale yellow Plymouth, so faded it was almost white. Rust from twenty or thirty winters of salted roads had crept from the undercarriage to claim the metal right up to the door sills in some places. The streetlight overhead reflected brightly in the windshield, hiding the driver from view.

I got within six feet from its front bumper when a loose fan belt on the Plymouth let out an unholy squeal and the car launched out towards me.

I jumped a few feet to my left and the Plymouth was past me, rocketing down the deserted street and whipping around the first corner in a skreetch of agonized tires. I was left standing in a blue-black cloud of acrid smoke. I saw neither the license plate of the car nor its driver.

Taking Bex home, I kept a careful eye on the the rear view mirror, hoping to be able to tell if we were being followed. All I could see were the general shapes of headlights behind me. I got a terrific headache from the eyestrain, but that was all.

Back in her neighborhood, I made a circuit around her block for caution's sake and found the rusted-out Plymouth parked down the street at the corner. I cruised past as though I hadn't noticed and parked at the curb in front of her friend's apartment building.

Bex said, "That was him, wasn't it."

"Same car, yeah. And he was out her last night, too?"

"Until 2:30. Once I turned out the lamp to go to sleep, I heard the car start, looked out the window when it drove away."

"I don't like this."

"It's them, isn't it? Those bastards who were going to shoot me."

I didn't answer.. Avi and Uri had a saying. Once is bad luck, twice is coincidence, but three times, it's enemy action. I've had a pretty uneventful life these past few years. All this shit had to be related.

"I keep feeling a cold spot where that man pressed that gun to my forehead."

I covered her hand with my own.

"Nobody's going to shoot you while I'm around."

I wished I felt as confident as I sounded. The back of my mind was already beginning to buzz with demands for action. I've never been good at concealing my thoughts, and Bex watched the side of my face with eyes that didn't miss a thing.

"Sam, what are you going to do?" she asked in a stern voice.

"We can drive away again, see if he follows. Catch him out on some lonesome stretch of road and have a little talk." I couldn't believe I was thinking like this again. Or that I hadn't ever really stopped.

"What if he doesn't? Kate and the baby are up there." Her voice was flat and final and made me admire her more than ever.

"Then there's only one thing to do. I'm coming up with you."

She shot me a mischievous grin.

"Kate and the baby, remember? I'm the one on the foldout couch."

"Good to see you've still got your sense of humor, but that's not what I meant."

Bex let us in through the security door at the front of the building with a spare key her hosts had given her. I followed her up the steps to the third floor. If there was anything finer than standing behind Bex and watching her walk up a flight of stairs, I didn't know what it was.

It was a small building, only two units running the length of the building on each floor. On Bex's floor two front doors stood facing each other across a carpeted hallway. One door was labeled 31, the other 32.

She stopped and rocked back on her heels, gestured to 32. "Well, this is me."

Her gray eyes were soft and luminous. The tiny ring of gold around the edge of the pupil seemed to sparkle with a light all its own. Her mouth softened. Her head tilted up toward mine.

I put my hands softly on her waist, thrilled at the touch of warm bare flesh there, and bent down into the most amazing kiss of my life. Soft, delicate and full of barely restrained fire.

A hundred years later, I came back into my body and my eyes swam back into focus. Bex freckled me an impish grin. She twined her hands around the back of my neck.

"Stupid sleeping baby," she said. We kissed again.

"Bad form for me to bring a strange man home, I suppose." She had the most adorable way of biting her lower lip when she said it. I kissed the spot she bit, felt the round steel ball of her labret with my own lower lip.

"Don't forget, you've also got a stalker looking up at the windows."

That cooled both our moods. Bex stepped back out of my arms and placed a gentle hand on my cheek.

"Be careful, Sam."

***

Once Bex was safely locked inside her friend's apartment, I headed down the hallway and took the back stairs out to the alley. These buildings were all built to a standard plan with only minor variations, and the back alley is an important feature of life here. On every block in the Twin Cities, the back alley is where the trash is collected, where the homeowners garage their cars, and quite often where a neighborhood reveals a funky, fun, colorful side that lends a bit of humanity to the pristine street faces.

The back alley also makes it possible to leave without being seen from the street.

I used the alleys to circle around the corner where the Plymouth was parked and come up on it from behind. No dirty exhaust cloud rose from the exhaust pipe, and the dark head behind the steering wheel was hunched down by the dashboard, peering intently through the windshield at apartment 32 in the building across the street.

The driver's door was unlocked.

I managed to get right up to the door without being noticed, settled my weight down nice and low, eased my left hand out until it rested on the door handle.

Even as I snatched open the car door and reached inside for its occupant, everything went sticky and slow again. I could hear the thunk and tumble of the door mechanism as it opened, feel the stubborn resistance of rusted hinges. I saw the slow-motion ripple that flowed through the skin of the driver's neck as fear and cold and the terrifying certainty of his own doom sped through him.

He tried to launch his weight forward, upward and backward all at the same time, and all in the confined space of the front seat. The result was a sort of spastic flailing of limbs. I had about a day and half to watch my fist close on the neck of his black nylon tank top.

The leverage was all in my favor. The chinless little man came flying out of the Plymouth and collided awkwardly with the sidewalk in front of me. I got a knee into his spine and my left hand on his throat to stifle his cries and crank on the pressure any time he tried to move his hands. My rapid search turned up an enormous cannon, a Desert Eagle in some large caliber, stuffed down the front of his pants. There was also a folded straight razor in his pocket.

I bent right down until my lips very nearly touched his ear, smelled dandruff and oil and that awful burnt-styrofoam scent. I whispered the truth about his situation to him, felt the fight go right out of him.

We both got into his car then, moving slow and gentle. I kept the Desert Eagle trained on him. He kept his hands in sight at all times. The Plymouth started on the third try and we drove away, minding the speed limit and obeying all the stop signs.

We headed north, away from the city and its lights.

Sixteen

As the city lights faded behind us, the chinless little man began to cry. At first, his hands just knotted and twisted on the steering wheel and silent tears tracked down his cheeks. Then the sniveling began. It grew in intensity until he was crying in big gusting sobs. A string of drool hung from his lips. Despite the two-day beard and acne-scarred cheeks, he resembled nothing so much as an overgrown child.

I racked the slide on his pistol and wasn't surprised to find he already had a live round in the pipe, same as his partner the other night. The sound broke right through his crying. I don't think he even heard me snick on the safety afterward for some measure of safety.

"I don't wanna die, man." His voice, rough and furry, was very different from the one he spoke with a couple of days ago.

The lower half of his face had a lumpy deformed look. His cheeks were swollen and inflamed, and the the loose gobbling line from the base of his nose into his shirt collar had a puckered detour where he'd lost teeth up front. He was a mess.

"What's your name?" I kept my voice devoid of the animal pity and dirty shame I felt.

"T, T-Tommy...Tommy Green."

"Listen to me, Tommy Green. Shut up and be a good boy, you might just walk out of this yet. Take this next exit up here, then turn right at the crossroads."

He followed my directions, whining to himself and hiccuping softly. Sometimes he punctuated it with a loud snort, wet and snotty, wiping his nose on his bare forearm with its matted black hairs and tough-guy Grim Reaper tattoo.

Once we were off the highway, the country night was black around us. The Plymouth seemed to float in place. The road rushing beneath the headlights was nothing but a shabby illusion. We were going nowhere, and Tommy Green's weeping was the perfect soundtrack for the trip.

Avi and Uri, the two Israeli killers who were my role models growing up, were the two hardest men I ever knew, but also two of the most honorable. They were both soldiers before they began their careers with the Mossad, and they still retained a strong sense of patriotism for their country, despite the way it had treated them. The Desert Eagle in my fist was Israeli-made, popular in the States mainly because it looked bad-ass on film and so found its way into just about every movie made since the mid-90's. I knew what they would say about it, could almost hear Uri's dismissive sneer. *"Too much gun."* Both of them were necessarily fluent with a wide variety of civilian and military weapons, but they felt that anything more than a .22 was 'too much gun', and that cocked-and-locked was a gunfighter's death wish.

It didn't take much imagination to know what they would think of Tommy. The little toad wanted so desperately to be a tough guy he'd probably do any amount of evil just to make himself believe it. But maybe I was making him more complex than he really was. In Avi's words, *"Why wonder? If you must shoot, you shoot. If not, not."*

I didn't want to kill Tommy Green, but I needed him to believe that I might. I felt grimy and shabby for the way I was about to abuse the sad sack of shit, but I reminded myself that he was the one intruding into innocent people's lives, not the other way around.

Eventually, I had him kill the headlights and turn into a cow pasture. By the time the car was hidden out of sight of the road, he began to wail all over again. I turned off the car, took the keys out of the ignition.

He made a mad scramble for the door handle, didn't even get it unlocked before I rabbit-punched the base of his skull, just about hard enough to take the strength out of him, not so hard he went into convulsions. Against my better judgment, I took a fistful of his dirty hair. The muzzle of the Desert Eagle would have seemed a yawning gulf held right in front of his eye. A long string of drool fell from his mouth and puddled in his lap.

"Sit down, stay still and shut up, Tommy. You make another play, I just might blow a chunk of meat out of you. This is a mighty big gun you got here. What do you think, would it actually blow your leg right off at the knee, or would you still have a little flap of skin or something?"

He sat petrified in the driver's seat. I slowly sat back on my side again. I kept the barrel of the gun trained on him. I knew from experience it made an impression.

He slumped forward until his forehead rested on the steering wheel. His voice was a despairing croak.

"I don't want to die..."

"Tommy, listen to me. Why did you and Jack come into my shop? What was the plan there?"

"I don't know," he said. "Jack said. It was Jack's thing. He had the gun, he was gonna do it."

"Do what? Rob me? Kill me?"

Tommy made a diffident little shrug. Didn't know, or didn't care.

"Tommy..."

"We were supposed to do you. Anybody with you. Jack, he, he said we'd get a thousand."

"Were you armed too?"

He didn't answer until I prodded him with the toe of my shoe.

"We didn't mean nothing by it. We were just, just, I don't know. Jack said we were gonna get a thousand."

"Were you armed that night, Tommy?"

He shook his head yes.

"Who hired you two? Who was going to give you the thousand dollars for murdering me and an innocent girl?"

"I don't know."

"*Who,* Tommy?"

He shrugged, spoke so low it was hard to hear him. His broken front teeth gave him a terrible lisp.

"Don't know," he said. "It was all Jack's idea. He made the deal, brought the pieces. It was all his idea. We didn't mean nothing."

"Where can I find Jack, Tommy?"

"Like you don't know."

"Where, Tommy?"

"Fuck you!" The tears started streaming hot and fresh again. "B-buh, bastard, you know you did it. Why are you doing this to me?" There was more, but I lost the rest of it in his blubbering.

"Where. Is. Jack?"

"Right where *you* left him, asshole! I didn't call the c-cops or nothing. He was my goddamn BROTHER, you motherfucker! We didn't mean nothing. Honest." He paused to wipe his nose on his sleeve again. "Please man, please, please, please. I don't wanna die. Please."

"You saying your brother's dead?"

"Like you don't know." Now he was sullen, bitter, but he gave me the address anyway.

"You two have different last names," I pointed out.

"After our dads."

"One last thing, Tommy. You've been following that girl who was in the shop that night. Why?"

"Saw you with her, after. You fucked me up pretty good, but not so's I couldn't still follow the two of you back to her house. I was gonna, I don't know."

In the back seat of the Plymouth, Lisa Torres sat with her arms locked across her chest, glaring daggers at the chinless little man up front. I wondered what was up with that.

"Your brother know you found her place?"

"Nuh. Never got a chance to tell him, ask him what we oughta do."

I thought a moment, made a decision.

"You're out of this now, Tommy. You understand? Out. You got a second chance here, something not everyone gets in this life." My eyes flicked to the backseat before I knew they'd done it. "Get out of town, Tommy. Go visit relatives, friends, check into rehab, whatever."

Originally, I meant to leave him out in that pasture to make his own way home as best he could. Instead, I left him at the Greyhound station in Norston with fifty dollars.

I got a lot of sloppy thanks as he got out of his own car. I offered him one last word of advice.

"Tommy, before you go, there's something I just want you to think about. Whether you believe me or not, I'm not the one who killed your brother. I don't know what all else you two might've been into, but if I had to make a guess, I'd say you might want to look at whoever hired you two to murder me. Pissed off at poor performance or just covering his tracks, I don't think the Cities are too safe for you right now."

"You got it man. Anything you say."

"And Tommy?"

"Yeah?"

"Come around Bex again, and I'll blow out your liver. Got it?"

Seventeen

First thing I did driving off in Tommy Green's now-stolen car was to pop the clip on the weapon and throw it out the window. I managed to break down the gun itself and wipe my prints on my tee shirt without having to pull over. I threw both the upper half and, twenty seconds later, the lower out the window. I was still licensed for concealed-carry in Minnesota, but the last thing I needed was to be pulled over and find out the pistol had been used in a string of murders or something.

I got back to the Cities, left the rusted-out Plymouth in the parking lot of a twenty-four hour bowling alley on a bus route that would take me back to Dinkytown and my car. The bowling alley was seriously down-market: Tommy's Plymouth didn't look a bit out of place.

When Hamish showed up to give me a ride back to my car, I was sitting in the grass at the far end of the lot savoring the warm summer night, the smell of the fields, the bright spill of stars in the summer sky.

I felt alive.

On the way back, I filled him in on the events of the night and my conversation with little Tommy Green. After I finished, we sat together in silence. In the glow of the dash lights I could see the knot of muscle at the corner of Hamish's jaw flex and bunch as he digested all that I told him. His face looked like it was carved from hardwood.

When he finally did speak, the first thing he asked was, "No shit, she's really been dreaming about shit out of your past you haven't told her?"

"I just about freaked. It was like being around my sisters or something."

"You seriously think she's got that witchy-thing?"

Actually, there was another alternative, but I couldn't talk about it with Hamish without bringing Lisa Torres into it. We shared everything, but not that. She was my private burden.

"She's got something," I said instead, "maybe not as much as my sisters or Grandma Roark. Or even my mother, what little I remember."

Hamish steered the conversation away from the subject of my mother with admirable tact.

"Who'd have thought?" he said. "Only one *I* would have picked for a bit creepy was old Tash. Always something more than a little bit off about that one."

"I tell you she was at Joe's last night? Angie says hi, by the way."

"If I know Tash," Hamish said, "there'll be just two things she can't stand. Hearing the word 'no' and not having you on her string." He grinned and chucked me on the shoulder. "You've done both. Good for you."

"You never did like her much, did you?"

"She's poison."

"You never said anything."

"You wouldn't have listened."

"Might've."

"Wouldn't," he said. "And there wasn't any need. You were so fucked up and lonesome, there was no way you were going to hear sense from anybody. I might've made an issue out of it, but one look at her and it was obvious she wasn't going to last. That girl played with you till she got tired and the only one didn't see it coming was you." He cut his eyes over to me in the dark. "Just seemed best to wait it out, be ready for you when you need it."

"You're a good friend, Hamish."

"Yup."

"Modest, too."

"I was born in Texas. We don't do modest down there."

"Ask you something?"

"Nope."

"What do you think of Bex? Be honest."

"Nothing like ol Tash. Truth to tell, she actually gives me a little bit of hope for you yet."

"I have to tell you, it's intimidating as hell sometimes. She so obviously deserves about two steps better than my very best. She's that special."

"Just remember, whatever she's looking for, she sees it in you. Just be yourself and you'll be fine."

"Thanks."

"That'll be eight dollars." His smile was infectious. I was feeling fine and warm and happy until Hamish brought me back to earth.

"Sam, you do realize those two meltdowns were there to kill you that night?"

"Yeah."

"And that whoever hired them already got rid of the one who might've told you anything about his employer?"

"The thought has occurred, yes."

"This is serious. Even more than we thought."

I didn't say anything.

He said, "Don't do anything stupid, Sam. You understand me? You're not in this alone."

***

The lights were still on at Bex's when we pulled up, so I risked a quick blip on the buzzer for apartment 32. The intercom squawked and the security door unlocked for me.

Bex met me on the stairs and threw her arms around me. She held on tight, put her whole body into it.

After a time, I said, "Not that I'm complaining or anything, but what have I done to deserve this?"

As nearly as I could make out from the tiny voice buried in the side of my neck, she saw the whole thing from the living room window and was sure she saw a big shiny gun, but we drove off and she wasn't sure who drove off with who or what happened and she was worried about me the whole time. I held her and stroked her back and assured her that everything was fine and that the dirty little creep would never bother her again.

She pulled back her head until it was six inches away and held my face between her palms. Her eyes were huge and searching and lovely and afraid and full of concern.

"Sam, what did you do?"

"He's just a fuck-up who got in way over his head. I gave him busfare and left him at the station. A new start might do him some good."

Feeling those gray eyes look right into the meat of my shabby, screwed-up, honest little soul, I was grateful the encounter played out way it did.

I couldn't lie to this woman, and I didn't want to lose her respect, either. The only way through it was to live up to who I could be and hope my best was good enough in her eyes. There are worse fates.

"I'd invite you up," she said, "but Paul just got the baby down to sleep again when you buzzed."

"A little tense up there?"

"I don't get it. I made such an effort to go out of my way and stay with them because they were so keen to have me, they don't have a bit of time for me when I get here, then they get upset that I'm enjoying myself anyway."

She waved a hand in front of her face, clearing mental cobwebs.

"I don't mean to whinge. It's not your problem." She put her arms around my neck again, more gently this time. Her lips were full, impossibly soft.

A long time later, she pulled back.

I saw her nipples hard and straining at the thin white tee shirt. A bright red flush bloomed across the center of her chest. She seemed as worked up as I was.

"Tomorrow," was all either of us could say.

Eighteen

The next morning I made a run down the street for sandwiches and a pulpy cardboard tray of coffees. When I came back, Hamish looked up at me and gestured with his chin to one of the couches in the waiting room.

The kid sitting on the couch had a mop of hair hanging down into his eyes and a lean pinched look to his face. Long-fingered hands at the ends of thin wrists. Clean tee shirt, 50's pin-up queen Bettie Page dressed up as a devil girl. The bottom edge of some big, gray, out of focus tattoo peeked out from under his shirt sleeve.

His name was Pete, and he had a brown cardboard portfolio, the kind they make you buy in art school, propped between his feet.

The kid looked up at me, full of expectation. He stood up to shake my hand, stumbled when he knocked his portfolio over. He made a couple of bends and dips reaching for it. For a minute, I was afraid he was going to knock something over. Up close, I could see networks of blue veins under the surface of his pale skin, dark smudges under bloodshot eyes. We sat down on the couch together and checked out his art.

He put a fair amount of thought into the portfolio he showed me. No botchy tattoos done with homemade machines or clumsy tribal designs in magic marker. Instead he showed me still lifes in pencil or charcoal so that I could see he understood light and shadow, had the ability to make his hand render what his eye saw. He had watercolors and pastels on a variety of subjects, giving me a sense of how he worked with color. A couple of pencil portraits done from photographs. Once he knew how to make the needles do what he wanted them to, Pete was going to be a terror in the world of portrait tattoos.

But it was with the cartoon characters he really shined. Blue-pencil roughs finished with bold sure strokes of dark graphite. He had a real feel for it. The kid made Spongebob, Donald, Bugs and the Powerpuff Girls stand, sit, move, interact and seem believable.

"Not bad, Pete, not bad. Where'd you go to school?"

"I got my two-year from MCAD in May." The Minneapolis College of Art and Design was one of the best in the country, with a bit of a reputation.

"I heard it's a real pressure cooker there."

"Yeah, almost half my freshman class dropped out that first year." He shrugged. "But once you got through that, the rest was a breeze."

"Why not go the full four then?"

"Money. I ran out, figured it was time to see what I can do for a living."

I sat with the cardboard portfolio on my knees, picking up one sheet of paper after another.

"Tried it out with the needles yet?"

" Dark Rites." He squirmed when he said it.

"You where sitting next to Marcus that night."

"Two days I'm there, the guy puts a machine in my hand and turns me loose on the clients. It wasn't pretty."

"I started out the hard way too, self-taught. It takes time to make the machine behave and your work to look the way you want it to. Something I don't get," I said. "The way you draw, it just doesn't fit with what I've heard. Even without knowing what you're doing technically, I still don't see you doing a five-legged horse or misspelling a name."

He put his hands together, elbows between his knees. "I remember both of those, couple more too. Marcus... I don't know what to tell you. Guy's loaded half the time, right off his face. He turns me loose with no idea what I'm doing, but some girl comes in he thinks is hot, all of a sudden he's God's gift, insists on doing the work himself. He's done some real shit jobs on them."

"So how'd a guy with your talent end up with that meltdown?"

"He comes in to the video store I work at. One night he offered me a job."

"And now you're looking to jump ship on him."

"Look, Mr..."

"Sam, just Sam."

"Sam, I've had all I can take from that guy." Pete looked upset, almost to the point of tears. "He's moving a lot of meth and shit out of his shop. Sucks so much of his own shit up his nose his head glows in the dark. He gets violent, paranoid, delusional. You know what it's like to come to work, find your boss so fucked up he doesn't know his own name?"

"Actually, yeah. I remember one guy I worked for used to come in drunk at like ten o'clock in the morning, sit there getting drunker and yelling insults at the customers. Back then, I was dumb enough to think I was paying my dues or something."

"I can't live with this crap," he said. "I'm ruining my sleep looking over my shoulder. I worry every day he's gonna get raided or something and it'll be *my* ass takes the fall. Guy I grew up with is doing six to eight in Stillwater just for sitting in the car while some guys he was with robbed a Seven 11. He thought they were in the store buying beer."

"It's that bad, why wait til now?"

"I've been thinking about it awhile now. Really. But it was last night decided me. You take me or not, I'm not going back there."

"What happened?"

"God damn paranoid asshole decided I was spying on him for the government or the phone company or something. He put a fucking *gun* in my mouth."

He rubbed his palms on his upper arms.
"Fuck that, man. I don't need it."

***

That same Friday morning, two young girls in nearby Shakopee, Minnesota lied to their parents. Fourteen year old Joanne Tolaffson and fifteen year old Denise Nudenberger both sang in the choir at First Lutheran and both made last year's honor roll at James J. Hill Junior High. Their yearbook photos showed a sunny blonde with a jaw a shade too strong and a freckled pixie self-conscious about wearing braces. Both smiling, happy and full of life just the same.

Their parents were expecting them to be with the rest of the choir at a weekend retreat.
Instead, they caught a bus into the Twin Cities.

Nineteen

Later that day it was Hamish's turn to make the food run, and I could almost taste the hot and sour soup from the Chinese place down the street. It wasn't Grand Shanghai, but it was still several notches above anyone else's best. While he was gone I did a tongue piercing, then put on fresh gloves and changed the trash.

I came out drying my hands on a paper towel, saw movement in the waiting room by the flash rack. Someone had come into the studio while I had been in back. When I stuck my head around the corner to say hello, I was met by Marcus Winton's distinctive silhouette: that shapeless black garment gave him such a hunched weird look. His gleaming bald head made a slow turn in my direction.

"Mr. Roark, a pleasure seeing you here."

"It's where I work," I said. His eyes were dark and glittering, his smile small and secretive.

Something in that smile made the heat rise through my chest into my neck and my palms sting. I ran a hand through my hair and leaned back against the corner of the reception desk.

"I should probably tell you, your old apprentice, Pete, he was in here this morning. Looking for a job."

Marcus moved the flesh on his face that would have cocked an eyebrow, if he had any. The glitter danced in his eyes and nothing else changed in his expression.

"I decided to take him on. Didn't figure you should hear about it some other way."

"Thank you. I do have to admit, I am surprised."

"So what brings you out, Marcus?"

"Tasha. She... worries you might have a problem with our... relationship." He had a voice like used motor oil. "I assured her she had nothing to worry about."

"What Tash does is her business. Always was."

He lowered his head a fraction of an inch, widened that tiny little smile another imperceptible fraction. His upper lip curled when he did it.

"She tells me you come from an occult background, sole warlock in a coven of witches."

"She's lying. Tash does that a lot."

"Pity. I had rather looked forward to...measuring our respective abilities."

I couldn't help it. The idea of this strange little man trying to start a psychic pissing contest was just too much. I laughed.

Marcus stiffened as though he had been slapped.

"Sorry man," I said, "it's just, you have *got* to be kidding."

The small man raised himself up to his full height and rolled his eyes in their sockets. He moved his hands away from his body, palms the color of wheat paste turned towards me. I felt a hot prickling up my arms like legions of ants crawling over me.

The prickling intensified. I refused to brush at my skin. Inside the closed studio, an unseen breeze plucked at my hair and shirt.

His teeth were small and sharp in his mouth when he hissed at me. The unseen wind blew pages off the drawing table, began to move the framed sheets around in the flash rack.

Marcus moved his hands further out to his sides. I felt something like sharp nails along the back of my neck.

Ever since I can remember, my anger and violence have held a powerful sway over me. I've struggled all my life to control them, to recognize my wrath as the enemy it is. Unfortunately, my violence has always been a double-edged sword. It's hurt me plenty, but it's also saved me and those around me on more than one occasion.

I didn't even think about what I was doing. I just did it. I came up off the desk and slapped Marcus's face.

The sound of it rang in the waiting room walls, answered the sting in my palm. Marcus rocked back on his heels, his eyes out of focus and filling with tears. A bright red stain the size and shape of my palm and fingers burned from the corner of his mouth up the side of his head.

"Two things, Marcus. One, I'm *not* psychic and don't give a rat's ass about any of that voodoo mojo bullshit," I said. "Two, you *ever* try anything like that on me again, I will truly and thoroughly kick your ass."

I saw his upper lip pull back and those sharp teeth part, but the voice I heard seemed to hiss inside my own head.

"You'll pay for this..."

The chimes over the front door tinkled and Hamish walked in with a bag of Chinese takeout. Hot and sour soup and other dishes I couldn't identify. The good smells filled the studio. Hamish put the bag on the desk and began setting out the containers inside it.

In that moment, I felt a sense of defeat and disappointment. I remember wondering whether I had resolved anything or simply made a bad situation worse. I suspected I knew the answer, but didn't see what I might have done differently.

"Hey Sam, what's going on?"

I pushed the hair out of my eyes, rubbed the ball of my thumb into the opposite palm. "Nothing. Me and Marcus here just trying to set a few things straight."

He looked over my shoulder.

"Sam, there's no one else here."

Twenty

When I pulled up at Bex's that night I saw her silhouette in the living room light duck away as I got out of the car, so I wasn't surprised to hear her coming down the steps by the time I got to the front door.

She stepped into the arm I offered around her bare waist and reached up to kiss me lightly, but I saw her eyes were tight and strained.

"Everything okay?" I asked.

"Fine."

"Whatcha got there?" I gestured to the paper bag under her arm.

"Wine for dinner. Can we get in the car now please?"

She said nothing through the five minutes it took to drive to my house. Once we got there, she went straight for the living room bookshelves. I make a fair living and don't have any other expensive habits, so most of what I do spend goes into books. I uncorked the wine she brought and started unpacking the groceries I picked up on my way over. From the living room, I could hear her happy sounds as she explored my library.

I'm no great cook, but I got a pan of frozen lasagna in the oven, set the garlic rolls on the counter to be ready for the last ten minutes of baking, came out with a glass of wine in either hand. I found Bex kneeling on the floor with a small stack of books already beside her. Her face was like a little kid's at Christmas.

She accepted the glass I handed her, took a sip, closed her eyes and took her time enjoying it on her tongue.

I tried a taste myself. "Yummy," was all I could think to say.

"It'll do."

"You know your eyes twinkle rather nicely when you say that?"

"I do *not* twinkle."

"I beg to differ, miss." I had another sip of wine. "This really *is* good."

She shrugged. "It's Australian. I was hoping I could find you some of our New Zealand wines, they're really much better. But the man in the bottle shop looked at me like I was crazy. He told me there was no such place."

"What'd   you   do?"

"Assured him there was, since I'm *from* there, and do you know what he did? He actually *congratulated* me on how well I speak English."

"What can I tell you? I hear about half of us in this country can't find Mexico on a map."

I sat down on the couch beside her. I wanted to reach out and stroke the sleek dark spill, but it was such an intimate gesture. I saw her face.

"What is it?"

A frown tugged at the corner of her mouth.

"Want to talk about it?"

"Just stuff with Kate and Paul," she said. "It isn't getting any easier with them. They both found out they have to work tomorrow, so we won't get to do anything together. They were already getting ready for bed by the time I left, but they also acted like I was somehow running out on them by coming here."

For once in my life, I knew enough to keep quiet and listen.

"And *you*. Kate acts like there's something dirty about me seeing you, like I'm some kind of whore for dating the tattoo man."

"A lot of people have their prejudices."

"She doesn't deserve them! Kate's the one took me to get *my* first tattoo, for fuck's sake. And don't think I don't remember some of what *she* used to get up to back before she turned into Little Miss Perfect with her handbag and pearls." She shook her head, and her hair threw horsewhip shadows on the hardwood floor. "Like I said, it's just stupid."

"When you're apart from your friends for a while and they have some big changes in their lives, it can feel like you're strangers. It's not easy."

She looked at me then, her eyes gray and direct, the gold flecks in them alive with a light of their own.

"I told Kate I was staying here tonight."

"Oh."

The moment seemed to stretch and pull until time was different altogether. The space between our bodies grew warm, almost palpable. The scent of her skin was everywhere in the room with us.

The flat, loud, harsh buzzing of the oven timer was not immediately separable from the coursing of my heart's blood or the energy crackling through my skin.

I ended up letting the lasagne cool while I waited for the garlic rolls.

After dinner, Bex stood up from the table, came around to where I sat and stepped out of the shoes she was wearing. Barefoot, she was small enough to put us almost at eye level.

She put her hands on my shoulders, and I brought mine around her waist.

Her skin had the warmth and texture of rose petals in a summer greenhouse, a place where the air was thick and misty and full of the smell of growing things, rich and dark and green, rising from dark fertile soil.

A short time later, I stood up with her in my lap and carried her upstairs.

Twenty-One

We had no way of knowing that while we tumbled and moved together in blood-ancient sea-rhythms, a fourteen year old girl named Joanne Tolaffson wept and screamed into her gag.

The TV news would describe her as an honor student, active in the choir at First Lutheran. In the yearbook photo they would air, a sunny young blonde with an Alice band and enormous blue eyes would smile out at the camera, fresh and happy and full of life, tragically confident in her own immortality. Longer news accounts on the web would offer many grisly details but no explanation for how it happened.

She did not know where she had been taken, only that she woke up unable to move and in terrible pain. Wherever she was, it was isolated, private. Dark clouds hid the bare fingernail-sliver of moon that hung low in the starless sky. Much of the night, intermittent rain kept people indoors and muffled any sounds she might have made.

Lit candles threw a constantly moving riot of dancing shadows along the ceiling in Joanne's view. By lifting her head, she was also able to see part of the wall beyond her feet, but the further sides of the empty room were lost in darkness.

The young girl's wrists and ankles were each punctured with sharp square objects at least five inches long and made of iron. From the overall wound profile the forensic team understood that she was crucified while lying on her back. Her vocal cords were raw from screaming into the gag in her mouth. It was made from her own underpants, held in place by a cord of soft fabric, possibly silk from a tie or sash.

Despite the warm June evening, it was bitterly and unnaturally cold where she was. Her hands and feet showed signs of frostbite, as did her buttocks and shoulder blades where they came in contact with the bare wood floor beneath her. Authorities would never be able to account for it.

In the course of her initial struggles, she had driven a number of wicked splinters into her buttocks and the muscles of her back. Some of them over two inches long. Many had been oozing and suppurating for hours.

All at once, gooseflesh rose all down the length of Joanne Tolaffson's pale body as a foul wind gusted throughout the unseen confines of the room. The candles were blown out, plunging Joanne's prison into total darkness.

Her captor began moving around the room just out of Joanne's sight, circling her staked-out body until all thirteen candles were relit. At that point, Joanne Tolaffson's gag was removed. The ligature marks began to fade, but the soft tissues at the corners of her mouth remained badly bruised.

The young girl who sang in the choir at First Lutheran was too hoarse to scream by then, and it didn't matter. There was no one within half a mile on that brutal night to hear her cries.

At some point soon after, Joanne Tolaffson's captor began to methodically torture her. The honor student from Shakopee whose parents still thought she was at a weekend event with her church was scourged with a length of barbed wire.

When she lost consciousness, common household white vinegar was applied to her nose and mouth. Whether to revive her or to intensify the pain, rubbing alcohol was liberally splashed all over her torn and ravaged body.

Inch by inch, the barbed wire whip tore away tiny shreds of skin and meat, over and over, until Joanne Tolaffson was flayed alive.

When at last the sharp-edged blade of a razor, knife or scalpel sliced her open and an unknown hand pulled the still-beating heart from her body, death was only the beginning of her torments.

Twenty-Two

Bex and I lay together late into the night, listening to the gentle rain at the window and making those small and tender explorations of each other's bodies, that first honest inventory of what made the woman beside me uniquely herself, and vice versa.

She had a tiny scar at the corner of her right eye, from an accident with a firecracker when she was little. A tattoo of a bluebird on her belly the size of a quarter. Glittering barbell in her navel long-healed, the new piercing I put in her lower lip the night we met.

Smooth pink marks flecked her hands, physical memory of the tens of thousands of espressos she poured to afford this trip. She had ten of the most adorable toes it had ever been my honor to encounter, and the whole length of her foot fit in the cup of my hand.

Those were only a few of the marvels I found that night. For me, some alchemy in the act of love turns strangers into individuals. Even the most random encounters had left me with a sense of the woman, not as a generic object for my use, but as a person in her own right. And tonight had been anything but random or between strangers.

For Bex, looking me over was a longer, more involved process. Not only were there a lot more hard miles on the odometer, the story was heavily illustrated as well. She found all the knife scars worked in with the imagery on my sleeves: battling samurai from 18th century woodcuts on my right, my favorite cartoon characters on my left. My legs were a collage of pulp magazine covers from the 30s and 40s - Doc Savage, The Shadow, Tarzan, Sheena and all the rest.

Her fingertips softly traced the puckered knurl on my thigh and the peppering of tiny white stars around it. Visible memories of a near-miss with a shotgun before I was twenty-one years old, casually concealed in the curling smoke from The Shadow's twin .45s. She kept rolling me over to follow the illustrations to her satisfaction, and I wasn't complaining.

"They're beautiful," she said at last. She slid up the length of my back, kissed the star-shaped hollow over my left shoulder blade. "And what's this?"

"Fell out of a tree, um, let's see, age probably seven or eight."

"Onto what? Jagged rocks?" "Onto another tree branch, smarty." She was in range now, so I kissed the top of her head.

"That's it? That's the story?"

"What can I tell you? Not every mark on me was put there with intent."

She climbed a little further up my body, kissed the end of my nose, my cheek and temple.

"Well, you've certainly done the hard yards, haven't you? No wonder you sorted those two out the other night."

"Shucks, m'am. Tweren't nuthin. Anyone in my place'd dun the same."

She giggled, and we made ourselves more comfortable.

"Samuel Matthew Roark, you're like no one I've ever met before, and you must promise never, never again to put on that ridiculous accent."

***

I was seventeen years old when I got my first tattoo. I was fascinated and terrified. It was just a small thing, as much as I could afford, and my heart's dearest desire. It was the word SAFE written above my heart.

Two weeks later, before my own ink had even fully healed, I did my first tattoo. I was fascinated and terrified.

Full of youthful knowledge of my own immortal destiny, I ordered a starter kit from the back of a catalog and haunted dentist's and doctor's offices until I found a sterilizer for cheap. I told everyone I knew I would be tattooing soon and immediately found myself surrounded by dozens of new best friends.

Seventeen year olds all know with a certainty the rest of us can only pity and envy that the whole world is a magnificent stage set placed there as a backdrop to their perfect destiny, and I was no exception. In tattooing I saw everything my heart desired. A chance to actually make art for a living, the independence to leave my family behind me forever and the attentions of those exotic unapproachable goth and punk girls I found myself drawn to.

And tattooing did give me all those things. But as the old saying goes, when you pick up one end of the stick, you pick up the other. I was part of a world of alcoholics and drug addicts, where speed-freak bikers with chains and bats tried to end my career as soon as it began. Where every one of those same exotic and unapproachable young women invariably raked broken glass through my head. Where every morning I checked that the blue-black .38 was loaded with 220 grain hollowpoints before I had my first cup of coffee.

Tattooing eventually paid for the college classes I took part time until I finally got my art degree, and it allowed me to travel all over the world. It also inevitably led me into a situation where I shot an armed assailant who wasn't out of puberty yet.

In all its best and its worst, my art form was a perfect fit for my personality. On some deep level I knew that if I hadn't found it, it would in all likelihood have found me.

I can still remember the moment of my first tattoo as if it were only yesterday, and not over a decade gone. It was a punk girl two years older than me. She had a small bluish spider in the center of her thigh. She had picked it out by hand a year ago with a safety pin and India ink, and I reworked it with nice sharp lines and true black color. I was offering free tattoos at that point, and Sara was the first to take me up on it. I was a seventeen year old virgin, and when she stepped out of her camouflage pants my mouth went dry.

With my gloved hands stretching the skin of her long bare thigh, the tip of the machine's tube filled with jet-black ink, the sharp point of the needle humming up and down as I lowered it to her skin, the swelling heavy awareness that we were swiftly passing the point of no return filled me with a sense of promise and hope, of the beginning of a brave new adventure.

Lying in the dark, with Bex's sleeping flesh warm against mine and sweet across my chest, I understood why I kept remembering that other, earlier moment.

Twenty-Three

Saturday morning, I woke early, languid and at peace. I felt relaxed, refreshed and, unusually, untroubled by the ghost of a sixteen year old runaway.

There was a stirring beside me, and I looked over to see a hair like a spill of dark silk and a single perfect forearm. The skull beneath the hair gave a little shake and one elfin face was revealed. The eye in view remained closed, or opened so little there was no difference.

I kissed the smooth forehead, got the start of a smile.

"Coffee?"

With a childlike gravity, the pixie-head nodded vigorously, then fell back away and vanished under a general tumble and arranging of sheets. Somehow, I found myself standing beside the bed, the whole of the top sheet wrapped tightly around the tiny New Zealander curled up in the center there.

Downstairs, I loaded the coffeemaker and set it to its perky morning business, scratched and yawned and wondered about breakfast. Birds were singing, squirrels chased each other through the trees in my backyard, and the sky outside was like a great blue bowl set over us all.

It had been a good night, and I was feeling fine.

I opened the fridge, bent down to reach out the new milk I put in there yesterday. I thought I as alone in the kitchen.

I stood up, closed the door and let out an involuntary yelp. The new carton of milk fell to the floor and burst.

A young girl stood in the corner. She was covered in blood and she looked terrified.

I couldn't guess anything about her, not her age or even the color of her hair. So much blood streamed down her body that it looked like a mantle of red and white lace. Lengths of black iron chain were draped around her.

She drew her arms tight around her torso in an effort to cover herself. Bulging blue eyes rolled from side to side in her red and white mask. She was terrified. The sound of her breathing was loud in the kitchen, fast and high and shallow and terrible in its silence.

I thought of Bex upstairs, looked toward the ceiling.

I only looked away for a second. When I looked back, the ghost was gone.

I was alone again.

***

Two apparition-free minutes later, I brought two tall and steaming mugs upstairs. The mess on the floor was cleaned up and the event with the ghost was locked away in the same box where I kept Lisa and anything at all to do with my family. I was feeling much more myself.

"I dropped the milk. Black okay?"

"You're forgiven this once."

Bex sat up in her small tent of sheets and accepted hers with small sounds of delight. Cupped in both hands, her mug looked the size of a paint bucket. She closed her eyes as she took her first sip and sat with them closed for a short time after. It was a sentiment I agreed with.

"Morning."

"Morning."

We made eye contact for the first time since waking up together, and Bex turned her head away, blushing a lovely rose color.

I stroked the skin of her arm with the backs of my fingers, let my hand fall back to the rumpled surface of the bed.

She put one small hand on top of my scarred knuckles. Her fingernails were perfect little ovals, unpolished, a quarter inch of white tipping the healthy seashell pink. The morning light fell across the curve of her cheek and the fine classic line of her nose, streaked her hair with colors of caramel and gold.

Her eyes gathered the light in and gave it back as something rare and powerful. They put me in mind of the clean air after a summer storm. A small secret smile played at the corners of her lips.

I think she saw something in my eyes, because she hopped up from the bed with the sheet held high around her chest. When she took a step toward the bedroom door, I reached for her.

She was fast. My hand closed on nothing but cloth. She was free of the sheet and down the hall into the bathroom, laughing. The cotton bedsheet was still warm and carried a trace of her scent.

I sat back against the pillows and sipped at my coffee, listening to the sound of the shower running and thinking about the delicious shape of her bare legs flashing down the hall.

A beautiful day indeed. If only I knew what to make of the ghost in my kitchen and the small, blue spot in the center of my chest that looked for all the world like frostbite.

Twenty-Four

Same as I dealt with growing up in a family of witches, I treated the ghost attack that morning with a hefty dose of denial. Besides, after the night I had with Bex it shouldn't have been a surprise that Lisa Torres would have to come up with new tricks to get under my skin. I lost myself in the cleaning, got it all done in record time.

By the time Hamish came in half an hour before we opened, he found counters, lids, cabinets, upholstery, every surface in the tattoo area and both piercing bays wiped down with germicide. The gear was all cleaned and sterilized and the floor mopped.

"Are you *whistling*?" He put two tall coffees in a brown cardboard tray down on the desktop, picked up the white envelope I left there after finding it under the door this morning. He sipped at his coffee and read the note, his eyebrows rising impossibly high up his forehead. I knew what The Brethren said.

REPENT Sinners.
The FINAL DAYS Come as a Thief in the NIGHT.

"This shit for real?"
"Full moon, global warming, new moon... Who knows."

He dropped it in the bottom drawer with the other note, looked up with a lopsided smile.

"Good night last night?"

"Sure. I guess."

"It's just, you got a kind of, whatchacallit, a glow going on there."

"You're seeing things."

"No, you got a definite *glow*, my friend."

"What am I supposed to say to that?"

"Seeing her again?"

"Tonight. This time, she's doing the cooking." I pretended not to see the smile stretched across Hamish's face as I wiped down the desktop. "There. Everything's all clean for you."

"We about ready to open, then? Must be five, six kids out in the hallway already."

"God bless Saturdays, eh? Bring them on."

With practiced ease, Hamish and I fell into our standard routine. He took care of most of the piercing business coming through the door. I did the tattoos and any extra piercings I might be free for. Since we were without a receptionist again we kept the cordless at hand, wrapped in fresh plastic with each different job to prevent cross-contamination. The day flew by in a blur of needles and ink and endless changes of latex gloves. By 7:30 I was so keyed up I had trouble keeping my mind on the job at hand.

By ten after eight, we had the place locked up and the alarm set. I had left Bex a house key that morning, and she said to plan on dinner at nine sharp. I only had to stop and pick up some wine. I had a hunch I knew a place might just stock something from New Zealand.

Heading to Surdyk's for the wine, I chose a route that took me down 14th, Dinkytown's main drag. Assuming a neighborhood of shops three blocks long could be said to have a main drag. The choice seemed random until I saw a neon flicker of a word as familiar to me as my own name. I couldn't be certain, but it interested me enough to park at the curb and walk back to check it out.

Sure enough, down a dark hallway of storefronts struggling to claim it was a mini mall, I saw an erratic purple tongue of neon spelling the word TATTOO. Dark Rites was open.

It was in the strangest block of shops I had ever seen, a concrete passageway stretching between the middle of the block and a sort of back alley parking area all the other buildings in the block backed onto. The passage was wide, with a low ceiling barely an inch above the top of my head. No lighting but what the shops threw off, and the main decoration was a heavy chain link gate at the end facing the street, drawn open and padlocked to the wall to invite shoppers to pass through. It was hard to imagine a more forbidding retail environment.

I passed two New Age bookstores and a place whose hand-lettered sign said only 'Military Collectible Stamps'. All were closed. Every time the wind would shift, it fluted and moaned down the barren concrete tunnel.

Dark Rites's windows were done up in photocopied flash sheets taped up across the glass like wallpaper. I wondered which of the place's previous tenants tinted the windows looking out onto that dark tunnel.

The front door opened with a hush and I stepped into some kind of tomb or temple. The light was such a deep blue twilight that it was difficult to see the corners of the room. The air was thick with spicy incense smells: musk and patchouli, undertones of vanilla and cinnamon.

The room had a counter through the middle to separate waiting room from workspace. At the back wall of the studio, a closed door. There was no one in sight, nothing but silence to greet me.

I moved around the room looking at the flash sheets scotch-taped to the bare walls and the snake in its glass tank. It was a big boa constrictor, no way to guess its length but as thick as my leg through the middle of its belly. I heard a feminine giggle from somewhere in back.

The only light in the shop came from a couple of swing arm halogen spotlights on the desk beside the dental chair. The stillness, the dark, the incense and the quiet combined to give the impression of temple or tomb.

I was about to leave when the door knob to the storage area rattled. The door stuck in its frame and made a protesting sound when it opened.

"Dead man. Come to get some ink?"

It was the hard-faced blonde from Resurrection Joe's, the one sitting on Marcus's lap. She wore scraps of black vinyl and combat boots and moved like a cross between a ballerina and a lumberjack.

"Just thought I'd be a good neighbor, pay a friendly visit. Marcus in?"

She stood across the counter from me, hands on her hips, smile twisted up on one side of her mouth, tongue moving around inside her cheek.

She moved her weight from one hip to the other and the chain around her belly made a small sound. I could see the flat hard muscles there like iron plates under her skin. Raw crusted scabs clustered around the large vein in the cup of her hip. Track marks.

"He's in back. Private session." Her voice was low and husky, like maybe she had a cold, or smoked a pack and half a day. She scratched at one wrist and shifted on her hips again. "Anything I can do for you?"

"I just wanted to let Marcus know there's no hard feelings at my end."

"You sure about that?" She looked me up and down, ran the tip of her pink tongue around small pointed teeth.

She leaned into the counter with her upper arms framing her breasts, did something speculative with her eyes, and finally shrugged.

"Suit yourself then. Pussy."

The pigtailed blonde turned on one foot and stalked back to the dental chair like a tiger pacing its cage. From the back I could see the part in her hair, as straight and white as if it had been cut there with a razor. She lay back in the chair and looked at me with that twisted wound of a smile again. From the back room, I heard another feminine giggle.

"Tell you what," I said, "I can see it's a bad time. Just give him my message, and you all take care okay?"

"What's your rush? Marcus won't be long." She stretched her arms up over her head to reveal more crusted grime, wrapped her hands behind the headrest and leveled a look at me with one eyebrow arched high. "Marcus *never* takes long."

I stepped out into the warm summer evening, stood on the sidewalk pulling clean warm air deep into my lungs and thinking about what I had just seen.

Footsteps behind me boomed and echoed from the belly of the tunnel. Two teenaged girls staggered past me, pale and dazed. Muscles knotted at the corners of their jaws and their eyes were chemical fires burning in the twilight.

Twenty-Five

My night with Bex was fantastic, and she was without a doubt the best cook I had ever met, better than some chefs I knew. Waking up with the lovely warm length of her curled against me, I thought I could get used to this. But she was spending Sunday with Hayley and Paul. It was the one day that week she and her friend would have together, though she said she might come over later that night.

I didn't go straight to work after dropping her off that morning. There was something bothering me, something I wanted to see first.

Tommy Green was a weak little coward, a hard-luck sad sack who let the other people around him write his script for him and then blamed them for the roles they gave him and the way the results turned out. He was an addict, a liar and a thief, with no detectable moral sense. He would have blown out my lights without a flicker of remorse if he could have gotten away with it, and all responsibility for the act or its consequences lay with his brother for asking him.

Nothing an addict says can be trusted. Nothing. I learned that from my mother-- I knew it well by the time I was old enough to walk. The youngest and weakest Rose brother was very convincingly distraught Thursday night. He was truly afraid, convinced that I had killed his brother.

I was ashamed to admit that, in all the excitement, I had believed him. I woke up that Sunday morning nagged by the knowledge that I'd had terrible dreams, unable to remember anything about them except that they concerned Lisa Torres and the Rose brothers.

That morning, in the cold light of day, I knew better than to trust his story on nothing more than a junkie's word.
I needed to make sure his brother had in fact been murdered.
There was something else bothering me too, and I spent the morning kicking myself for not thinking of it earlier. It was Hamish and his keys brought it back.

The night the Rose brothers first came in to my studio, I distrusted them immediately. After they left that first time, I distinctly remembered turning the deadbolt to lock them out.

So how did they get back in to point a gun at Bex's forehead?

I wished I'd thought of it while I still had my hands on Tommy, but he would be long gone by now. The best I could do under the circumstances was to see what I might learn from Jack.

I had no way of knowing if I could even trust the address Tommy had given me for Jack. Or rather, Jack's body. It wasn't the same as the burned-out shell listed on the driver's license I took off the older brother, but Tommy maintained throughout the ride from that isolated pasture to the bus station that it was the place he was supposed to return to with his brother, where they would split the money and party.

It was just possible the second address was set up as an ambush. I could arrive to find a room full of speed-freaks with shotguns, or cops looking to grab the first suspect they could lay hands on, but it didn't seem likely. Too many variables, not enough pressure to lure me into the trap. And quite frankly, the Rose brothers didn't strike me as being capable of even that much sophistication.

It was probably safe, but I would keep my eyes and ears open a little bit wider, just in case.

The address Tommy gave me turned out to be a rundown building in a marginal part of town. It was half a step up from as bad as it gets: the sort of place people pass through, on their way up or, more likely, down. It wasn't the sort of place anyone stays long.

It was the sort of place where a certain number of tenants every month would take their own lives.

The front door had the standard security buzzer and intercom setup, but a large scorch mark showed around the faceplate of the intercom, and the keyhole to the door looked like it had a piece of twisted metal snapped off inside it. I pushed the base of the security door with my foot and it swung open.

The foyer was dark and gloomy, even on a sunny morning in June. Discarded junk mail lay scattered on the threadbare carpet and the rows of tarnished brass mailboxes still showed pry marks from the days when welfare checks used to be mailed out instead of deposited onto a WIC card.

A quick look at the mailboxes gave me an idea of the layout of the building. 1A, 1B, 1C, 2A, 2B, 2C and so on. Stood to reason 2J would be upstairs and toward the back. Lisa Torres stood on the stairs: silent, accusing as always. We shared a brief moment of eye contact before she vanished.

I touched the spot on my chest where the second ghost, the girl in chains, hit me the day before. I started up the tired and worn steps.

The hallways were thick with the smell of bad greasy cooking and cigarette smoke. It looked like it was lit by 40 watt bulbs, every third or fourth one burnt out and not replaced.

The apartment I was looking for was on the second floor, at the end of a hallway carpeted in dirty gold shag. God alone knew what color the walls were supposed to be under all the nicotine stains.

The halls were hushed and quiet, even after eleven on a Sunday morning. Not a family building. Here and there, the sound of a television carried through the thin walls, floors and ceilings. Somewhere in the complex, a woman sobbed.

Rounding the corner of the hallway, the first thing I saw was the door to apartment 2J at the far end. It hung slightly open. A black sliver four or five inches wide showed between its edge and the jamb.

Now was the time for the gloves. I always keep a few pairs in my glove compartment, memory of days when it was pretty likely I'd have to make some running repairs to whatever shitheap I was driving. Nobody wants a tattooist with motor oil ground into his skin. There was no chance of that with the anonymous piece of gray plastic I drove now, but the gloves still came in handy often enough I got spoiled to having them around.

Never for breaking and entering, though...

I pulled back close to the wall, where I would be harder to see moving up and I would be out of the line fire if it did turn out to be a trap. My feet were reasonably quiet on the grimy shag carpet and I moved with a great deal of caution.

Three feet outside the door I stopped. Listened. Heard the same distant TVs, the same woman's brokenhearted pain.

Nothing from inside 2J.

I stood motionless and tense as a coiled spring for three long minutes. Somewhere in the back of my head, some very ancient mammal machinery was figuring odds based on lack of yellow crime scene tape, likelihood of any neighbors noticing me out in the hall like this, the possibility of Tommy using a phone to set something up last night and a thousand other variables.

When three minutes passed with no scrape or rustle of cloth, no grunt or wheeze or cough, no shift or movement from the other side of that door, I was pretty sure I was safe.

And by the end of three minutes, my nose was well enough accustomed to the smells of the building itself to admit that the sniveling little addict was probably telling the truth.

Beyond that door I would find a two day old corpse.

The door swung gently open in front of my foot without the roar of a shotgun filling the morning, and I moved through the doorway sharp and careful for tripwires, pullcords, any sight or sound of a trap. At least, I was as sharp and careful as I could be in the face of the sick sweet stench of decay in that room. The rotten fog closed around me, crept into my nose and mouth and down my throat. The summer heat was intense, and the smell even tried to get in through my eyelids.

I lifted my hand and my tee shirt to my mouth, tried breathing through that. It wasn't too terrible, as long as I also pinched my nostrils shut and only took shallow breaths through my mouth. I managed not to gag.

I found the TV smashed and lying on its side with the cord pulled out of the wall. Saw the plastic kitchen chair with pink and purple flowers printed on its vinyl surface. It had been moved away from its normal spot to sit directly facing the duct-tape patched easy chair in the center of the room. Beside the chair stood a wood-grain plastic end table with two nearly empty pill bottles and a bottle of tequila with maybe three fingers left in it.

The only thing missing was the corpse.

The easy chair was crumpled and shrunken in the seat, sodden with blood and torn at the back by four gore-packed bullet holes. Whoever sat there lost a fair amount of meat with all the blood. An absolutely enormous chipped dull gray revolver lay wedged between the cushions on one side. A folded newspaper lay halfway across it.

So much blood saturated the cushions that it dripped down to form a dark puddle spreading out from beneath the legs of the chair.

The puddle hadn't completely dried yet. Every drop that fell from the belly of the chair set the whole mass of the syrupy puddle to quivering and shaking. The plik, plik, plik sound was a loud slow drum beat in the deathly quiet. From far off, I could still hear the woman crying.

I felt cold breath curl along my arm, like an ice burn in that stifling heat. Lisa's shade squatted beside me over the pool of blood. From ancient Greece to Russia, China to Japan, the

Cherokee to the Navajo, all the folklore agreed on one thing--
ghosts have a hungry fascination for blood.

Lisa Torres certainly did.

I wanted to be anywhere else right about then, but I moved
into the kitchen anyway. It was the color of a poisonous mushroom
and as bare and soulless as the living room. One look at the
countertops, and I had a new reason to be thankful for the gloves.

Nothing in the drawers or cupboards gave me any idea how
Jack Rose might have come into possession of my yellow pages
ad, sixteen crisp fifty dollar bills and a key to my shop.

I was becoming increasingly aware that I was in an
unwholesome environment and had maybe outworn my welcome. I
took one last look around me and left the way I came in.

On my way out I passed Lisa, still staring rapt at the
dripping puddle.

***

The clock on my dashboard said it was already eleven, past
time for me to get back to work. It was one of the ironies of the
storefront that I could set my own hours and change them at will,
but if I let myself get in the habit of too many late starts or early
closes, it would be no time at all before I was ducking calls from
the landlord and wondering what happened to all my customers.

The sunlight was dazzling after the gloom of that building,
and the heat of the summer day was in full swing. As soon as I
turned the key in the ignition, I flipped on the A/C too. It's not
something I use often, but I wanted the cool air to wash over me
and take away some of that hot charnel reek that clung to my flesh
and lingered at the back of my throat.

Once the car started to cool down a little, I dropped it in
gear and pulled away from the curb. I got as far as the corner stop
sign before I was no longer alone.

I figured her for somewhere in her early teens. It was hard
to guess Lisa's age, stamped as she was by the signs of her own

substance abuse and her cruel wisdom about the human capacity for evil: it made her seem old beyond her years.

With the girl sitting beside me now, it was the opposite problem. Braces on her teeth, an Alice band and an unmistakable sense of wide-eyed innocence made her seem really young. She had dark blonde hair and enormous troubled eyes. Only the adolescent length of her jawline and shy coltish awkwardness kept her from looking even younger.

More coils of black chain wrapped around her, cruel and heavy. They were roughly made, maybe even hand forged.

She turned to me with eyes strained from crying and seemed as surprised to see me as I was to see her. The fingers she had been twisting and knotting together in her lap reached out for me without being able to touch me. Where her hand passed through my arm, I felt icy flesh rise.

A horn blared behind me and startled me into turning my attention back to my driving. I crossed the street and pulled over into a Target parking lot a block further down.

The girl tried to speak, but no sound came. The effort looked like it put a strain on her: she appeared flat and vaguely grainy, somehow just not as *there*. Finally, she gave up and sat in the seat across from me weeping into her hands. Her full presence returned, but it kept slipping.

The child sat beside me in her chains, sobbing and shaking in her misery. Here and there, in blinks and flashes, she was once again the way she had appeared in my kitchen, naked and vulnerable, covered in blood. It seemed like a long time before she cried herself out.

"Why me?" I asked. She looked up, opened her mouth to speak and instead sent me a look eloquent with the futility of what I was asking.

"Tell you what, just nod your head yes or no, okay?"

The girl nodded, tears reduced to sniffles by now.

"Is this about your death?"

Innocent brown eyes went wide in shock and horror. Her mouth went slack and trembling. She reached out to me with both hands...

And the only thing with me was a cold stinging wind swirling through the car.

Twenty-Six

When I finally got in to work that day I told Hamish everything about Marcus, including my visit to Dark Rites the night before, but that was all. For one thing, I didn't know where to start.

Also, I suspected those images would haunt my sleep for some time to come. No sense dragging my best friend into it too.

He sat back in his chair listening to me, with his feet up and his hands laced behind his head, a smile growing on his face the whole time. By the time I finished, he was shaking his head back and forth, his eyes merry and bright.

"This the same dude shaves his eyebrows?"

"Very same."

"Seriously, no shit. Man shaves his eyebrows, his eyebrows now, he's acting like this?"

"The guy's an idiot, what can I tell you?"

"Delusional too, he thinks he's got any claim on ol Tash."

"That too. I don't know what he thinks he's doing with his studio, either. His shop's buried off from the street, the interior's straight-up creepy as hell..."

"Makes sense, if Pete's telling the truth. That shady kind of shit, you don't exactly want regular folks feeling too welcome. And don't forget that back-room funny business."

"No way those girls were eighteen, either one of them. I didn't hear a tattoo machine, but even if he was just doing a piercing, he'll lose his license."

"You honestly think he was piercing back there?"

I rubbed my palm across my knuckles, felt the calluses whisper and scrape.

"No."

***

With a can of Sprite in hand and Hamish taking his time reassuring a middle aged couple with a thousand questions about genital piercing, I flicked the work computer over to local news. The top of the page was splashed with a headline was large and simple: *STUDENT SLAIN*.

The girl in the first photo was the chained ghost in my car this morning.

Two color photos taken from their school yearbook ran alongside a larger photo of a dazed and crying mother, prostrate in her grief. It was an intimate image, powerful. I felt like I was somehow invading their lives just looking at it. The less disturbing photo of a wooded area roped off with yellow crime scene tape and filled with standing cops ran further down the web page, along with two more copies of the yearbook photos.

The story was basic, so rather than let the pictures go to waste the writer found new ways to say the same few facts over and over. The two girls were best friends, their parents hadn't known they were missing. Joanne's mutilated body was found in an undeveloped part of Anoka County by a Saint Paul Boy Scout troop. Christine was still missing-- police expected the case to break any time now.

The scout reference was a hyperlink. I clicked, found out that when they found the body the first thing the kids did was start snapping photos with their phones. The photos had since been taken down from Facebook but had gone viral on Tumblr.

I clicked back to the yearbook photos, called them up side by side. Something about them nagged at me. It took me a minute to remember.

Two young girls, too young for the bellybutton piercings they wanted, but trying anyway. Hamish and I saw dozens of kids every month, heard every bizarre excuse imaginable for why they didn't have ID. These two came in, giggling and nervous and more polite than some. They left unpierced and disappointed, trying not to show it.

I had met them both, alive and well Saturday afternoon. And turned them away to their deaths.

***

It turned out to be a slow day for tattoos. My afternoon booking cancelled and I had no walk-ins. I spent some time trying to think up a solution to my problems, without too much success. Finally, I gave up and buckled down to catch up on my drawing.

Astounding catered to regular people, usually getting their first or second tattoo or piercing. Over the last six years, I had built up a small base of regular customers and did a good amount of business by word of mouth. I was proud of that, but it meant just about everyone coming through the door wanted something small.

I loved tattooing, even if the work I did was almost entirely limited to guys who thought an armband was the ultimate in bad-ass and girls afraid anything bigger than a quarter would make them look ugly. I did my absolute best with each one, enjoyed them too. All the same, I felt limited.

Which made it puzzling to me that when I did get a customer asking me for something big, exciting or different, something to challenge me, I invariably stalled on doing the art for it.

My usual excuse was that I was too busy doing all those small walk-in tattoos to draw the big fun stuff. Problem was that on days like this, I had to admit I really had nothing else to do *but* draw the fun stuff.

So I put the stack of folders on top of the reception desk, got out pencils and erasers, sat down with my oversize drawing pad propped in front of me and actually started to draw.

When clients wanted custom work, I made detailed notes talking to them, traced out measurements where I needed to, did rough sketches, and gratefully accepted any reference photos they brought in, anything they had to help me see what they wanted. I also took down their contact information and put each project in a separate manila folder.

First was for an exotic dancer who wanted a piece across her shoulders drawn from classical mythology. It became apparent pretty quickly that she had her myths mixed up. She wanted me to show Zeus, father of the gods, lying broken and bloody on the floors of Olympus while Aphrodite, goddess of love and beauty, was pulled from inside his forehead. Aphrodite had come out of the sea. Hera was the headache who needed to be smashed free.

I did two versions in pencil. One much like she asked for, without anything to identify the mystery goddess in question, and another based on Botticelli's *Birth of Venus*. It would require a vertical format and preferably her whole back, but it would also be nothing short of breathtaking.

And not nearly so creepy.

Growing up, drawing was a way for me to escape. In a way, nothing about that has changed. Drawing still puts me in a little world of my own, and not much reaches me there.

I was vaguely aware that the phone rang now and then, and that if Hamish was piercing I would answer it, but I never paid any attention to the calls themselves. I was more involved with the page in front of me than the world outside.

Hamish put a sandwich in front of me, and I ate it, but I had no idea what it was.

A body piercer working out of a specialty shop Uptown wanted me to put together a floral half-sleeve to make a strong feminine impact and cover a few sloppy pieces she got before she knew better. She knew Tasha and had seen her sleeves plenty, so she knew what I could do for her. I had the tracings I made of the tattoos to be covered, the total tattoo area and where the old work sat. She had also gone from 'anything you want' to bringing me a thick stack of printouts from botanical websites with choice flowers circled.

There were a few tricky spots, but mostly it went smooth and I was happy with the result. My aim was to keep the viewer's eye moving from one burst of color to another, give it no time to wonder what might be behind the cool green foliage or hidden under the ladybug on one leaf.

Just one folder left on the desk. I flipped it open, read my notes. They were for a young guy named Jim, came in weeks ago. I had really dropped the ball on this one.

Jim wanted a naughty nurse, and nothing he had seen in the flash was quite right. The folder was a slim one, photocopies of other pictures from the art in the flash rack with my handwritten notes on them about what elements he liked and what he didn't. I spread the copies out in front of me and sat looking at them for a time.

I began to feel the gradual pull of the drawing taking shape down inside me, took a sip of cold, stale coffee and began to draw again. I started with big looping strokes, feeling my way in, growing slowly tighter as I grew more definite.

She strode forward with a panther's grace, her figure seen from mid-thigh to the top of her little white hat. There was a rolling power in her shoulders and hips, in the deft lock and release of haunch and waist and rib.

The white nurse's uniform was open down the length of her sternum with a ring-pull zipper. The hem rode up to just below the juncture of silky tanned thighs.

Her breasts were not the comical absurdities common to pin-up art, but still round and firm. I knew that when the zipper purred further down, it would reveal faint ridges of scar tissue along their bottom curves from where the saline bags were inserted when she was twenty-two years old.

Hair the color of ice spilled across her shoulders and throat. Her bangs fell low across her face, shadowing her cat-green eyes from view and throwing attention to her satisfied and predatory smile. A shadow fell across my page.

Like some primitive sorcery was at work and the creature was summoned by the act of creating the image, Tasha stood before me in the flesh.

She still smelled of cinnamon and musk and soap, but her hair had lost much of its gloss. There were black smudges under her eyes and a strain around her mouth when she smiled.

She touched the tip of one finger to the top of my page. The nail was perfectly manicured, the exact color of the congealed pool beneath Jack Rose's chair that morning.

"Last Halloween. I'm flattered you remembered."

"I never forgot, Tash."

For probably the first time, her eyes lowered first. Her lashes fell across her cheeks like feathers.

"I'm afraid I wasn't very good to you, was I Sam?"

"Ancient history. What brings you in today?"

"You were quite clear before. If I want to reach you, you'd prefer it's here, at work." She cut her eyes toward the back room, where Hamish was rattling some forceps in the cleaning sink, and licked her lip. "Could we maybe go someplace, just, you know, to talk?"

I saw a muscle twitch under her right eye when she sensed my hesitation.

"Please?"

I didn't want to see her, but like that other ghost, I knew I had no choice.

"I guess I could use a coffee."

***

Tash and I sat in a quiet booth at the back of the coffee place down the block. Nights, the place jumped and buzzed with chatting students and local jazz bands. Middle of a hot afternoon, the U in summer session, we were the only customers.

Tasha huddled in on herself, latte cupped in both hands. There were small scratches on the backs of her fingers.

I sat across from her and sipped at a tall iced coffee. Except for the dark circles under her eyes, Tasha's skin was flawless. The muscle under her right eye jumped, temporarily distorting her good looks into something very different.

"Aren't you going to ask what's wrong?"

"We've played that game a little too often."

"That's not fair, Sam. It just isn't."

I rubbed my palm across the knuckles of my right hand. The callouses scraped like sandpaper.

"I'm just as bad as you are in my way," I said. "Grow up around crisis and messed-up personalities, fucked-up gets to be all that feels comfortable. Hard not to climb the walls when everything's smooth."

Her eyes took a dangerous glitter and her mouth was a flat line. With my usual social grace, I pressed on.

"Tash, you need drama like a fish needs water. If you're not the center of attention, you don't know who you are."

She opened her mouth, that fire that's always burning inside her ready to spill out, and did another first.

She stopped.

Stopped, pressed her lips shut again, and sank down into her arms in a sulk. I sat back in the booth and took another sip at my coffee. I had been over too many hurdles with her. We sat like that while I finished half my glass.

It was good coffee. The espresso shot was rich and sharp when it was poured over the ice, the milk that topped it sweet and cold. Soon as the drink was gone, so was I.

Softly, then gathering strength, Tasha'a shoulders began to hitch up and down. Her chin crumpled and her breath came in ragged little jerks. Her thick bangs hung down over her eyes, but I could still see individual tears mark long slow tracks down her cheeks. The drops fell in soft pats onto the tabletop. One splashed into the foam on the surface of her untouched latte.

Beneath the pad of my thumb, the knuckles on my other hand felt like the iron lumps at the back of a ball-peen hammer.

When she finally dabbed at her wet and glistening eyes with a paper napkin, Tasha's smile was rueful and shy.

Finally, she heaved a sigh, delicate and nuanced. "I guess I deserve this. I've been too *cruel* to you in the past to expect you to show concern. I've just taken you over too many hurdles."

"You some kind of mind-reader now?"

"I've *always* known what you're thinking, Sam."

"Scary thought."

"I know what you're thinking right now."

"You don't think very much of me." Her right eye twitched again. "And *yes*, I know I've done a lot to deserve it."

"This is new for you,. I'm not sure how to react."

Her eyes took on a quick dangerous glitter before the lights inside them clouded again. It was like watching impurities in the wax make a candle flame dance behind smoky glass.

She reached across the table, took one of my hands in both of hers. Her skin hummed with a quivering energy, like there were high-tension wires too close to its surface.

"You told me you loved me once, *remember*?" Her eyes were tortured, anguished. I took my hand back.

"Did you Sam? *Did* you love me?"

I kept my face flat and my eyes empty, even when the hurt came bubbling right up to the surface of that soft and flawless skin.

"Let it go, Tash. I'm with someone now"

"I know." She gave me big guilty eyes and her lower lip quivered. She looked back at the table again.

"Arthur know you're here?"

"Arthur." She made a dismissive wave of her hand. "That was *never* serious, you know that."

I did know: with Tasha a relationship usually lasted until the sweat cooled or the money ran out.

"Marcus, then? He seems to think you two have something going."

She lowered her head and rocked her shoulders back like a fighter taking a blow. She came back up out of it with some of that old witchy light burning in her green eyes again, a smoldering shot of it from up under those thick lashes and a flicker of her tongue across her bottom lip.

When she spoke again, her voice was soft and husky.

"He *hit* me, Sam."

"So leave."

"I mean it. He's *cruel*, Sam. Unspeakably cruel."

"Again, leave."

Her answer barely reached me, a scratchy little whisper.

"I'm afraid, Sam. He frightens me."

"Now *that* I find hard to believe."

"Marcus is spooky, seriously *spooky*. I've seen, he can do things, get in your *head*, make it seem real." That was a better fit with what the Tasha I knew. It was hard to imagine her afraid of any man, whether he lifted his hand to her or not, but I knew there were things in her head that came skittering after her when the lights went out.

"And he *hates* you," she said. "I mean it. He's terribly jealous."

"And you wouldn't have anything to do with that, of course."

She tucked a lock of ice-colored hair behind the shell of one ear and gave me the eyes again.

"He does know how I feel about you. How I've always felt."

"I did mention I'm with someone."

"Don't tell her then." She tried one of her naughtier smiles. It made a strange contrast with the wet eyelashes and tear-tracked cheeks. "Unless maybe you want to bring her along? It'll be like last Halloween, all over again."

My face felt as though it had been peppered with hot ash blown on the wind from a nearby fire.

"This is bullshit and you know it. I'll admit, you've pulled me in with this kind of crap in the past. Remember those times you thought you'd been drugged? Or how about that guy you were sure was following you? Or the time that famous musician was supposed to be putting a contract out on you?" I pressed both palms flat on the table.

"If you're really so damn afraid, go to the cops. Or a women's shelter. Just leave me out of it. I'm done."

Her lips flattened to a short sharp line. White spots stood out on the points of her cheekbones. Her facial tic jumped again, completely distorting the beautiful mask on its surface.

She rose stiffly, head and spine erect. Her body radiated a dry scorching heat like standing too close to a woodstove.

She bent down to me with a painful slowness. The hand on my shoulder thrummed with a mysterious and powerful energy, and her lips were so close to the shell of my ear that I felt the wet flick of her tongue when she spoke. Her hot breath was like a violation.

"You had your chance. I tried. You *had* your chance. Everything that happens from here is all your fault. *Everything*."

The sound of her heels on the tile floor made me think of Roman soldiers hammering nails. It took a long time to fade in the afternoon quiet.

Twenty-Seven

I had promised John I would finish the shading on his thigh piece this weekend, and that night seemed as good as any. Aaron and their latest piercer agreed to cover for him, so he showed up at six and we made an early start.

Like a lot of tattooists, John had some real ugly crap on the fronts of his thighs, was building up some really fine work on the backs and sides. It's just one of those things. When you're young and starting out, the top of your thigh is the single easiest place to reach on your whole body. Later on, the backs and sides are some the best areas you've got for big and interesting work.

The tattoo we were finishing today was real cheesecake stuff. Fifty years after she was the queen of the pinup, Bettie Page was still popular with illustrators, cartoonists and tattooists everywhere. Her career never advanced much beyond the stage of what they used to call 'artist's model' but she had achieved a level of fame far more enduring than any of the minor Hollywood starlets she had once aspired to be. As a little old lady, she was endlessly amused at the persistence of those old photos.

For John's thigh, I had used a black and white nude of her kneeling before the camera, one finger lifted to her mouth in a gesture of erotic speculation as she turned to face the viewer. Her eyes had that surprised and mischievous innocence she could conjure on command. The black robe fell away from her shoulders and lay puddled around her, the two sides clasped together by one hand held between her breasts. Her other hand caressed the shaft of the scythe leaning against her bare shoulder-- its blade gleamed wicked and sharp. Mostly, Bettie showed up as a jungle girl or a little devil, but she made an excellent Reaper too.

I had the whole side of his thigh to work with, and the design used it to the best advantage. The front of his thigh was already taken up with a dead baby/voodoo doll motif he'd used to cover up the mistakes he'd made starting out. His cover-ups were a lot better now: I could still see glimpses of the words underneath, even if I couldn't make them out.

I liked tattooing John. A lot of people in the industry, they'll try to backseat-drive the whole tattoo. John's got the sense to sit back and relax, not always the easiest thing to do in a trade given to control freaks. This was our fourth and final session on this piece. Linework and black tones had been done, the blue highlights in her robe, hair and scythe another. A month or so earlier I laid in a field of solid white throughout the figure's skin and finished the white highlights on robe and blade. Now that the skin was properly healed, we were doing the finished skin tones. To keep the Spooky Dead Girl feel he wanted, I used a lot of blues and purples

"More innocent times," John said. I looked up, realized I was tuning in at the end of a longer sentence. I had been concentrating on blending shadow tones in the figure's neck and shoulders. He caught my blank look, gestured at Betty's head up by his hip.

"I was just thinking, those were more innocent times. Life was different then."

"People were still people, fucked up as ever."

"Yeah, but think about it. Back then, a little kid found his dad's stash of dirty magazines, most he was gonna see was some topless women, maybe spanking each other or something. Now, you got free websites showing little kids sodomized by farm animals."

I sprayed the tattoo and wiped it down. The healed white underneath gave the colors I laid in over it a clear jewel-like quality. As I watched, tiny drops of blood welled back up out of the skin.

"You might have something there."

"Damn straight. When *I* was a kid, we had to pay good money for that shit." The grin that broke out across his features made him look like a demented leprechaun.

"You're sick, you know that?"

"Funny, that's what your mom said last night. Didn't stop her, though."

I worked on the planes of the face, shading my way from the hollows under the cheeks to the shadowed areas around the eyes and nose. I dipped the needles in a pale pink I was using sparingly, just enough warmth to keep the flesh from looking too cold and dead.

"Know what I like about this piece?" I began to move the warm tone down through her throat and across the center of her chest.

"Hot and creepy? You do kinda go for that sort of thing."

"Truth to tell, I think I'm a little bit over that."

"That little foreign girl's reformed you? I'll believe it when I see it. Meantime, I say you're all about the creepy hot chicks."

"No, what I like about your tattoo's the size of it. With her kneeling like that, and the size of your leg, the picture's big enough I can show some real detail."

"I know what you mean. Guy came in yesterday, wanted a wizard in front of a castle, summoning a giant dragon out of some magic cloud, holding a crystal ball, even knew what expression he wanted on the wizard's face. And he asks me, can I do the whole thing maybe two inches square?" John shook his head side to side in silent laughter.

We were quiet for a time while I concentrated on some of the soft blended effects across the rounded surfaces of thighs, forearms and breasts down to where they disappeared behind the black cloth of the robe. When I stopped to wipe down the skin and decide where to go next, John twisted around, checking out our progress. He let out a low whistle.

"Not bad."

"Given any thought to what you're gonna do with the back of your thigh?"

"Won't be easy." He slid in the chair, hiked the leg of his baggy shorts and turned so I could see.

"Fuck," was all I could think of to say. Streaks and whips and worms of scar tissue crossed over and laid alongside each other in a thick ropy lattice from midthigh up into the seat of his pants.

"Yup, good old Dad, all the way up past my kidneys. An extension cord was his favorite, but the old bastard could really get creative when he put his mind to it."

"I'm sorry."

"Hey, fuck it. At least it kept the asshole off my sisters. For awhile, anyway."

"You did what you could," I said.

"Don't go all Oprah on me. It's not like the Old Man's still around. A whore in Port Arthur stabbed him in the neck years ago." He stabbed one finger at the Bettie Page/Reaper along his thigh. His smile wouldn't quite stay in place.

"Told you I come from a fucked-up family."

Twenty-Eight

The tattoo finished late that night. With Tommy on a bus out of town and his brother Jack missing and presumed dead, there wasn't much I could do to find out who hired them. I hadn't seen the ghost of the girl in chains since that morning, and even Lisa Torres had been strangely silent.

I hated how much I missed Bex.

Back home, I tried to stretch out on the couch with an old-fashioned paperback book, without too much success. When I realized I'd read the same page a couple times already and still had no idea what was on it, I gave up and flipped on the TV. A hundred-odd channels and not a damn thing to watch.

Nothing to distract me from the fact that Hamish was right.

Six years, spent as peacefully as any man could ask. Long enough that I grew increasingly certain I'd put the bad old days behind me, until now. Three violent encounters in four days, even for me that had to be some kind of record. I wanted to point to the other guys, to say 'not my fault', even though I knew better. It *was* my fault. Something about *me* was at the heart of all of it.

I just didn't see what I could have done differently.

***

I remembered standing on the steps to the 19th century station house after the New Orleans cops finally kicked me loose for shooting Lisa Torres. The summer sun stung my eyes: everything seemed too bright, too colorful. A dead sixteen year old's face still hung in front of me whenever I closed my eyes, but the claustrophobic tightness eased across my chest. I didn't see how I was ever going to sleep again.

Michelle Labeaux, the local lawyer I had on retainer, kept one hand on my arm to steady me. She assured me that barring some paperwork, and her fees which she tactfully didn't mention, it was over.

I stopped on those worn sandstone steps and shielded my eyes against the glare. What I saw waiting for me on the sidewalk struck me so forcefully that the strength sagged out of my knees and Michelle's hand on my arm stiffened to support me.

Slouched against the side of their rented sedan, smoking those black French cigarettes both favored, Avi and Uri looked as comfortable and serene as rattlesnakes sunning themselves on a hot rock.

"Come on back inside with me," Michelle whispered next to my ear. "We'll wait there while I get a couple of gentlemen I trust in the FBI to come on over and give us a lift home."

I was impressed. I would have expected someone so inexperienced and from such a wealthy family to still retain a certain naivete, but my lawyer knew exactly what Avi and Uri were.

"It's okay," I said, "they're with me."

I crossed the sunstruck sidewalk to my adoptive fathers. It had only been five years since the last time I saw them. Somehow in that time both men had grown shorter and older. I was unprepared for the flood of emotion when it hit me: I wanted to run to them, to seek shelter and protection as a child. But I wasn't a child anymore, if I ever really had been.

I stopped in front of the two men, slim dark Avi and wide bullet-headed Uri, and held out my hand to them. Uri wrapped my hand in his own hard and enormous paw, shook it gravely with his other hand on my shoulder. It was the first time I noticed he had to reach up to do it.

I looked from one to another, trying to frame the question they must have seen in my eyes.

"Your grandmother," Avi said, soft and simple. Of course.

I introduced them to my attorney, and they were grave and polite with Michelle in that Old World way of theirs. I assured Michelle that I was safe with them, though I could see she still didn't quite believe me. Or she was reassessing how I came to find myself with a teenage hooker shooting at me.

I remember sitting in the back of their rented sedan, watching a cigarette spin a long curl of blue smoke up to the roof of the car, having no idea how it got into my hand. I spent the ride staring out the windows at familiar streets that were somehow different now. I didn't want to close my eyes, didn't like what I saw when I did. No one said much.

On the way back to their Garden District hotel from the police station, we were stopped at light when a couple of hard-eyed young men spotted the rental plates on the sedan and headed over. One came around the front of the hood while the other approached the driver's door. It was a good bet someone else was ambling up behind the car: car-jacking was a popular crime at that time, and tourists were always a favorite target.

The one blocking us in from the front was nervous, inexperienced. He kept looking around as though afraid to be seen, more understandable for a daylight assault/robbery than the stony calm of his partner. He also drew his pistol too soon, held it like he wasn't entirely sure what to do with it.

With a casual movement of the wrist, Avi flicked the car into reverse and sent it shooting backward. There was a sickening crunch, and he just as smoothly dropped it back into drive and swerved forward. He caught the other two, each with one front corner of the bumper.

"Not to crack windshield," he said as we rocketed out into the intersection and made several random turns before merging with the flow of traffic. He turned back and looked at me with his sweet smile and merry eyes.

"I cannot understand," he said, "why anyone get out of a thousand pound battering ram to make a fight."

These were the men who taught me.

Uri scanned the street, his eyes grim and the muscles at the corners of his jaw bunching and flexing.

"This place, it's no good."

***

They stayed in a beautiful nineteenth century hotel on St. Charles Avenue, a place I had gone a couple of times to sit with a drink and a book out on the veranda of the bar, watch the sunlight fall through the oaks and listen to the streetcar trundling by.

Once we were all up in their suite, Avi opened a bottle of wine and poured three glasses while Uri arranged a couch and chairs in a rough circle. What I wanted more than anything was a shower, but I took the seat Uri offered. Avi came over, left the wine back on the table. When we were all gathered together, he began to speak.

"For me, the first time, I was twenty years old. The first time I know, I mean. Before that, in war everyone is shooting. Maybe you hit, maybe you don't, you don't know. This was the first time I knew." He stopped to light another of those black French cigarettes, took a moment to inhale and savor the smoke in his lungs. I was glad to see I didn't have one of my own.

"I was the army then, parachuting. He was a sentry, I had to use a knife, to be silent." Avi drew more smoke into his lungs.

"He made no sound, but even with the knife in his throat, he fought in my arms. He wanted to live."

"I had only eight years old," Uri's voice was deep and rough, like something made to cut stone. "I grew up on *kibbutz* near Golan, a farm, very beautiful. We had sheep and oranges." I knew that kibbutzim were collective farms, as big a part of the Israeli psyche as cowboys are to Americans.

160

"In war, always the soldiers come, our side, their side. In peace, raiders sometime come from Syria, to steal, to kill. So always we keep a guard." He looked down at his hands for a time before going on. "I am guard from seven years old, two hours a night. I feel like I am a man when I do this. One night is very dark, no moon, I hear a noise. A raider, stealing food. We see each other, both so surprise. I shoot him," he tapped the center of his forehead to illustrate, "but I am small. Very different to paper target."

He was right. It was different.

***

The sound at the door woke me. I didn't even realize I'd fallen asleep. When I answered it, Bex came into my arms and held me close for a long, sweet, fragrant time. Her skin was warm and soft in my hands, her head a happy weight on my chest. I gradually realized my tee shirt was getting wet.

"What's wrong?"

She wouldn't face me, stayed pressed against my chest so I wouldn't see her tears.

"Nothing. Everything. Hayley."

I scooped her up, carried her to the couch and sat with her there on my lap. She tucked her forehead behind my ear and curled one small hand on my chest.

"And you, what am I supposed to do about you when this is all over?"

For a moment I thought of the gleaming black .45 in Jack Rose's hand, its barrel pressed to Bex's forehead. Everything was so much more fragile than any of us wanted to let on, and these moments were all we ever had.

I kissed her once and carried her up the stairs to my bed.

***

After telling their own stories, Avi and Uri waited silently for me to speak. Slow and halting at first, then gathering momentum until I was barely aware of my own words, I told them what I had done. Every detail.

Avi brought the glasses of wine over, and we drank a toast. It was a mark of solemn respect for the fallen, a celebration that we had lived to walk in the sun another day.

They made it a rite of passage. Only later, I realized it was also a farewell.

Twenty-Nine

Thomas Sven Green never made it onto a bus that night. It was one of those situations that made me at times wonder about the persistent power of human stupidity, or to suspect that we each do have an inescapable fate that awaits us all.

He only had to wait two hours for a bus to take him out of state. With the money I gave him and the thirty-five dollars in his pocket, he could have traveled as far as the West Coast. Or he could simply have landed in Ames, Iowa with cash to spare.

Instead, as he had all his life, Tommy Green fell in with bad company. He met up with two local glue sniffers, one slightly retarded, both brain-damaged from their habit.

With just two hours before the arrival of the bus that could have taken him away from the worst of his problems, at least for a while, Little Tommy started buying forty-ounce bottles of malt liquor at the convenience store across the street. The proprietor still remembered him weeks later, identified the 'chinless little weasel' immediately from mug shots. Tommy and his new friends started drinking, drank until the dark craving for greater highs was like an animal clawing at him from beneath the skin.

An hour later, that same proprietor called 911 to report an abortive robbery by Tommy and the glue sniffers, who tried in some fashion to rob the same store on average once a month. As always, Tommy had an uncanny ability to connect with people who would lead him further along his stupid and self-destructive path. Same as with his brother, I imagine he felt their leadership absolved him.

After he fled the store, nothing is known about where he went or what he did for the next several hours. At some point that night, though, he changed company again, seeking something he could feel but never define.

An addict, trailer park hooker and single mother of three eventually admitted to police that she remembered seeing 'that creepy little freak' shortly before three that morning, when she went to Lot 18 of the SunBreeze Mobile Estates to score the substances that would send her sweeping out of her life and problems in an omnipotent rush, to make the things she did to afford the drugs seem like a movie she was watching about someone else's life.

She remembered the gallon jug of wine in a paper bag kept close between Tommy's feet, the smear of electric blue spray paint on his upper lip. She remembered that he sat in a ragged chair in the trailer at Lot 18 with his pants down around his ankles skin-popping into his thighs. He wore brightly colored boxers printed with pictures of beer cans.

For the next seventy-two hours, Little Tommy went on a massive spiraling binge. By three o'clock Sunday morning, Tommy huddled naked in a knot of blankets in one corner of the trailer, his heart's blood coursing with cheap bathtub crank.

At 3:25, while I slept with Bex held close in the protective circle of my arms, a tall bald man in black leather walked into the SunBreeze Mobile Estates looking for Thomas Sven Green.

The SunBreeze was not a gentle place to live. It was a place where rape, incest, crimes against children and the elderly, violence and murder were all bleak facts of daily life.

Its residents lived in daily terror and sad intimacy with the depthless capacity for human cruelty, and no one who saw the bald man shuffling among the trailers that night failed to see that he was trouble walking, trouble it would be better not to get involved with. From police interviews the following morning, nearly every trailer in the SunBreeze was full of soundly sleeping occupants or had a TV turned up a little too loud to hear the shrieks and screams of the dying.

Strangely, those same sleeping television watchers were eager and disturbingly gleeful to tell their stories on the local and national news feeds as vividly as possible.

They told of the tall man, over six and a half feet, bald, dressed head to toe in black leather, making his stiff halting way through the trailer park to Lot 18. There, he was intercepted by two ex-cons acting as guards for the drug house. They carried shotguns. The bald man tore their throats out with his bare hands and shuffled into the trailer.

The SunBreeze shuddered with sounds of gunfire, crashes and screaming. Muzzle flashes and broken glass went unseen by nearby neighbors to Lot 18. They huddled on the floors of their own trailers and prayed no stray bullet would find them.

By 3:35, several witnesses saw the tall man walk out of the SunBreeze Mobile Estates the same way he walked in, as slow, unconcerned and unstoppable as cancer.

In the trailer at Lot 18, nothing was left living. Little Tommy Green, whose brother had been murdered less than a week earlier, who had been given one hundred fifty dollars and a second chance, was found still wrapped in his blankets.

His head was turned all the way around on his body so that he faced behind himself. His expression was surprised, as though what was happening must be some terrible mistake.

Alone among the dead in that place, his heart was never recovered.

Thirty

Monday was my day off. A day off, with Bex. No woonder I woke up bright-eyed, bushy-tailed and ready to wrestle tigers. Toweling off after my shower, I caught myself whistling. Standing at the sink to scrape my overnight beard down to a pale blue shadow along my jaw, I saw the guy in the reflection grinning like a fool. My good mood was unshakable.

The dead girl in my shaving mirror had other ideas.

I turned on the hot tap, lathered up my face, and looked up to see Lisa Torres standing against the far wall. She stood with her thumbs hooked in her low-riders, her eyes on the ground at her feet. There was no trace of the three entry wounds like drops of scarlet wax on the yellow tube top or the chalk white skin below it. She almost looked like a normal teenager.

I looked back behind me, but she wasn't there. I could only see her in the mirror, so that's how I addressed her.

"What's on your mind, Lisa?."

She shook the fall of stringy bleached hair from in front of her eyes but still refused to look at me. I dipped the razor under the hot tap, cleared a line of shaving cream from the corner of my mouth.

She stayed right behind me. I could see her reflection in that part of the mirror not yet completely fogged. Her opaque dead eyes finally flicked up at me over my shoulder.

She had no breath to fall on me, but a cold as deep and black as subterranean water radiated off her skin.

I think I fucked up.

No way I was stepping into that one. I scraped the stubble away from my upper lip instead.

Remember I said it was coming, and you couldn't stop it?

The razor paused over the far corner of my mouth.

Well, it's started, and...

"What have you done, Lisa?"

She dug the tips of her fingers into her pockets and looked back down at her feet.

"You telling me you're behind all this shit in my life right now?"

The dead girl tossed her head and snorted.

That stuff so far's all chickenshit. This is bad, *real bad.*

"I don't know what to tell you, Lisa. Why don't you tell me?"

She shook her head hard from side to side, her arms wrapped tight around her body. The bathroom was clouded with steam and bathed in buttery summer light, but the ghost rubbed her palms against her upper arms as if she finally felt the biting cold that radiated from her own skin.

"Same as the night you tucked that pistol in your jeans. It's not working out the way you thought it would. My question is, what are you going to do about it?"

She bit her lower lip, pain and fear close to the surface in her eyes, but said nothing.

In the mirror, I could see her hands rise up behind my shoulders and feel their clasp, soft as flesh, cold as something hidden a long time under the ice.

I looked down and still saw nothing, but felt her ghostly fingers dig into the flesh at my shoulders and spin me around.

If I say anything he'll know. He'll know and he'll hurt me. He can do it too, bad enough to make me wish I was alive again. It's worse than I thought, lots worse.

"Same as the night you tucked that pistol in your jeans. It's not working out the way you thought it would. My question is, what are you going to do about it?"

She bit her lower lip, pain and fear close to the surface in her eyes, but said nothing.

In the mirror, I could see her hands rise up behind my shoulders and feel their clasp, soft as flesh, cold as something hidden a long time under the ice.

I looked down and still saw nothing, but felt her ghostly fingers dig into the flesh at my shoulders and spin me around.

Without the mirror for help, I couldn't see any sign of the spirit in the bathroom with me, only feel her bony icy hands grasp the sides of my head and pull me down to her with unnatural strength. I was suddenly and deeply afraid.

It was like plugging my face into a light socket. I felt my spine buckle and thrash. White light, and darkness.

I came back to myself, rubber-legged and holding myself up by leaning against the bathroom sink. All I knew was that the hot water was still running, and that something smelled like shaving cream.

And--

And the incredible pain of chunks of metal tearing through my body at almost twice the speed of sound. I knew what it was like to feel my body slipping into shock, icy and numb. I felt Lisa's anger, bitter and hot, a black iron brand on her soul.

And something else. A beast out of childhood nightmare, a ravening bristling thing of dripping teeth and insatiable appetite, dragging behind it a dark clanking chain. Caught in the chain's coils, sometimes two and sometimes three teenage girls. Their dead skin was pale and blue in the darkness. Their faces, sometimes their own and sometimes Lisa's, were masks of pain beyond my imagining.

For the first time in the years I had known her, I saw a new side to the runaway street kid from East Texas. She regretted the suffering of those innocents her revenge had harmed.

A whole kaleidoscope of Lisa's emotions rioted through my head. Six years after her death, she was finally becoming a real person to me.

I looked at my reflection in the mirror, saw the injury in the center of my forehead. Fright-white, fading to cyanide blue, angry red at the edges. It looked like a bullseye.

I knew what I had to do, and I could only hope Bex would understand.

***

When I came back into the bedroom, Bex was awake and propped up on one elbow. Her twinkling, elfin smile changed when she got a better look at me.

"Sam, what on earth?"

"Frostbite. At least, I'm pretty sure it's frostbite."

She sat up in bed with her knees tucked up under her chin. I don't think she knew what an erotic picture she made. I sat down on the bed with her.

I swallowed and searched for the words I wanted.

"This might sound kind of messed up, but I decided I'd rather be honest with you and have you think I'm crazy or something than hide this from you." I looked down at my hands. "Remember I told you about shooting that girl down in New Orleans?"

"The one I dreamed about? Not bloody likely to forget." She rubbed at the gooseflesh rising on her bare arms.

"For the last six years, I've been haunted by her ghost. At first, I thought I might be hallucinating, visible manifestation of my guilt, that sort of thing. But then, I do come out of a real spooky family. Psychic, witchy stuff, the kind of thing might make you keep an open mind about being haunted."

Beside me, Bex was all ears and big attentive eyes. At least she didn't run screaming out of the room.

Instead she surprised me by putting a warm hand on my arm. Her fingers softly covered the image of a kimonoed warrior tumbling through the air, shielding him from the demon he fought.

"That must have been terrible. I only spent a couple nights with the poxy little hag, and I already hate her."

"It gets worse."

I told her what life was like for me the last six years. She listened well, and asked lots of questions. I didn't have many answers.

Finally she said, "Well one thing's obvious. She's in love with you. Maybe not as much as she hates you, but I'm sure of it."

"You got that out of what I just told you? Six years, I never knew until now." I touched the burning spot on my forehead for emphasis. Bex gave me the sort of look that said she wasn't surprised.

"Anyway," I said, "that's what I'm worried about. She's done some pretty terrible stuff to get me away from people she's had a lot less reason to be jealous about. I'm afraid to think of what she might come up with for you."

Bex dimpled at me.

"So she's got a lot of reason to be jealous, hm? Why Samuel Roark, I do believe you're blushing. I didn't think anyone so dark could turn such a bright shade of red."

"So, you do still want to keep seeing me?" I couldn't believe how tentative I sounded.

"Are you kidding? I've known you less than a week, and so far we've been attacked by ruffians, you chased off a stalker and now we're on a hunt to lay a ghost to rest before she takes her revenge from beyond the grave. I think it's safe to say that this is my most exciting holiday ever."

"You're the greatest, Bex."

She came forward into my arms then, her lips warm and soft on the frost burn Lisa left behind.

Thirty-One

We had breakfast at Mickey's. Bex loved it, kept comparing it to a place back in New Zealand called Drexels. The way she talked about her home, I wondered if I might one day see it.

"You come out, we are so going."

It was a simple remark, offhand. But it stopped us both, held us with eyes locked across the table.

Without another word, or giving me a chance to reply, Bex swept our check off the table and stepped up to the counter.

While we waited for the waitress to ring us up, Bex changed the subject.

"You don't seem to like your family very much."

"My mother was a total write-off, but my grandmother and sisters aren't so bad. Just creepy."

The phone rang behind the counter. The waitress picked it up, said 'no customer calls' and hung up.

"Creepy how? Did you mean what you said before, your grandmother can really move stuff around with her mind?"

"Yup. Dowse for water or buried treasure too. Tell your fortune, past present *or* future, and generally scare the pants off everyone around her."

"Sounds *cool*." It struck me that with her shoes off, the little Kiwi wasn't much taller than Grandma Roark.

"Try living with it. My sisters are just as bad as she is. They'd sit around that big old house in their rocking chairs, just staring off into space. Nobody'd say a word for hours, then all of them laugh at the same time like they just heard a funny joke."

"That must be where you got your ability to see ghosts."

We were out on the sidewalk now, headed for the car parked on the street a block away. We passed a ringing pay phone.

I made no move to answer it.

"Possible, I guess. My sister Agatha used to say I had the talent and refused it. Guess I've always preferred to deal with the world of things I can see and touch."

"Except now, something from their world is touching you." Her fingers touched the mark below my hairline. The skin was mostly just red there now, like a sunburn with a gray spot in the center. I would probably lose that skin.

"So where do we go from here?"

"I thought I'd take you to Stillwater," I said. "It's this really beautiful town on the St. Croix River, right on the Wisconsin border. It's like stepping into a time warp, one of America's prettiest prisons too, if you're into that sort of thing."

"That's not what I meant, Sam. This ghost isn't done with you, and you know it. Or do you think she's already done the worst she can, maybe she'll give up now?"

"No."

Not by a long shot.

Thirty-Two

It was a gorgeous morning. Once my anonymous little piece of gray plastic whisked us past the used car lots and outlet stores east of St. Paul, it was a lovely drive too. Bex held my hand and looked out the window and hummed along with the songs playing on the iPod in my car. I had trouble keeping my mind on it.

For some reason, I kept remembering a time years before the death of my mother. I would have been four or five, playing some solitary game in my grandmother's front room. I remembered the draft of the door opening, and my older sister Agatha coming into the room on her way upstairs. She held herself very straight and tall as always, didn't look right or left or straight ahead but off to some far-distant point. She walked up to me, placed one hand on my left arm, then turned and mounted the stairs.

Seconds later, I felt the draft and heard the door, and Agatha came in again. With the same, slow, sleepwalking motion, she crossed the front room to me, put one hand on my left arm, turned and started up the stairs.

I was terrified.

When I found her a few minutes later, she lay unconscious on the ground under the tree she had been climbing, her left arm twisted awkwardly beneath her. She'd chosen an isolated spot to climb in, and my grandmother's property offered a wealth of choices, but without feeling in any way guided, I knew where to look.

Uncanny things happened around my sisters all the time. They were a fact of life until I left home at sixteen, but none made the impression on me that that one did.

I had always chalked that episode up to Agatha and her powers. Now I wondered.

After I left home, my life's trials and challenges were all bounded by the customary laws of physics. It wasn't always the happiest life, but it was something I understood.

The week I'd had, maybe it was only natural that I found myself thinking again about all the dark fruit that fell from my family tree.

I only have one coherent memory of my mother. There are other things, pieces and fragments: the way she used to hum to herself when she would get ready to go out, the smell of the powder she wore, the memory of a smile or a touch, the smell that filled a room when she was high.

But one memory of long enough duration to be called an episode.

I don't know how old I was, except that I was just about the same height as the arm of the chair she sat in. I don't remember what I had been doing before she called me over to her, only that I stood beside her with that curious admixture of fear and hope that characterized my childhood. It seems to be a fact of life for anyone sharing their home with an addict they love.

My mother was given to unpredictable expressions of wild generosity, maudlin tenderness, harrowing rage. I never knew what she might do next, probably because she never had any idea herself.

So I stood beside the arm of my mother's chair, more scared than anything else because I even then knew without words that when the dark fires burning inside her sang out for blood, there was no safe place for any of us.

I remember her staring off into space, ignoring me, her head nodding in time to some slow and soundless music only she could hear. She ignored my presence for so long I began to hope she had forgotten me entirely.

Then her shining dark head swung around on that long powdered neck and a sloppy smile spread across the lower half of her face. She brought one hand , smooth and cool, up to my cheek, seemed to savor its warmth.

"You're a good boy," she said, the only words I actually remember her speaking to me. Every other memory I have of her is silent.

Her eyes went wide and black and filled with a glitter that had nothing to do with the single lamp burning in the room with us. I was dry-mouthed, afraid that something I might say or do, or fail to say or do, would spill her over the edge. When her eyes were like that she could cry for hours, sneer cruel insults and laugh at my tears, or send her magic roaring through the house to tear our home apart in a fit of black wrath. Those times, I tried my best to protect Tabitha, the baby.

When I could find courage enough to swallow and find my voice, I asked if I could please go color in my room.

All light and movement fell out of her face like a switch had been thrown. Her mouth was slack, the eyes empty. Worse than empty. They were pieces of clear glass set in a doll's head, windows to a vast, chilling and frightening expanse. They showed me a dark void where nothing could ever survive. Not life, not warmth, not love. Not even hope.

She turned away from me without saying anything. I left the room as fast as I could.

I remember rubbing at my cheek where she touched it, offended by the taint of whatever residue had been on her fingers.

I remember being afraid, sure that in that last moment I had seen something about my mother, something she kept hidden, something she feared and tried to hide from herself.

I was sure I had seen the truth.

Thirty-Three

The little town of Stillwater was just as beautiful as promised, on a sunny summer day in June even more so. If the main street was a little bit too obsessed with antique shops, it made up for it with bookstores, great places to eat and drink and architecture that started in the mid-1800's and largely stopped by the 1930's. I liked the way those old buildings were so intimate and personal, not a Superstore in sight.

All the same, our visit here wasn't entirely the sightseeing expedition I made it out to be.

W.H. Smith was large, airy, well stocked and well lit. Like every bookstore, used or otherwise, most of their trade was in the sort of novels people read at the beach or in airports. Unlike most, Smith's refused to let the fiction take over. Whether ancient history, geology or the memoirs of prominent regional citizens, they were the best place I knew to find nonfiction on any subject.

Their range of works on the occult beat anything I'd ever seen on the shelves of those dim little places smelling of incense.

When she saw the floor of the shop and the stairs leading up to the collection on the second floor, Bex sparkled up at me, kissed the corner of my mouth and scampered off. Up at the register, Dave had something to show me.

"Not the sort of thing I'd normally stock," he said as he brought a cardboard box up from under the counter, "but when I saw them, I thought of you first thing."

Inside were old Peanuts books from the 50's and 60's, first editions collecting the early newspaper strips of Charlie Brown, Linus, Lucy and all the gang. In the oldest ones, Snoopy still walked on all fours like a dog.

"Not too shabby," I said. "How much?"

"Two fifty." I raised my eyebrows and put the book in my hands back in the box.

Dave was tall and thin, scholarly from the tips of his long pale fingers to the top of his curly gray head. He looked like discussing money physically pained him. "I know it sounds like a lot, but look."

He peeled back the front cover of the book I had been holding. Time had yellowed the fountain pen scratch, but the signature was as distinctive as the day Charles Schulz made it.

"Every one of em. I could get three, three fifty on eBay, easy as anything, more if I sold em seperate. But I wanted to show you first there."

"Okay Dave, you got me. Sold. I'm also after whatever you've got on ghosts, exorcism, that sort of thing." I hoped Lisa wasn't listening in on me right now.

"Not much in the way of ghost stories since that LeFanau I sold you last year."

"I'm thinking more... nonfiction. If that's not a contradiction in terms." I still couldn't admit it in public.

"I know what you mean. Come on back, let's see what we got. Jody, you want to watch the counter a minute?"

***

An hour later, Bex and I were deeply involved in burgers and malts at Rexall's, a drug store whose soda fountain had edged out the pharmacy fifty years ago. Not much had changed since they took out the last of the shelves and display cabinets to put in more tables in 1956. Not much except the world outside.

The bookstore had been a bust. There were simply too many titles, no way to tell which were worth the trouble. Plenty of talk about 'psychic imprints' and 'visitations', not a word about how it worked or what to do about it. Useless.

I looked up at the tiny New Zealander across from me. Her burger looked enormous in her small hands and her dark hair glowed in the sun like filaments of burnished gold.

There was no pay phone on the back wall between the restrooms. It had been removed at some point in favor of an old-fashioned bubblegum machine. A well-dressed woman pushing a baby carriage through the door lifted a ringing iPhone to her ear. She listened a moment, said 'fuck you' in a bored tone and put it back away.

Bex caught me looking at her, wrinkled her nose in a smile as she chewed. Her eyes were a promise of hope, a visible reminder that for all its ugliness and brutality, the world was also a home for much that was good and fine.

"What?" she said.

"You're pretty awesome, you know that?"

She smiled, full of sunshine from across the Pacific, and started to say something. No words came out. She took a deep breath and tried again.

"I wonder if we're doing the right thing."
"What do you mean?"
"Well, those men, the ghosts,all this crazy stuff in your life..." Her gaze landed on my frost-burned forehead. "It doesn't seem right somehow, being out on a date like nothing's wrong."

"It's not that nothing's wrong, it's..." I ran one hand through my hair, searching for the words. "It's like that old proverb. This guy, right, he's chased over the edge of a cliff by a tiger, just manages to grab a handhold. Now, he's clinging to the side of this cliff, hundred foot drop below him, hungry tiger snapping and waiting right above, and he sees this strawberry growing out of the rocks beside him. Certain death in every direction."

"What does he do?"

"He eats the berry. And it's the sweetest thing he's ever tasted."

She gave me one of her smiles, reached over and kissed my chin.

"I'm no berry, Mister Roark, but point taken. *And* compliment returned."

I held Bex's hand and smiled at nothing in particular.

Out on the sidewalk, we got ice cream cones and walked with them in the sun. Our steps took us in the direction of a pair of pay phones at the corner. I turned, brought us back near the display window of a chain bookstore before I could be sure I heard them ringing.

We finished our ice creams, thrashed over the very short list of my possible enemies and fruitlessly discussed ways of finding The Brethren. Our conversation as we walked back to the car was mainly about dinner options.

A man on the sidewalk walking toward us began to play Moon River in chiming electronic tones. He brought out his cell a few feet away from us and the music stopped. He stood motionless on the sidewalk, one finger in his ear to block the background noise. I noticed he kept looking at me.

"You Sam Roark?"

I stopped in front of him. He held his phone out to me.

"It's for you."

Thirty-Four

I brought the stranger's phone to my ear. Wary as hell, but curious too.

"Hello?" As though things like that happened to me every day.

"Sam?"

The voice at the other end of the line was soft and breathy, with a slight hint of a lisp. A little girl's voice, though its owner wasn't so little anymore.

"Tabitha. I guess I should have known."

"Then why didn't you answer me earlier?"

"What's on your mind?"

"We're worried about you."

I pinched the bridge of my nose, said nothing. I didn't know what I could possibly say.

"You stopped wearing It." That was how Tabitha always referred to whatever sidearm I wore: It.

"I would have thought you'd sound happier about that."

"It protected you."

I waited but there was only silence on the other end of the line. Not the crackle, hiss or hum of an open line. Not a single sound in the background. Just perfect silence.

"Why'd you call, Tabby?"

"Something bad is after you. Something really bad."

"Tell me something I don't know." My cheeks burned. I was ashamed of my childish behavior, but I couldn't seem to stop it, either.

"Sam, I mean something *our* kind of bad. Not the kind you're used to."

"Then how would a gun protect me?"

"Symbols." She said it as though being patient with a child. Which to her, about these things, I was. "Magic is all about symbols. Same way I'm talking to you right now. The iron didn't hurt either."

"I don't know what I'm supposed to say to that, Tabitha."

"I liked it better when you called me Tabby. It was like old times."

"We're not little kids anymore." I hadn't seen my family in eleven years, long enough for the knobby-kneed thirteen year old I left behind to grow into a twenty-four year old woman.

To avoid the staring eyes turned my way, I looked up at the sky and its slow push to a blood-colored sunset.

"We've missed you, Sam."

"I bet."

"*I* miss you. I know Agatha does too. She talks about naming one of the babies after you."

"Babies?"

"Twins, due any day."

Of course. They had to be three: with Tabby the maiden and Grandma Roark the crone, my older sister wouldn't have room to manuver.

"You should come. Be here for the birth, meet your neice Audra, she's four now."

"Fuck." Agatha named her oldest after our mother.

"Don't be like that. She's just a little girl, and she's adorable. Bring Hamish, and your girl, we'd love to meet her. Please, Sam, say you'll come."

Bex and the man whose phone I held to my ear looked worried. I felt like I'd taken a punch to the heart.

"Something's out there, stalking you in the night." Tabitha's voice in my ear fell to something a hair above a whisper. "A black beast dragging an iron chain, thirsting for your blood."

The same beast Lisa showed me this morning. My skin prickled, but I said nothing.

"Old Rosie showed it to us. She was in our dreams, all our dreams. She says, an innocent died to birth it, and another will die to feed its master's hate." There was a pause: perfect, still and soundless. "Sam, there's something else she says. She says *the child is yours*."

"I don't have children, Tabitha. You know that." But my first thought was of a child born in East Texas, died on the floor in front of me in New Orleans.

"It's what *she* says."

"Yeah well."

"Sam, we're worried about you. Down here we can protect you, but where you are now there's nothing we can do."

I closed my eyes and took a deep breath, trying not to say the wrong thing, knowing I probably would anyway.

"Sam?"

"I'll think about it, Tabby. Okay?"

I was surprised to hear her giggle into the phone.

"You called me Tabby."

"Hey, this guy wants his phone back. I gotta go."

"Come see us. And Sam? What's her name?"

"Huh?"

"Your girl. She seems sweet. Heart like a lion. Tell her that for me, will you?"

"Alright, I will. Look, Tabby, I really gotta go."

"Love you."

"Love you too," I said, but I'm pretty sure the connection was already broken.

I handed the phone back to its stunned owner, turned into Bex's raised eyebrows.

"My little sister says hi. She thinks you're sweet."

***

Bex was quiet after the call from Tabitha. I'm not entirely sure she even noticed the restaurant we chose, or what she ordered once we were there. Her gaze was soft, unfocused, searching among the lost and private worlds in the clear depths of her untouched chardonnay.

"That was your sister?" She didn't look up when she asked.

"One of them, yeah. Tabitha, the baby."

"I thought you didn't talk to your family."

"I don't, really. Tonight was the first time in years."

She looked up from her glass then, her eyes as clear and full of light as a pure mountain spring.

"How did she *do* that? *How* could she possibly know to call *that* cellphone at *that* moment?"

"I told you my family's a bunch of creepy witches. Stuff like that's just the tip of the iceberg for them."

"But, she couldn't just know that man's number, could she?"

"I think... I think what that was, Tabby was only using the *idea* of a telephone." This was a subject that made me uncomfortable, had ever since I was a child.

"I think it's more like, she wanted to talk to me, she just thought about it real hard and picked up a phone. The one nearest to me will ring. I've seen all of them do it before: they never dial a number, never get a long distance bill."

She shivered, ran her hands up and down her arms to warm them again.

"I see what you mean by creepy."

"My Grandma Roark does the same thing, but with a pan of water and a needle. Don't ask me how that works."

"What if they rang through to voice mail? Would they have to wait in a queue?" I saw the hint of a smile at the corner of Bex's lip and played into it.

"What I want to know is, where on that basin of water do you press 5 for more options?"

It was the moment more than anything we said, but we both burst out laughing. Pure stress relief. We ran the whole gamut, phone banking on a crystal ball, does she tap on a real mouse's head when she wants to use the internet, every stupid gag we could think of. We laughed until our sides hurt and tears ran down our cheeks. True to the Minnesotan character, the other diners were scandalized at the spectacle of public laughter but too polite to say anything.

Bex was the first to recover. She leaned into the table and wiped her eyes with the inside of one blue-veined wrist.

"Christ, Sam, but I needed that. You certainly know how to show a girl a good time."

"You're not so bad yourself," I said, "and when you laugh your ears blush a most fetching pink."

"Do not."

"Do too."

She stuck out her tongue at me. "Tell me something, Mister Samuel Roark. Is dating you always like this?"

"Not a bit." For some reason I couldn't identify, even to myself, I felt the question deserved a serious answer.

"I've never met anyone like you, Bex. You and me together, it's like nothing I've ever done." I looked up, caught her eyes. "That, and people aren't usually trying to kill me."

She reached across the table for my hand, gave it a squeeze.

***

Unfortunately, throughout the rest of our dinner I kept wondering if I had been completely honest with Bex, or with myself.

Violence had been a much more frequent visitor into my life than can possibly be considered normal. By the time I was old enough to drink, I had already been shot, stabbed, sliced, bludgeoned, pummeled, and in one case, narrowly avoided being blinded by an acid-throwing pimp I had never before seen in my life. I had a longer, uglier combat record than a lot soldiers, cops or criminals, people whose careers were supposed to throw them in harm's way.

The years since I shot Lisa Torres had been quiet ones. I hadn't done anything heavier than throw the odd drunk out of a party now and then, and I told myself loud and long that this time of peace was due to my putting up my gun, or to some growth in wisdom and maturity.

But here it was, back and worse than ever. I was unarmed and closing in on thirty, and I found myself back in the center of the raging storm. Like I never left.

I had to question the truth of my rationalizations.

***

After dinner we stepped out onto the sidewalk into the warm and gentle breath of summer, looked out a sky more dazzling and dramatic than anything Winslow Homer ever painted.

Thick towers of cloud, lit from beneath by a sun no longer visible on the horizon, glowed lavender and gold as though spun out of strands of candied light. The sky above those clouds was a deep inky purple, already showing a first peppering of stars overhead. Below the cloud line, in a band the width of my hand along the horizon in the west, nine different shades of red followed the sun below the earth, from deep crimson to the bright pink of a salmon steak.

At the center of the tunnel down which they seemed to travel, the sun's light still lingered as a pale yellow smudge beckoning and drawing the surrounding reds.

It was breathtaking, and Bex and I stopped there on the sidewalk and allowed our breath to be taken. She put one hand around my waist, and I put an arm on her shoulder. Every now and then, this place truly shows itself to you.

I heard complaints all the time, and all too often joined in with them, about the heat and mosquitoes in summer, winters that fall upon us like the curse of some Old Testament prophet, a populace bland and narrow-minded to comical extremes. But the people here are also courteous, kind and generous, and the land here at any time of year was possessed of such majesty and dignity and utter beauty, it was capable of restoring even the most broken faith.

I looked down at Bex, saw the arch of her cheek and temple illuminated in burnished, rosy gold. Something inside my chest seemed to break and melt at the same time.

***

We drove back to the Twin Cities, silent in the twilight. My mind kept returning to my sister's words, and to the essentially pointless nature of premonition. Not the shameless scam artists working psychic hotlines or doing cold-reading to auditoriums packed with the lonely and gullible. My sisters were very much the real deal, each in her way as powerful as Grandma Roark at her best. The way my mother might have been if she hadn't burned her gifts in the flame at the end of a pipe.

The women in my family were all powerful witches, generation after generation. My old ghost, the new arrival, whatever the hell it was they were both so afraid of, it wouldn't stand a chance against my sisters and grandmother in their coven of three.

With the tires humming on the road and night falling on the prairie around us, the temptation was there to nose the car south onto I-94, to head for my family and the shelter they could provide.

So why didn't I go to them? Partly it was pure stubborness: This was my mess, *my child,* as Old Rosie put it, and I wanted to handle it myself. Part of it was Old Rosie herself, and the nature of prophecy. I grew up surrounded by prophetic dreams and divination and all of that. I knew how those messages might prove uncannily accurate in hindsight, but next to useless beforehand.

Dreams and visions are the lyrical poetry of the mind. The predators in my life were coming with the cold precision of a math problem involving terminal velocity.

Thirty-Five

Hamish looked terrible. I stood at the side of his hospital bed, trying to keep my face brave. He seemed somehow smaller, shrunken. I held his big knuckly hand and tried not to think about the tubes and drips and needles, the lights of electronic screens and the silent movement of nurses in and out of the room.

He looked at me with his one visible eye, managed to tug a wry little smile from under all those bandages.

"So much for playing shortstop for the Twins." It was hard to understand him with his face so badly swollen.

"You know, there are easier ways to meet nurses."

He laughed more than my joke seemed to warrant. The effort seemed to tire him out.

"What happened?"

Hamish licked his lips before replying. The rich golden brown of his eye seemed too pale and weak in that setting.

"They were waiting for me at the shop this morning... Caught me coming through the door."

"Marcus?"

"Don't know, I never got a look." He stopped again to lick his lips. They were cracked and swollen, and on one side a misshapen knot of dark purple vanished up into the bandages that hid the rest of that side of his head.

I gave his hand a reassuring squeeze. "Don't worry about it. You came out of it in one piece, that's what matters."

Hamish managed to pack more disbelieving anger into that one unbandaged eye than I would have thought possible.

"Get a good look at any of them?"

"I came in to open up this morning, stepped around the corner into the waiting room. Saw someone move, thought maybe it was you." He closed his eye, and I saw his mouth tighten in pain.

"What happened next?"

"I don't know. They had a ringer with them, *serious* fucking karate geek. I didn't even *see* half the shots coming." The effort of talking seemed to tire him out and he fell back against his pillow.

"Want to tell me what he looked like?"

"Hoodie and jeans, that's all I got. Fucked me up and busted my leg and left me there to die, just like that. Like I was nothing."

He turned his head away from me and closed his eye again. He was quiet for so long I began to worry he had lost consciousness. His hand burned between my palms as though filled with hot sand.

"I'll square this," I whispered, my heart in my voice.

***

No matter what they do to hospitals to try to cheer them up, what colors they paint them or what cheery murals decorate the walls, it still doesn't hide their essential nature. They remain tile and disinfectant, pain and sickness. The longer I stayed, the heavier the air became with the smell of death.

Greg caught me in the hall. For some reason, the coat and stethoscope and scrubs made it look like the guy I knew was dressed up as a doctor. Maybe because today was the first time I'd seen him at work.

Greg caught me in the hall. Maybe it was the youthful face. Maybe because today was the first time I'd seen him at work. Either way, the coat and stethoscope and scrubs made it look like the guy I knew was playing dress-up as a doctor.

He stood in front of me with a hand out in front of my chest.

"Hell of a thing, Sam. I'm sorry."

"Yeah."

"Look, the break is clean and his other injuries are not as bad as they look. Even the smoke inhalation wasn't all that serious. The only reason we're keeping him overnight is the risk of concussion." He ran a hand through his hair. "You know, in the grand scheme of things, this wasn't that bad."

I said nothing. Not twenty feet away my best friend lay broken and in pain, victim of an attack meant for me.

"Reason I'm telling you all this, yeah it sucks, but you need to focus on what's important: Hamish is going to be okay."

"You know he was the first person I met here? Couple of dumbass kids, fresh off the bus, been looking out for each other ever since."

"The police are going to want a statement--"

"I was a wreck when I came back to town. Hamish got me back on my feet, made me start the new shop. I owe him my life."

"Do you have anyone to stay with you tonight? Jim and I were going out, but I'm sure he wouldn't--"

"I'm fine."

"Sam, you never could play poker worth a damn. Every thought you've got is written all over your face. You need to let this go."

I did brush past him then. I had to get out of that house of death.

Thirty-Six

Back at the studio, I ducked under the crime scene tape and passed through the door the police had left standing open when they were done. Broken glass from the door panel crunched underfoot.

The fire had turned the foyer, reception desk and front half of the waiting room into a lifeless alien landscape. It was like stepping into some bombed-out urban combat zone. The smell of smoke and signs of water damage were everywhere.

Back in the studio area the damage wasn't nearly as severe, but the place felt different now, funereal. It wasn't just the burnt smell that clung to everything like an ancient curse.

Part of it was the still hush. For the first time I could remember, Murphy's was closed. Everything was closed.

Part of it was the darkness, the dim wash of orange light from the street below. For six years of my life, Astounding Tattoo had been more home to me than any of the places I had lived, and it had been violated, all but destroyed. Now it felt subtly dangerous, enemy territory.

I told myself that entertaining those feelings played right into the bastards' hands, that off-balance and powerless was exactly how they needed me to see myself. But I still didn't know how to stop.

The desk was scorched and broken. It lay on its belly against the back wall, thick gouges in the linoleum where it landed. The waiting room couches weren't where they belonged either, and I couldn't account for why they looked why they had been thrown across the room. Everything about the scene told a bloody story of violent struggle.

Looking at the room around me, those couches being away from the blaze was probably the only thing that kept the building from burning down.

There were fist-sized holes in the drywall, and when I saw the feathery whips of my best friend's blood high on the walls and ceiling, I felt a stinging in my palms and saw black spots in front of my eyes.

I wanted to see Bex. To hold her. But she was out of harm's way, safe back at Hayley's, dropped off before I found out about all of this. The thoughts in my head right now, it was just as well she was nowhere near me.

I stood in the darkness, alone with my thoughts, more alone than I'd ever felt in my life.

"Motherfuckers."

I didn't think I said it out loud, but from outside the shop came the sound of a door opening, a soft knock on the charred doorframe..

Mr. Nguyen stood in the doorway, looking uncomfortable. The hairdressers across the hall were usually shut and gone long before now, but this was not a usual day.

"I want to thank you sir," I said. "You saved my best friend's life."

From what I understood, his appearance frightened Hamish's attacker's away, and his wife's phone call to 911 prevented the fire from doing more damage than it did.

Mr. Nguyen was dignified and formal. I always felt awkward around him. I didn't know whether to shake his hand or bow, and I was afraid of offending him by doing the wrong thing. He looked around him with the corners of his mouth drawn down, his eyes eloquent with a deep sadness.

"A terrible thing." He shook his head. "A terrible thing."

He turned his face toward the glass on the carpet, looking instead into some intensely personal and utterly private place inside himself.

It was then I noticed that his right hand was so swollen that the knuckles vanished into dimples on the back of his hand. This man had been injured pulling my friend from the fire.

When he absently flexed his fist closed, the swollen knuckles stood away from the bone like iron bearings the size of quarters.

***

My basement was an ordinary place, bare concrete floors and a cool damp feel all year round.

Moonlight slid through narrow strips of window glass at ground level, up around my head. It was impossible to see any distance. Objects more than a few feet away became dark hulking masses without any distinct shape of their own.

The basement was where I did my laundry, where the central heat and central air worked their magic on the rest of the house, where I kept my weights, heavy bag and other odds and ends I used in my workouts.

It was also where I kept a lot of stuff I don't use anymore.

I felt my way past stacks of boxes to the far wall. Some long-ago handyman owner built in a rough-cut workbench along its entire length. The pegboard behind the bench stood empty of tools. Cobwebs and dust lay thick along the work surface.

I bent down a couple feet to the right of the vise that long-ago owner hadn't thought it worthwhile to take with him, felt around along the dark shelf below. It occurred to me that the man who built this workbench was likely dead now. When his children sold off his tools in the estate sale, it was probably just more trouble than it was worth to remove the bench vise.

Or maybe a child or friend inherited and still uses the hand tools to this very day, and the vise got left for some other reason. No way to know, really.

Then my hands found it.

The box wasn't quite where I remembered it. That happens, enough years go by. I stood up, put the FedEx box on the workbench. The house above me was quiet as the grave. I flipped the box over, saw the white shipping form embalmed behind its plastic window.

The flimsy paper didn't show the slightest sign of yellowing or stiffening, but the plastic in front of it had begun to turn a milky color. The FedEx box still had its original seal intact.

I reached for the cardboard pull tab. Just as my fingers touched it, the central air rumbled to life, cooling the house back down to make the thermostat happy. Startled, I dropped the box. It landed on the scarred wood bench with a heavy clump.

I took a deep breath and pulled the cardboard tab. The closure ripped in two and the box stood open at one end.

I tipped the open end down, and the contents slid into my hands.

It was cold. Years in the basement's dark chill made it seem like some fragment of black ice from a distant alien world.

Its weight found my hand and the two knew each other perfectly.

It was cold, but it warmed as I held it.

Even though I was officially only 'held for questioning', the New Orleans PD had been dead-set against returning my .38. Out of little more than mule-headed stubbornness, I spent enough to buy several replacements before my attorney was able to recover it. A lot of time and money for a weapon I had no interest in ever seeing again.

When she finally did get it released, I chucked the box down here unopened. Didn't even think about it. Until now.

It was still encased in its old clip-on holster. I drew it, thumbed the cylinder release, spun the empty wheel. The NOPD returned it unloaded, which was just as well. I think it would have been too ghoulish to find it still contained three spent shells and two more still waiting for the hammer all these cold dark years.

I held it to the moonlight and sighted down the barrel. It was a disgrace. Six years with powder and carbon stuck to the barrel. I had always kept it clean as a mirror. After all, I thought my life might depend on it.

I flicked the cylinder shut, held it another minute longer. The gun fit my fist as though made for it. Until a few days ago, I hadn't held a firearm in years. Those recent times were like a one night stand after a long abstinence: you remember what to do, but it still feels awkward, unfamiliar.

Having the warm iron of the .38 in my hand again was like being reunited with a long-lost lover, familiar and intimate despite the strangeness thrown up by time and distance.

It was a squat little thing, with a barrel just an inch long. It had no front sight and the hammer curved down into the frame of the gun so that there would be no way for any part of the weapon to snag or catch on clothing if drawn at a crucial moment.

No safety to forget, either. I didn't carry the .22 Beretta Avi and Uri loved so much, but their lesson stayed with me: time lost thumbing a safety can get you killed. The .38 had a double-action pull so stiff it took a conscious effort to fire it at the gun range.

Or as was the case on that hot summer night, so much adrenalin in my system that I didn't even notice the act of firing, just saw the young girl jerk and fall in the spaces between three sheets of flame.

Knives, bats, clubs, chains, all are much like our own hands: tools that *can* turn deadly if so used. The gun in my palm looked like what it was, a durable little machine with only one purpose on earth: the ending of another human being.

You could drive a car over this gun and still pick it right up and blow a hole in a person's liver. Its only reason for being was death.

The reason I stopped carrying it.

I hadn't stopped being dangerous when I set aside my gun. I had just given myself more options when danger rolled back around. I thought about the commitment of carrying a gun, what it meant when things got scary.

It was a commitment to kill.

I ran one thumb down the top of its spine, trying to decide if I was ready to make that promise again.

Thirty-Seven

I ended up back at Hamish's bedside. Visiting hours were well past, but sometimes there are certain advantages to my job. At some point or another, I had tattooed or pierced more than half the staff I saw in the hospital that day. So many of the marked, and all them adamant that nothing show below the line of their short-sleeve scrubs.

If the world knew how many doctors, lawyers, judges, and people in positions of power were decorated this way, there might not be the prejudices there were about body art. But the world remained the way it was, and I didn't hold it against them. And the staff let me sit at my best friend's bedside long after everyone else had been made to leave.

I sat with Hamish in the darkened room, held his hand and tried to make any sense at all out of my situation. I was tired of running blind, letting other people write the script. It was time to clear the battle lines.

I couldn't quit thinking about an event that happened when I first started tattooing. I was a confused and unhesitatingly violent kid of seventeen when a local tattooist named Big Jim sent a crew around to shut me down. I wasn't the first person he did it to, and probably not the last before he finally admitted the genie was out of the bottle and accepted what he could no longer change. But that night, in the alley behind my building, it was a different story.

I was still a skinny little teen waiting on my full growth: an inch or two under six feet then, maybe 130 or 140 pounds. They came at me in the back alley when I went down to take my nightly trash to the dumpster. A classic three-way press, or as close as they could get in a narrow alley. Three six and a half foot, 300-plus pound, sweating, hairy, growling men clumping at me in a heavy run.

Two closed in front and back, swinging baseball bats. The third headed around my flank with a chain. They came barreling in at me, no hesitation, no mercy. It was a devastating attack. Since then, I've seen it completely destroy larger and stronger men than I will ever be.

But what they didn't, couldn't know was that I had grown up the weakest child of the town freaks, fighting my way out of worse odds among the most cruel and merciless savages of all - other children. I had been carefully and thoroughly trained by two who had come through much, much worse. And come through unscathed.

The struggle was short, terrible, intense. A dark and nasty business of stick and move, stick and move. I was never where they wanted me, never where they expected me to be. Every chance I got, I took my shot: hard and mean and merciless.

Seconds later, I dropped one of the aluminum bats onto the rough pavement. It landed with a ringing metal clang, bounced rapidly end to end until it settled and rolled under the dumpster. I opened the security door to my building, walked back up three flights to my studio loft. Left a blind man and two cripples behind me.

I was sure there was a lesson for me there somewhere, but I was just too tired to think what it might be.

***

By ten-thirty I decided to quit imposing on the staff's goodwill and head home myself. If Bex was going to stay with me tonight, the plan was that she'd call by twelve.

I stopped in the doorway, looked back at the bed where my friend slept. I made him a silent heartfelt promise and moved out into the night.

Thirty-Eight

I told myself I was just going to go home and get some sleep. That I'd wait for Bex if she was coming. That I'd be in better shape to address my problems in the morning. That's what I told myself, but the reality was that patience has never been my strong suit.

The memory of the way Hamish looked in his hospital bed was still too fresh. It made my palms sting and the flesh of my face tighten against the bone. The blood in my body felt as though I had stood too long staring into a furnace.

When I saw the purple flicker of the neon sign for Dark Rites, I knew that no accident had diverted my route home this way.

The interior was as deserted as it had been on my earlier visit. The fluorescent shop lights glowed pale through the tinted film on the window glass, and only the fact that the door swung open to my touch indicated the shop was in fact open.

I walked into the center of the main room, stood with my feet planted and the blood pounding in my wrists. Within seconds, Marcus came through the door to the back room.

His scalp and eyebrows were freshly shaved and gleaming. The shapeless black garment he wore rose high on his neck and rounded his shoulders to the point of making him look hunchbacked. When Marcus moved up to the counter across from me, I saw that the garment's hem dragged the floor. The overall effect was of an egg extruded from a tumorous black column.

"Dead man. To what do we owe the pleasure?"

He unfolded thin bony hands from the garment as he spoke, and his eyes had a bright unnatural glitter. Behind him, the hard-faced blonde emerged through the door and reclined on the dental chair.

I took a deep breath, tried to think before I acted. I knew that when faced with a problem I couldn't directly fight, I had often yielded to the temptation to attack the first problem I could lay my hands on. Marcus was an ass, but he wasn't the thug who'd burnt my business and attacked my friend.

"I don't get it," I said. "What's your problem anyway?"

"It hardly matters now. The curse is in effect. Your life will whither, and all you love will suffer before it claims you. It's all over for you, dead man."

I clenched and loosened my fists and fought my natural urges.

"Marcus, I don't know what your problem with me is, but it's over. Let it go. There's nothing between you and me."

In their dark sockets, his eyes gleamed like small chips of stone. I could hear his back molars grind as the speed coursing through his blood sang its black song to his deepest heart.

"Your woman danced in the groves the night we laid the curse. Her body was the altar. My seed will *burn* all you hold dear." He spoke the words in a little singsong voice, to himself as much as me. In the background, the hard-faced blonde snorted, though I couldn't tell who she was laughing at.

I should have known better than to try to talk sense with a speed freak.

"Marcus, you and Tash have yourselves a fine life, just leave me out of it."

"There are riddles in the blood, dead man."

"This was a mistake. I'm out of here."

I turned to go. His voice sang out behind me, clear and lucid this time.

"And how *is* your big black buck tonight? It's all anyone's talking about. Perhaps the curse will visit your little foreign slut next."

That was it. The hot bubble of anger I'd held down floated loose, rose up in my chest and burst. Its fires lit up my veins and stopped the world.

I spun on one heel and punched the junkie directly below his small, red, smirking mouth.

Marcus flew head over heels, hit the battered grey linoleum of his studio floor and skidded along its length for several more feet before coming to a stop.

The burning anger evaporated like a flash fire out of fuel, left me with a sadly familiar mix of exhilaration and shame. Marcus wasn't the only addict in the room.

On the dental chair, the blonde stretched out her full length, gave a little wiggle. Her expression was deprecating and merry.

"He wakes up," I said to her, "tell him I find out he *wasn't* just talking a lot of shit, I'm coming back."

She tinkled her fingers at me in a little wave. The poison inside her showed bright and oily on the surface of her smile.

Thirty-Nine

Bex and Hayley were fighting. They kept their voices low so as not to wake the baby, and the sound of their fierce hissing whispers curled around Paul's bones like the sharp air before a lightning storm and sent him fleeing into the bedroom with his laptop.

He was a Minnesota boy, large and blond and diffident, squirmingly uncomfortable with any conflict that didn't take place on a sporting field. At intervals, he would stick his head into the front room and offer the women drinks or snacks, make comments about being sorry he had so much work to do in the back bedroom. He was desperate to maintain the fiction that his wife and her friend were simply catching up on old times, what they called 'having a natter'.

In a sense, Paul was right. The two hissing women *were* catching up on old times. Or rather, old times were catching up with them. Bex and Hayley had not seen each other in two years, hadn't really been close in three. Time enough for their lives to become wildly different places, for old loyalties to strain to the breaking point.

Once, the two were as close as sisters. Now, instead of bringing them back together, their reunion was showing the girls that they had little, if anything, in common anymore. Hayley was a young mother and a married woman: her favorite topic of conversation was her concern at getting little Jamie in the preschool she'd chosen, four years before the boy would need it.

Bex hated that her best friend had been taken away from her and replaced with this Americanized Stepford Wife. Hayley was disappointed and angry that her friend was not more supportive of her new life: she took it as a rejection that Bex didn't want to sit for Jamie.

"Is that what you got me to travel halfway around the world for, to babysit?"

"You *knew* I had a son, don't pretend you didn't."

"But I didn't know you gave up your whole life to do it. I mean, come on Hailz, you work all day, come home exhausted, you're in bed by nine o-fucking-clock and up again two or three times a night with the baby. Why the hell did you *ask* me to come here?"

Hayley started crying then, and Bex leaned in on her, crying too. Maybe once the two old friends got it out of their system, they would be able to make up, reclaim some of the closeness they once had. That hope made Bex hold her friend tighter, cry that little bit harder.

They were interrupted by a loud echoing boom from the back of the house. Bex at first thought Paul must have dropped a piece of furniture or something. Until they heard it again.

Hayley and Paul's apartment had two doors fronting out on the hall for fire safety: the main one in the living room opened onto the front stairs and the one in the kitchen opened out by the rear stairs. It sounded like someone was knocking on their back door.

With a sledgehammer.

Hayley stood up and moved halfway across the room, where she stood poised in mid step. The curve of her spine took the shape of a question mark. From around the curve of her best friend's hip, Bex saw Paul move from the back bedroom to the kitchen door. His heavy irritated tread lumbered over the floorboards.

Bex leaned back in her seat to see Paul, blue flannel bathrobe held closed in one hand, reach for the knob with the other.

Just as he set his hand to the doorknob, another enormous boom sounded from behind the door. Paul jumped back as though burnt, looked around him with an embarrassed smile, and shook himself like a wet dog.

"Who's there?" he called out in the deep tone he liked to think of as his badass voice.

From the other side, silence.

"Who is it?" Paul warmed to the role he played. "I've got a gun!"

Bex thought he did a pretty good tough guy imitation, even with the bathrobe and slippers.

For a long and time-stretched moment, silence.

Tentatively, Paul touched the tip of one finger to the doorknob again. When no sound shook the apartment, he folded the whole knob in one large, soft, pink hand.

Silence.

He looked back at his wife, shrugged, and reached for the latch on the deadbolt. It slid back with a brisk clack. The door made stubborn sounds as it opened.

As Paul stepped out into the hall and vanished from view, Hayley moved cautiously forward into the kitchen. Bex found herself getting to her feet too. She stood beside her chair, her heart's blood pounding in her chest.

"Anybody there?" Paul was a big heavy man, a gridiron football player in his younger days. His every step and movement screeched and squeaked in the floorboards of the hall.

He stepped back into the apartment's kitchen, the shuffle and slap of his bedroom slippers somehow at odds with the weight of his tread.

"Must have gone." He was unable to hide the relief on his face.

That was when it hit him.

Bex saw Paul fly backward through the doorway, arms and legs trailing behind him as though he had been sucked into a raging storm.

That moment stayed with her: Paul hanging frozen in midair, blue bathrobe billowing around him, one slipper hanging suspended inches from his bare pink foot.

Then he was gone, disappeared into a dark hallway full of terrible sounds and the smell of rotten meat.

Strange things happened to her memory then. The next thing Bex knew, she had the kitchen drawer open, rummaging in it with both hands, looking for a knife and not knowing where they were kept.

Something heavy crashed into her from behind, slamming her hands in the drawer. The pain made the world slide sideways and the gorge rise in her throat. She lay bent over and pinned to the counter, both wrists still trapped in the drawer by her own hips and the weight on her back.

She shook violently from side to side, full of rage and unwilling to meet her end in that way. The weight slid off her, and she looked over her shoulder to see Paul's broad back moving from her.

She spun away from the counter, spilling the drawer to the kitchen floor and slewing the utensils inside all over the linoleum tile.

In the center of the gleaming confusion was the cheap serrated knife the couple used for their vegetable chopping and roast carving. Its blade gleamed, and Bex dove.

Her hands were numb. She could feel nothing in them but a throbbing ache that seemed too large for her body to contain. She had to use both hands to scoop the knife up off the floor.

A black boot crashed down next to her fingers. She crabbed backwards across the tile, kicking eggbeaters and spatulas in every direction before she found the safety of the corner.

There, with the wooden faces of the kitchen cabinets at her back and one brass handle digging into her shoulder, Bex concentrated on forcing her swollen and painful fingers to grip the plastic handle of the knife.

She was aware of smashing and crashing sounds above her and the movement of large male legs on the tile. Paul's bare foot, his slippered foot, and his attacker's thick black boots crushed everything they landed on into mangled metal and splintered wood. The smell of rotted meat was everywhere.

She heard a ringing in her ears and wondered if her head had hit the countertop harder than she thought. She got her fingers to close around the knife, but they refused to hold it tight.

Bex was finally able to get a grip on the knife by using her other hand to hold her fingers in place around the handle. She got her weight under her, looked for one oil-smeared black denim leg to come near her.

As soon as she saw her target, she launched herself, sinking the blade deep into the meat at the back of the thigh.

The flesh was hard, as if it was too thickly corded with muscle to work a blade through. Bex fought the resistance, shoved hard against the hilt of the knife until she felt the blade hit bone.

From above her came a sound like sheets of wet newspaper being torn in half. Paul's feet left the floor and began to flail at the air. A heavy fall of warm rain obscured her vision, and Bex twisted at the hilt of the knife with all the strength in waist and spine.

The back of one hand, dirty and silver-ringed, swung down at her face. Something like sheet lightning exploded in the room.

Forty

The next thing she knew, Bex was on her back and several feet away, with no conscious awareness of time having passed. It was like someone had cut the tape in her head and spliced it back, when? A couple seconds? More? Less? She couldn't tell.

Bex did know that when she pushed herself back up onto her arms there was carpet underneath them, so she was at least partway in the living room. She saw white tile at her feet, so yes, only partway. She definitely lay between the two areas.

The ringing in her head was loud, the sounds in the room around her were muffled and quiet.

Hayley stood down the hall in the bedroom doorway facing the intruder. She held a blue-black pistol in both hands and stood with her feet wide apart.

Hayley's mouth was wide open and the veins in her neck stood out as her jaws moved. Bex heard her voice as a sound like the ocean's roar.

Paul's blue flannel robe lay in a heap on the kitchen tile, too sticky and splayed out at too many angles for the thing inside it to be Paul. It had to be some mistake.

Bex struggled to her feet, used the smooth white wall for support. The room dipped and swung, but she got her legs to stay beneath her.

She wanted her knife, saw it still stuck in the dark man's thigh. It was hilt-deep in a wide ragged wound. The man swung his leg awkwardly as he took two lurching steps in the direction of the bedroom.

The pistol in her friend's hands began to gout fire from the muzzle. It exploded over and over, flat claps under the ringing in her ears. The man in black staggered and fell backward. The stink of gunpowder filled Bex's nostrils.

The man in black tumbled back over the kitchen counter and came to rest on the living room carpet. Bex felt but didn't hear the tremors in the floorboards when she landed.

Hayley came to her then. Bex could only stare blankly at her friend's face, unable to understand the words being spoken to her. Fresh tears streamed down Hayley's cheeks and the two women put their arms around each other.

Together, they moved around the side of the counter to take a closer look.

Even in death, the man looked menacing. His black leather jacket was torn and stained, with snarls and missing teeth on many of its zippers. His tee shirt slid halfway up a lean emaciated belly covered with gray jailhouse tattoos broken by round purple puckers.

His left leg was hitched up off the carpet, propped by the blade of the kitchen knife. Hayley turned her face to her friend's shoulder and Bex felt hot slick tears against her skin.

In the center of the intruder's chest, five clustered bullet holes had torn a ragged hole in the shirt's black cloth. Tiny wisps of smoke still curled upward from the wounds, joined the blue haze of gun smoke throughout the apartment.

Bex distantly wondered if the smoke alarm were going off. None of this seemed real.

Hailz was pantomiming something to her. Finally Bex understood what it was. Phone. They would need to call the police, and the landline was on the far side of the body.

Bex understood that she was to retrieve the cordless while Hayley covered the intruder's limp form with her pistol. She didn't like the idea, but there didn't seem to be any alternative. She nodded her head yes.

One bare foot touched down on the floorboards closer to the body. Another.

She took a tentative third step.

The man's black eyes popped open. His face split into a wicked grin full of the worst teeth Bex had ever seen on another human being.

Teeth she had seen before.

She leaped back. The man's hand was snake-fast: it closed tight around her foot and Bex fell into Hayley, fouling her shot.

Hayley put one arm around her friend's waist, reached around her body and fired one-handed. Less than three feet away.

Bex didn't see the damage the bullet did to their attacker, but her foot popped loose from his grasp. She did hear the gunshot itself, a small flat sound like someone cracking their knuckles.

Hayley fired again. Then she was pushing Bex in front of her, hurrying and shoving and herding her into the other bedroom.

The nursery.

A great bubble of sadness rose in Bex's chest then. Hayley took three determined strides across the room. She bent over the crib and came up with the kicking, red-faced infant. It howled its fear to an uncaring world.

Hayley thrust the child into Bex's arms, looked at her with a silent understanding that made Bex's eyes brim with tears.

The man in black was already less than six feet from the nursery door.

Hayley turned and fired two more rounds into him. He fell back into the living room again.

She kissed Bex on the cheek and little Jamie on the forehead, said something to him that Bex couldn't hear and didn't need to.

She hustled them to the kitchen doorway. Already Bex could feel the vibrations of the heavy booming footsteps coming closer.

Hayley looked at her friend, her sister. Her face was full of something she couldn't find the words for in the time that remained to them.

Then she turned her back and filled the doorway with her body.

Bex didn't hear the shots as she ran down the back steps and out into the alley.

Forty-One

I was tempted to swing by Bex's house on my way home. It was only five minutes away, not too far at all. But I felt guilty for monopolizing so much of her time on what was supposed to be a visit with her friend from back home. I suspected that she and Hayley needed to spend some time tonight setting things right between them. There was no way stopping under her window and mooning like a lovesick teenager was going to help.

I told myself that if Bex did decide to stay with me tonight, she'd call when she said she would. More likely the pair would end up laughing and reminiscing over a pitcher of margaritas. I resolved to prepare myself to sleep alone.

Having done nothing but sleep alone for quite awhile, I didn't see why the prospect seemed so daunting now, after just three nights with Miss Bex Temple. I told myself it had to be something in New Zealand's water supply and forced myself to drive home without going anywhere her apartment.

Which is how I came to be driving past the park on the Hennepin side, drumming my fingers in time with the iPod, singing badly and making up the words where I didn't know them, when a ghostly white figure came racing out of the park directly in front of my headlights.

I stabbed down on the brakes, sure I heard something clip the edge of my bumper as I skidded to a stop. The fleeing figure, either a small woman or a large child, did not stop or slow down, did not even look in the direction of the car that just struck her.

She was off and running at one hell of a fast limp down the street I lived on.

The painful motion of her run was off balance, and the cloth bundle in her arms obscured her face. But something about the set of her shoulders, the action of her waist and scissoring of those calves was enough to show me the woman I knew.

I blasted my horn, but Bex didn't turn around or do anything to slow her desperate pace. I looked across the darkened field, but I don't know what I expected to see. The park was so badly lit, I wouldn't have known if she were being chased by a pack of dogs or a marching band.

She was barely across Hennepin Avenue before I gunned the car around the corner and pulled in ahead of her.

I reached over, threw open the passenger door and called out her name, but it wasn't until she saw my face that Bex dove into the car.

She was lathered in sweat, gulping for air and wild-eyed with fear. There was crusted blood on her hands and fresh coppery stuff still flowing from her nostrils and the side of her mouth. Bright scarlet drops fell from her chin onto the fluffy white blanket in her arms.

The blanket extended one tiny hand and clutched doll-sized fingers at a dark lock of hair.

I'm often wrong, but never uncertain. I gunned the engine the rest of the way down the street to my home.

"NO! NOT THERE! NO!" Bex yelled as though I was across the street and not in the car with her. The baby in her arms began to cry, exhausted, without much heart.

"It's okay," I said, "just for a minute."

The way she looked at me, I realized Bex couldn't hear me. I whipped a quick U-turn in front of my house and stopped with one foot already out the driver's side door.

I held up one forefinger and mouthed the word slowly. I saw her frightened glance up the street before she looked back to me and slowly nodded yes.

I kissed her and ran inside. Thirty seconds later I was running back to the car.

Back behind the wheel, I keyed the ignition. Bex held the bundle of white cloth close to her and made little shushing sounds while peering intently down the street. I put the car in gear and started down the street.

Bex suddenly went stiff, one rigid arm pointing beyond the windshield.

And then I saw him.

He lurched forward like a steam engine left running and forgotten. Tall, thin, all in black. His bald head gleamed under the streetlights, and his eyes were featureless dark hollows.

His head swiveled on his neck and he seemed to taste the air around him. Then he stepped out into the street in front of the car and put his hand out like a traffic cop.

Avi's lesson came back to me: No one in mortal danger should willingly surrender the use of a two thousand pound battering ram. I didn't recognize the man in black, but the line between him and Bex was clear and simple.

I gunned the engine, felt the impact in my back teeth as he went sailing into the night.

I was out on Hennepin and right onto the ramp for I-35 faster than I ever would have given that silly gray piece of plastic credit for.

I never saw him land, never saw him get back up again.

But I was sure he did.

Forty-Two

IAn hour later, Bex sat on a crackling paper bib spread over Dr. Greg Lambert's dining room table. Her legs dangled over the side like a little girl's. The baby was quiet in my lap, looking like Winston Churchill. Greg had just finished treating Bex's torn and bloody feet. Spats and spots of blood Jackson Pollocked the tile floor. A metal basin beside him held a pair of sharp surgical tweezers and more pieces of broken glass and gravel than I liked to think about.

Before that, a quick checkup showed little Jamie was unharmed. Then there had been a lot of poking and prodding and shining lights and so on until he was satisfied her head injury might be okay without an MRI or CAT scan.

Greg and Jim had just been on their way out when I rolled in unannounced. As odd as it had been seeing him dressed up as a doctor this afternoon, it was just as surreal to see him now, acting all serious and professional in tight leather pants and a mesh shirt. Depending on how he turned while he worked, we could see the cadecus tattooed over his heart or the abstract black tribal design across his shoulders.

Not until he had both her feet wrapped in white gauze did he strip off his latex gloves and acknowledge my presence in the room.

"Well that's women and children, how about you?"

"Not a scratch." I unconsciously tucked the hand I bruised striking Marcus Winton out of sight. "I wasn't there, just found them after."

He looked at me a moment, nodded more to himself than to anyone else in the room. I had never been able to guess what he might be thinking.

"Hey Greg, thanks again for seeing us like this."

"What are friends for, right? Want to tell me again why you couldn't take her to a hospital?"

"I didn't tell you the first time."

The corner of Greg's mouth pulled sideways. He turned back to Bex and raised his voice so she could hear him.

"Dizziness. Nausea." He ticked them off on his fingers. "Blurred vision. Double vision. Vertigo. Slurred speech. Any of these, you GO to Cedar Riverside, OKAY?"

Bex nodded her head yes, and I saw the muscle at the corner of her jaw flex and bunch as she bit down on the pain. Greg looked dubious, nodded to himself again and touched me on the shoulder.

"Come out front with me a minute."

Bex wasn't any happier to be left alone now than she was when we first came in. The only reason I was in the room with her was that she refused to let me leave. We settled for stepping out into the living room with the door open so she could see us. Greg turned his tribal tattoo to the doorway and spoke with his voice low.

"Godammit Sam, what the hell did I tell you? Wasn't Hamish enough?"

"I told you, I--"

"Cut the innocent bystander crap. You left me today hungry for blood, show up with yet another victim. The fuck, man. What is she to you, anyway?"

I floundered, trying to find words. However, Greg had always been much better at reading my face than I was at reading his. He saw his answer there and nodded.

"The child hers?"

I nodded. His mouth tugged sideways and he looked tired.

"You never could lie worth a damn, Sam. You really shouldn't try."

I dropped my eyes and jogged the baby a little bit in the way that she liked and she curled in closer to my chest.

"Quit being so hard on him. Honestly, you can be such an asshole sometimes." Jim breezed in from the back of the house. He had changed from clubwear into pajamas, and his face lit up when he saw the baby. He took her in his arms, cooing and rocking her and telling her in a soft baby voice not mind mean old Greg.

"Sam, that baby needs its mother."

I held his eyes, let him see the truth I knew but couldn't speak. He dropped his gaze and blew air through his cheeks.

"That bad?"

I nodded.

The two men shared a look and Jim turned his face back to the baby.

"You know, there's a good reason I'm required by law to report this to Child Protective Services." I wasn't sure which of us he was talking to.

"She's a stranger here," I said, "not even in the country two weeks now. Someone's after me and she, I don't know..."

"Just like Hamish."

"She's had a rough night. I don't want to see her jammed up in a bunch of legal trouble too."

His mouth was a flat line. I couldn't tell if I was gaining traction.

"Here," I said, "I've got an idea. Hang on a second."

Bex's hearing was coming back, but for the moment it was still easier to pass notes back and forth instead of shouting at each other. She didn't have any contact information for Paul's family here in Minnesota, but she was sure Hayley's parents in Christchurch would. She gave me their name and phone number.

"You can the nearest living relatives through the New Zealand branch of the family. That work for you?"

"It'll have to, won't it?" Something that was supposed to be a smile played at the edges of his face but didn't stay.

"You two must be tired. I'll make up the guest room."

Jim smiled and nodded over the top of the baby's head. They were sitting together now on the couch, and she looked to be asleep. Certainly more comfortable than I'd been able to make her.

"Thanks, but better we didn't. I don't want you two in the line of fire."

"You're not taking this child." Jim's voice was steel, no argument. In truth, there was none to make. Greg and Jim were great parents. I was a walking free-fire zone. I nodded.

Greg puffed air through his cheeks and walked away from me down the hall. I waved to Bex and she came hobbling out of the kitchen on her bandaged feet, looking like an extra from a horror film. Her clothes were a bloody ruin and we had no others.

I put one arm out, and she stepped into its protective circle and covered my hand with her own. Behind their dark mask of bruises her eyes were tender.

Greg came back in with a paper Dayton's bag, the kind with twine handles on top. The first thing he did was pull out two shapeless gray pieces of cloth and hand them to Bex.

"I jog sometimes," he said loud enough for her. "You can change in there."

Once she was gone, Greg gave me a look down inside the bag.

"Painkillers, muscle relaxers, antibiotics. Some cortisone in case of burns. The pharmaceutical companies give out freebie packs to promote their products, no need to record that they're missing. I also threw in plenty of gauze pads and rolls, surgical tweezers, scissors, stitching needle and thread."

"Thank you."

"Just promise me one thing. It gets any worse than what's in that bag, you get your asses to a hospital."

I took it from him, clasped his hand when I did so. I was realizing I had more true friends than I ever knew.

Forty-Three

We made one more stop, this time at a 24 hour Walmart in the suburbs, before driving an hour across the St. Croix River to Hudson, Wisconsin. Bex fell asleep in the car and didn't wake until I carried her into our room at the Holiday Inn and laid her down on the king-size bed.

She looked around, bleary and still half-asleep, smiled up at me. With her two black eyes, she looked like a tiny cartoon raccoon.

"Sam," was all she said.

I went back out to the car, brought in everything we needed, then went down the row of rooms to the ice machine and got us a couple of vending machine hot chocolates. When I came back, Bex sat on the edge of the giant bed, looking small and bleak and far away.

She didn't look up when I came in, did acknowledge her cocoa with a soft little thank-you. I went through the shopping bags for some of the edibles I bought.

Food and drink revived her a bit. She sat on the bed with one foot tucked up under her, looking tiny in her too-big gray sweats, and began to talk.

Tears ran silently down her face as her story unfolded. She paid them no heed, pausing only when she needed to blow her nose on the motel tissues. When she finished, she let out a hitching little sigh and said, "I just can't believe they're both dead. Just like that. Gone."

"Any chance they're not?"

She shook her head and dabbed at her red-rimmed eyes.

"No. He killed them."

"That man we saw? The one I hit with the car?"

"That didn't stop it. Whatever that thing is, it isn't human."

"You saw... *it* take four rounds in the chest and keep on coming?"

"Eight. Eight shots. H-Hayley, she shot it four times the *first* time, then twice more when it sat up and grabbed me. Two more after that when it got up again. She shot it eight times."

"Bulletproof vest?"

"I *saw* the holes in its skin. Smoking little holes. I saw its cloudy white eyes, like they had some kind of film in them but they could still *see* me. I saw its," her voice broke and her eyes went wide. She put one hand to her mouth.

"I saw its teeth, Sam. I know who it was."

"Who?"

"It was him. That man with the gun from the other night. He was wearing different clothes, but I'll never forget those teeth."

Even as she said it, I thought back. The figure I'd seen could be Jack Rose. Height and build were close, even if I hadn't had a closer look.

"That does give us one problem, though." I told her about what his brother had said and what I found at Jack's apartment.

"Don't you see, Sam? This man, this Jack Rose, he isn't human. He's like a vampire or something. He can't be killed. Somebody shot him, but he didn't die. Now he blames us, probably because he was supposed to kill us and got shot when he didn't."

"That is, without a doubt, the weirdest damn thing I ever heard."

"I wouldn't think a man who sees ghosts and receives psychic phone calls from his witch-sisters would have a problem believing in the walking dead." She managed a smile.

"You're right. It's just a little hard to take. I've never heard of anything like this, not even when Grandma Roark was doing her damnedest to scare the pants off us."

"I wouldn't have believed it either. If I hadn't seen it."

I was full of nervous energy, anxious to be doing something. I moved around the hotel room, unpacking. Bex started pulling tags off the new clothes.

"Jesus, Sam. You must have spent over a thousand dollars in that store."

"Just a few hundred. It's Target, stuff's cheaper than you'd think."

"Have I found myself a rich guy?"

"Nope. Just a Boy Scout. Always prepared." I pulled the plastic out of my pocket. "I have a card with a ten thousand dollar limit, keep it in the freezer for emergencies."

"Clever."

It did raise a good point though. I looked good on paper, but simply didn't have that much folding money I could lay my hands on in a hurry. I wondered how much we would need before all this was over, and how much the shop would need to get back up and running.

There was no way to know. I opened theFedEx box instead.

When I lifted the cardboard flaps, it released a musty smell into the room, more like something buried in the earth than stored in a basement. I thought I smelled jasmine and wet brick.

And gunpowder.

***

"Sam, what is that?"
My own personal murder weapon.

She held my .38 in her hand like the pregnant little engine of death it was. I showed her how to tell if the weapon was loaded, how it worked. It took less than thirty seconds.

"Don't worry about anything you hear out in the hall tonight, you're safe in here. Anything actually comes *through* the door and *into* the room, I blow it to paste. For any reason you have to use this, just point it like a finger and pull. Anything in front of you will go away."

She dry-fired the gun a few times, looking uncomfortable. I knew that most of the rest of the world outside the U.S. was not as murderous and gun-crazy as we were, but I wanted to believe that if Jack Rose came through our hotel door or window, Bex would be able to pull the trigger.

While Bex showered and then drew a hot bath, I cleaned the .38 until its barrel gleamed like a mirror. It took forever to scrub six year old carbon from the snubnosed one-inch barrel.

When I had the weapon cleaned, loaded and ready to go, I could still hear Bex slapping and splashing in the tub. I thought a little bit about how she would look in better times, up to her shoulders in bubbles. I hoped we would both live to see it.

I hefted the gun in my palm. Once, the weight of it riding on my hip was as natural as wearing shoes. I'd practiced drawing and firing twice until the gesture felt as natural to me as brushing my teeth.

The idea with firing twice was that your first shot might go anywhere, might be nothing but distracting noise. By the second, you expected to be aiming. The night I shot Lisa Torres, I'd fired until she fell, and I hadn't missed.

It had been six years.

I thumbed the wheel into the body of the .38, all empty chambers. Standing in the middle of the room, feeling a little foolish and trying not to look at any of the motel mirrors, I clipped the holster inside my belt, right hip. Took a deep breath.

Back when I was young enough to worry about getting into bars and old enough to grow one, I wore a beard for a couple years. I felt like GI Joe, but I didn't get carded.

The day I turned twenty-one, I shaved it right off again. I remember worrying that after not using a razor for so long I might cut my face to ribbons, but my hand remembered as though I had never stopped.

Dry-firing the .38 again was like that. As natural as shaving.

I heard the water start to drain out of the tub and sounds that had to be Bex standing up out of her bath and toweling off. I made an embarrassed jump down onto the bed and started thumbing ammunition from the Walmart into the empty chambers before she caught me in my James Bond act.

When she did come out, wrapped in a towel and clothed in a halo of sweet-smelling steam from the bath, it occurred to me that Botticelli got The Birth of Venus all wrong. Her face, shoulders and arms were a mass of brown and purple bruises. She was still the most beautiful woman I had ever seen in my life.

"What?"

I didn't reply. Didn't look away either. She came around the side of the bed, one hand held up at the bodice of her towel-dress. The hotel towel was ridiculously long on her: it fell past her knees and emphasized how tiny she was. I saw that she had removed the bandages from her feet, but I didn't say anything.

Instead I held one corner of her towel in my fingertips. Rubbed the thick white cloth with my thumb.

Bex looked down at me, put her hands on my shoulders. Through the thin cotton of my tee shirt, her touch was scalding .

I pulled gently at the corner of the towel. The knotted cloth between her breasts held, eased, slipped away. The towel fell from her body.

Our love that night was grasping and greedy. A celebration of the life still pulsing inside us, hot and warm and fragile.

Both of us knew, somewhere out in the howling night, the black beast my sisters saw in their dreams sought us.

Step by shuffling step, the beast was coming.

Forty-Four

The next morning came gray and drizzling. Bex and I had a late breakfast at a Perkins, barely noticing the light rain sheeting the windows.

By ten o'clock, it had already been a busy day. The anonymous piece of plastic I drive looked exactly like I had hit something with it last night. No blood stains, but a wicked and memorable dent in the front quarterpanel.

A quick stop at the airport and we had a rental, an SUV only slightly smaller than a school bus. The beast handled the wet weather like it wasn't even there. If we saw Jack Rose again, I had a vague idea of smashing him to a fine paste.

By ten, we had also made a stop at a gun shop on Hiawatha and picked up more ammo. I hadn't said anything last night, and Bex hadn't known enough to ask, but from the sound of it, regular cap-and-ball ammo wasn't going to be much good against what chased us. I put more hope in the idea of 220 grain hollowpoint slugs flattening to the size of quarters on impact.

Now we sat in a red vinyl booth a mile down the highway from the gun shop. Behind her dark glasses, Bex did admirable justice to an omelette while I demolished my pancakes. She'd managed to find something that fit from the clothes I'd bought her last night.

She sat with my iPad, taking advantage of the restaurant's wifi. While Bex read, we drank cup after cup of strong coffee from the plastic pot the waitress left at our table. The girl had already refilled it once, and it was feeling light again.

Hayley and Paul were right there on the local Yahoo, *BRUTAL SLAYING: Couple Murdered in Own Home*. Two photos ran with the article: the coroners wheeling out a shrouded stretcher and a wedding photo of the happy couple in better days. Seeing the two together was like a fist around my heart. .

Bex was a fast reader. She dragged her finger down the touchscreen, tapped for the article's second page. Her eyes whipped from side to side. There was no mention of her name, no allusion to her presence in the apartment that night. Sooner or later, that would change: all of her things were in that apartment. She tapped one fingernail on a sidebar article with the legend *Trailer Park Slaughter: Possible Connection.*

Together we read about the fate of little Tommy Green.

***

We made our way to the rented SUV, moving slow in the thin weak rain.

With a couple pairs of tube socks and heavy boots a couple sizes too large, Bex could manage a decent walking pace. She wouldn't win any footraces, but at least she was able to move without pain.

"So what's next?" she said.

I knew the sensible answer. I was out of my depth, and we both knew it. The smart thing to do was to hop on a southbound onramp, stay ahead of the walking dead man until we reached my family.

Except.

The thought of running to my sisters and grandmother and hiding behind their skirts dug at me, a deep wound healing with shrapnel still embedded.

Except even if I grabbed Hamish and Bex and took them to safety, John and Greg and Jim, the baby Jamie and everyone else I cared about would still be here, still at risk.

Except the child was mine. An innocent had died to birth the beast that was Jack Rose, and another would die to feed its master's hate.

I looked beside me, empty space. Bex had stopped walking.

The few feet between us had become a gulf. A gray curtain fell in that space, water slicking her cheeks and wetting her hair. Her arms were folded and her mouth was a hard dark line.

"The bad guys have called the shots long enough," I said. "I'm going to take it to them with red-hot tongs."

"While I sit on the sidelines, huh? Tucked away all nice and safe like Hayley's baby?"

She had a hard hot anger to her. Her best friend's death was still a fresh open wound. Her eyes welled up with a bright shine and she pulled back, arms folded close around her.

"That thing came after you last night without me there. We're safer together."

"I'm in this, Sam. Don't for a second believe I'm not."

"Hey, united we stand, right?"

From the look on her face, I could tell she didn't believe me.

Forty-Five

I thought that the nasty weather and the U being in summer session might make things a little better, but parking in Dinkytown was still a nightmare. Probably because this was one day I couldn't park a few blocks out and just walk in. After a lot of circling, I finally found a loading zone half a block from where I needed it to be.

I got drenched walking even that short distance. Bex was back in the car, warm and dry and shifted over into the driver's seat. She wasn't happy about leaving me on my own, but she was able to do more behind the wheel than hobbling around on injured feet. I just hoped that leaving, she would remember to drive on the right side of the street.

My old flannel shirt kept me warm in the rain and helped to hide the lines of the pistol. After going unarmed so long, I had the old worries that its shape showed through. I also knew from experience that people just about never noticed that sort of thing. I figured the white latex gloves on my hands were a lot more noticeable. It made me glad of the rain. People were mostly off the sidewalk, kept inside and all focused on their own troubles.

Under the storm-dark skies, the interior of the shopping tunnel was an impossible gloom. The sounds of rain drumming down overhead and a thick torrent of water gurgling down the center of the concrete walkway echoed over and over on top of each other until they were deafening.

The purple tattoo sign wasn't lit.

There were no shop lights spilling out into the tunnel from any of the other three shops, either. I wondered if they were all closed for lunch or something, wondered again just what 'Military Collectible Stamps' did with his time.

Marcus was the key to this. I didn't know what his problem was with me, and I didn't care. I was through fucking around.

The tattoo shop, the thin slice of it I could see, was dark and still. I was ready to bust the door in. Instead, it gave gently under my fingers. Unlocked. I pushed the plate with the tips of my fingers and stepped through.

Once inside, I stood loose and ready, jacked on adrenalin and waiting for my eyes to adjust to the gloom. Behind me, the front door pulled shut on its spring. The sounds of flowing water were somewhat muted.

Except for the snake in its tank, I was alone.

I passed swiftly through the hushed and still front room. On a shelf behind the counter sat a pistol, a flat black shadow in the gloom. I wondered if it had been there the day before, when I punched Marcus. I hadn't even considered the possibility.

The weapon was a Glock, boxy and loaded and lethal. I didn't want it, didn't want to leave it behind me. Settled for clearing the chamber and sticking it in my waistband.

I looked around the tattoo area. The room was so bare and neglected, I couldn't believe anyone had ever mistaken it for a working studio, let alone me.

The lock to the back room was heavy duty. It looked like the type of thing that might stand up to sledgehammers or a shotgun blast.

The hinges, however, were normal old brass in a boring wood frame. I kicked them apart in two tries.

The door lock really was rugged. It had three steel deadbolts and needed a key to open from either side. Even with the door off its hinges, the bolts were set deep enough that the splintered wood still hung stubbornly in its frame. I had to pull it out by hand to get through.

When I did wrench it loose, the broken door fell away from my hands, tumbling away in an echoing string of crashes.

So much for the element of surprise.

A flight of concrete steps led down into a darkness so complete I couldn't see where the door landed. There was no light switch on the wall and I hadn't thought to bring a flashlight.

No choice. I moved carefully down the steps, testing for unseen obstacles. The layout was already familiar: I had looked at buildings just like this one all over the neighborhood before I signed the lease for my current space. I told myself all I was likely to find was the usual collection of ladders and light bulbs and various other crap the landlord stored there, maybe a primitive but functional toilet.

I didn't believe it, but it's what I told myself.

The .38 was warm in my hand. I still hated being blind and vulnerable.

I counted eleven steps down when something small and hard hit me in the eye. I batted at it, found a pull-string for the overhead lights.

The room flickered to life under banks of fluorescent tubes. This was nothing like any of those other basements.

It was big. The length of the three storefronts above, and outfitted like some kind of 1970's rumpus room. The floor was thick gold shag with swirls of what was probably white once. The furniture was a thrift shop collection of beanbags and couches. One was a brown geometric pattern, the other looked like it was made out of orange foam blocks. The air smelled wet and moldy, and also like a butcher shop on a summer day.

It was nightmarish, like the Brady Bunch kept a dungeon under that A-frame house of theirs.

There was nothing old or thrift shop about the TV or stereo centered on one wall, though. The TV was a mammoth plasma screen, the stereo a curved piece of black glass that looked like it was going a hundred miles an hour. It had speakers ranged around the room and no visible controls.

Three doors were set along the walls of the basement. One of them was open, so I tried that one first. No light switch in that room, no light to turn on if there was. But enough light streamed in from behind me for me to see.

The room was bare. A stained foam pad for bedding, green plastic bucket for a toilet. Walls and ceiling covered in the thick sheets of Styrofoam that a lot of people use for insulation or soundproofing. A sloppy effort had been made to paint the panels black.

The only other piece of furniture dominated the room. It stood a little below hip height, looked like a cross between a saddle and a pommel horse. Everything else in this place was squalor, but this thing had been lovingly cared for. Its leather gleamed, and all the snaps and buckles were oiled and polished.

Set in the middle of the floor in front of the saddle was a big iron eyelet. A length of heavy chain threaded through it, and at the other end of the chain an elaborate set of black leather cuffs.

They were wide and thick, made to hold the forearms from wrist to elbow. The lining was a soft black fur, matted and greasy with sweat, peppered with tiny flakes of skin.

A flicker registered out of the corner of my eye. I looked up to see Joanne Tolaffson standing in the cell with me. Her skin was gray and withered, patches of mold breaking out moss green and poison white on her flesh. She was too small for the black iron chains wrapped around her body. It made her look frail and sad and pitiable.

And very, very dead.

She watched me with wide pleading eyes whose clear blue color was filmed over with milky cataracts. I saw that she was crying, except the fluid tracking down her cheeks had an opaque yellow cast.

She tried to speak again, or maybe just to blubber. No sound passed those cracked and swollen, oozing purple lips. She saw I still couldn't hear her, and the knowledge made her cry harder.

"It was here, wasn't it? This is where you came when you got off the bus?"

She tossed her head from side to side, an emphatic 'no'. One bony mummified corpse hand pointed to the ceiling.

"I want to help, but you've got to help me understand you."

The ghost hung her head. Her shoulders shook with silent sobs and the thick yellowish fluid fell from her cheeks, vanished somewhere before it hit the ground.

I left that small terrible room with the shade of Joanne Tolaffson on her knees, weeping in the middle of it. Rage was a winter storm in the center of my chest. Shards of ice tore at everything soft inside me. Drifting snow buried everything warm.

The second door was a mop closet, three feet square with a big grated drain positioned over a waist-high faucet. That rusted iron grate was spattered and stained with dried blood. Perfect and whole, three teeth gleamed up at me out of the thick sticky puddle.

The third door was locked, but this time it only took me one kick to bring it off its hinges and send it flying into the room in front of me. I was right behind it, training my gun around the room.

I might have yelled something, but Marcus was beyond caring.

It had gone hard for him. I felt a guilty and savage satisfaction at the knowledge.

His hands were bound around the back of his black vinyl office chair with regular steel cuffs, and another pair bound his legs to the chair's center post. Both were ratcheted so tight the flesh beyond them was black.

He was naked, his skin fishbelly white and covered with coarse black hair and cigarette burns. I thought of the smell in the office air, revised that to cigar burns.

His jaws were stretched wide around his ruined mouth by a bondage ball gag and his eyes were wide open and bulging. He looked like he died screaming.

I saw that Marcus kept a bare office. It would have been messy if there had been more in it, just the chair he was shackled to, a battered desk and a stained old couch. Sick shit on the cheap.

He had another small television on the scarred and scorched wooden desktop. It was cold when I put my palm on it.

His desk had only three drawers, all down one side. I pulled them out from the bottom. Found a foul-looking stack of pornographic magazines in one. Opened boxes of condoms and a crumpled leaking tube of KY jelly in another. In the last, a number of used condoms, knotted at the end.

I pulled away with a shudder, glad I wore gloves.

Under the desk, down where his feet would be when he sat there, a tidy little gray steel safe sat hidden from casual eyes.

It also sat open and empty. Whatever it once contained wasn't there now. His keys sat in the lock, the ring attached to a strap with his name and a pentagram branded into the dark leather.

I passed through two locked doors to reach this room. None of them had been locked with Marcus's keys. Whoever killed him had their own set of keys.

The center drawer of the desk turned out to contain nothing more interesting than takeout menus from neighborhood restaurants, a couple of matchbooks from Resurrection Joe's and a three-inch glass pipe, the bowl caked with scorched brown sediment. My mother's had been much more elaborate, but it didn't make her any less of a junkie.

I had the feeling that when his killers left, they took away with them anything that might have helped me, along with the contents of the safe.

I looked over at Marcus's frozen screaming face, saw the stubble across his brow line and scalp and wondered when the last time had been he shaved.

It was a small office: the only thing left to do was look under the couch. It might have been white once, or maybe beige, but that was a lot of years and a lot of fluids ago. Now it was just about as broken-down as it was possible for furniture to get.

When I lifted it to look underneath, I found a patch of black mold the size of a garbage can lid. Nothing else. I stood up, gave it an angry kick.

From right behind me, electronic tones began to bleep out the tune to an old horror movie. I couldn't remember the movie, knew the song was called *Tubular Bells*.

The tune played for a few seconds, hesitated, played again. By that time I tracked it down to its source: an Android smartphone like a black plastic toy. It was on the floor, hidden in the folds of that shapeless black garment Marcus had on every time I saw him. The tune played twice more before I was able to dig the phone out of the mass of dark cloth, but at last I had it in my hand.

The incoming call screen said 'Unknown Caller'. I thumbed the button on the touchscreen, curious to find out who was calling the dead man. I put it to my ear and said nothing.

I needn't have bothered. My baby sister's breathy lisp came on at the other end of the line. No wonder the cell network was at a loss.

"Sam, what are you doing? Get out of there."

"Tabby--"

"It's the girl, Sam. She's in terrible danger, and so are you. You've got to get out of there. *Help* her, Sam!"

My first thought was a mental picture of my rental car in the rain, one door standing open, Bex nowhere to be seen.

I took the stairs four at a time in my rush.

Forty-Six

I hit the sidewalk at a dead run, the .38 still in my hand, the rain harder now, like stepping into a solid wall of icy water. Visibility was awful. I was barreling down the sidewalk faster than the objects in front of me were emerging from the shimmering gray curtain of falling water.

I was almost on top of it by the time I saw the rented SUV's rear bumper rise up out of the wet. My momentum carried me in a headlong slide along the wet pavement, crashing to a stop against the rear door. I shook my head and jumped in though the open passenger door without bothering to think about how it got that way.

I must have scared the hell out of Bex. She kicked the SUV into gear and floored it. We leapt away from the curb and into the street with more speed than I would have thought possible for such a large vehicle.

Her driving instincts were excellent. We tore down that street, throwing high plumes of water into the air behind us, and in less than ten seconds were down though the onramp and accelerating further to keep up with traffic on the expressway. Her posture was stiff and tense, but her movements at the wheel deft and perfectly timed.

"What is it?" she said. "What happened?"

I was so ridiculously glad to find her safe and sound and Tabby's warning groundless that the words caught all over themselves and none of what I was feeling came out.

I looked over at Bex behind the wheel, saw the lines of her arms as she wove the rental through the wet-weather traffic, the way her hair fell around her face, the cuts and scratches along her cheek and jaw. I still couldn't find the words.

"I wonder if you missed your calling," I said instead. "You'd have been a great getaway driver."

Bex swept us easily through the interchange from 35W to I-94. As she drove, it became steadily more obvious that nothing was actually after us. As she loosened up, I told her what I found in Dark Rites.

Traffic on the freeway ground to a halt outside of downtown, but we were in no hurry to go anywhere. There were emergency lights up ahead.

"Let me see the phone?"

I passed it over. Bex glanced briefly at it, clicked it to life and began moving one thumb across the touchscreen.

She flicked through a few pictures, shuddered and tossed the thing back in my lap. A bare-breasted Tasha smiled into the screen. What I assumed was Marcus's crooked narrow penis caressed her cheek. I tapped the arrow on the side, got a photo of a girl who couldn't have been more than thirteen or fourteen sprawled naked and awkward and stoned on the orange foam couch. Everything else I saw was more of the same, many of them trussed this way and that to the shining leather saddle in his home-made dungeon.

A sour metal taste coated my tongue, and a little more of whatever had been left of my innocence left. I impulsively stabbed at a button and the pictures vanished from the screen. I wished they could leave me that easily..

Bex looked up, saw that the tail lights in front of her were a few yards further along, eased forward to compensate

Outside the car window, several tow trucks were stopped along the side of the road, orange lights winking on top of their cabs. Up ahead, a row of orange plastic cones merged our lane with the one beside us. A uniformed cop in a plastic rain cape waved a red wand of a flashlight.

"Let me see the iPad again?" Bex said. I reached back and handed it to her while she rolled another couple of feet forward. She rapidly riffled through the cached pages, her finger skimming along the screen, searching.

I sat in the rental's leather seat and poked my way around Marcus's cellphone, was surprised to find that his number wasn't the one Jack Rose called the night he and his brother entered my life. I couldn't think of why he would hire them, but I knew that where addicts are concerned, motive wasn't always an issue. They might even commit suicide, leave a ten year old boy with no way to understand.

The SUV inched forward another couple of feet, and I tapped the Video tab on the tiny phone. There was only one, less than ten seconds long. I opened it.

"It's both of them," Bex said. "See?" She tapped the screen of the tablet for emphasis.

"What both? I told you, it's just the one ghost I've been seeing." In the palm of my hand, tiny figures and faces moved in a ghostly light. Whether by accident or recording option, they flickered in silence.

"One girl's dead, Sam, but two went missing. Remember, Joanne Tolaffson *and* her best friend Christine Nudenberger. Both of them ditched out and took the bus to Minneapolis last week. The other girl's still missing."

"I can't believe I didn't see that."

"When you sister called you, *I* wasn't the girl she was warning you about. I wasn't in danger." Bex pointed at the second girl in the news photo. "This girl, Christine, she's the one in danger. It means she's still alive."

Bex pulled out into the lane beside us, forcing cars hanging bumper to bumper to make room for her. She ignored their angry honks. In the wet light, she looked like a thing made of steel.

"Sam, there's a chance we can still save this girl."

I looked back at the phone in my hand, watched the short silent video all the way through. And again. The top of my scalp went cold and the ice crept down my spine.

"I know who's got her," I said. I gave Bex directions for where we had to go.

Forty-Seven

The storm was a bad one. The weather system brewed up somewhere out in the Dakota Badlands and crawled black and angry across all that flat empty prairie. It was the sort of summer storm that makes farmers afraid of losing their crops. Every few years you'd see news stories after a day like this, blow-dried reporters in city shoes and gruff men in overalls standing in front of fields of trampled pulp that had once been corn, wheat or sorghum.

Just past Brooklyn Park on our way out of town, we hit a belt of weather like passing through the belly of God's Wrath. Solid sheets of water lashed at the windshield, and gusts of wind rocked the heavy 4x4 on its springs. Our speed dropped, but not by much. Bex took us smooth and fast through the storm. Her face was a hard mask, focused on the road ahead.

I always thought my fear and distrust of the police was a natural product of the ways I'd always seen them act. I knew that a great many cops were decent, honest, hardworking people with an impossibly hard job to do. I also knew that when the school bully was given a badge and a gun, shotguns and riot gear and dogs and helicopter support, the potential for abuse was terrible to behold

I envied my more normal friends their ability to treat police officers as the civil servants they're supposed to be. For them a traffic stop was a minor inconvenience, not a potentially catastrophic encounter with people licensed to harm those they were charged to protect. I believed I had just seen too much, enough that it sickened me when audiences cheered the lantern-jawed steely-eyed cop on TV or in movies violating the scary minority's civil rights.

But then, I also read once that people raised by addicts commonly grew up with an irrational fear and distrust of police officers. Something about our earliest authority figures being volatile and frightening. The way that book described addictive behavior, it was like they'd been looking in my mother's windows twenty years ago. Grandiose promises and sudden groundless punishment. Emotional absence and smothering affection and frightening, insane, depthless wrath. All swirling out of some interior chemical state that has nothing to do with the children, though the kids often believe it does.

I certainly did.

So I had to confront the idea that the visceral emotional reaction I feel at the sight of badges and uniforms and that arrogant self-satisfied posture had more to do with my own background. But then, in that same book I also read that a great many self-destructive and violent adult children from backgrounds like mine are drawn to the power and control a career in law enforcement offers. The high rates of alcoholism, drug addiction, gambling problems and suicide among police officers as well as my own experiences certainly seemed to bear the idea out.

It was entirely possible that what might seem like an irrational fear was simply like knowing dangerous like.

Either way, I couldn't bring myself to call 911 and send *them* after Christine Nudenberger. I told myself that by the time Bex and I convinced them there was a problem, let alone to do anything about it, the two of us would have been locked up on general principles and the girl might well be dead.

We were the only ones who might make it in time. But if we failed, that *couldn't* be the end of it.

With a visceral feeling of revulsion, I picked up Marcus's cellphone again.

Just north of Anoka, we burst out ahead of the storm front entirely. The road ahead was still dry and clear, the broad prairie around us bathed in a yellow-green light the color of a week-old bruise. I called Hamish's cell and left a message on his voicemail. I told him where we were going and what we expected to find, tried not to think about what that said about the odds of us coming back alive. The connection hummed and crackled with static, some kind of interference from the storm.

Five minutes later, the cell lost coverage.

We rode before the storm front another ten miles when I spotted our turn. Everything looked unearthly in the eerie light.

The road twisted and wound and worked its way deeper into the North Woods. The whole time, black thunderheads piled high in the west, cold and angry and ominous.

We ran hard for most of an hour on the twisting rural roads. Once or twice we ran through an open stretch wide enough to get a good view of the storm front stalking our flank. The sky on one side was full of thick golden light. The other was a deep bone-bruise purple with flashing veins of lightning. The cold nasty rain we left back in the Twin Cities had built up to something much worse out here.

We made our way in silence, each with our own thoughts. Bex kept both hands on the wheel, capable and focused. I checked the Glock I'd taken, a 9mm in working order. I believed we were both doing the same thing, trying not to let the other know we were scared.

Finally, we rounded a curve through some trees and came out running along a slight ridge. A forest stretched out below us, pine so thick it seemed to catch and hold a faint blue light in its depths.

In the center of that deep green hush sat a lake with water so clear and still it was a perfect mirror looking back into the sky. It was easy to imagine how it would look on a clear day. Even Bex eased off her speed and murmured, soft and appreciative.

Right now, the sky reflected in that water was like nothing I had seen before. The air was a dirty grainy yellow, so gritty you could taste it. On three sides around us, storm clouds rose in great black anvils, tearing across the landscape for miles around, tethered to the earth by flickering quick threads of lightning.

As the SUV made its turn back into the woods and began its descent to the lake, I was certain I saw several telltale cones dropping down from the dark masses above. Those cones were always fragile, rarely surviving long enough to reach the ground, and never for more than a few seconds, a minute or two at most. But whenever and wherever those funnels managed to find a foot on the earth, however brief, they would visit a fury on those below like the very wrath of God.

***

Bone Lake was too small for a country club or the power-boat summer crowd. The last time I had seen it, the lake was frozen over and speckled with ice-fishing huts, the land around in every direction covered in a thick white mantle. I recognized it all the same. The general store was locked up tight, steel storm shutters over all the windows.

Bone Lake was a weekend place all year long: ice-fishers in winter, duck hunters in fall, walleye fishing in the summer. Middle of a weekday like this like this, the cabins and shacks around the lake were deserted.

Bex and I made our turn off the gravel and onto a dirt lane. Ten minutes later, I spotted the driveway we wanted.

The house was shuttered and dark. Tall pines edged right up to the eaves. Their blue depths and whispering needles made the forest around us seem wild, untamed and holy.

Bex kept looking over her shoulder down the dirt lane as she filled her pockets with ammo for the .38. I knew we weren't likely to get a chance to reload, but I understood the desire.

The .38 was the natural option for her. Easy to carry, nothing to go wrong. Just point and shoot.

The house sat still and silent in the dirty yellow light. Its heavy wood shutters left its face blank and expressionless in the moments before the storm.

"Now what?" Bex said.

I slapped the magazine into the butt of the Glock. The sound was smooth and deadly.

"Let's go get her."

Forty-Eight

"Sound will carry out here," I said into Bex's ear. "Don't slam the door when you get out of the car. The cabin we're headed for is two doors down: about two hundred yards--" I caught myself. "Two hundred *meters* in that direction. It's pretty much all trees between here and there. Not too much chance of being seen, just heard."

She nodded and checked the load on the .38, spun the wheel with her thumb and flicked it closed like she'd been doing it all her life. American TV and movies really were creating a global culture.

"Bex..."

She laid one small hand on my cheek, silenced me.

"Tell me later, Sam. There'll be time." She held my eyes a moment and climbed out of the car. I tucked the Glock into my waistband and followed.

Out into a world holding its breath. Light the color of an old bruise lay over the land. All around us, every living thing was hushed and still. The only sound was an eerie moan from high up in the trees, pine needles slicing the wind.

And something else. Bex heard it before I did: a faint sound, carried in gusts when the wind turned our way.

It sounded like a baby crying, or someone hurting a cat.

A few yards into the woods, we were in another world. Rough black trunks rose on every side. The forest floor was thick with fallen pine needles and dead. The air was dark and green and pure and still. No bird or squirrel or anything else moved or sang or made any sign of life. Bex was like a ghost, bent low and moving in silence a several yards to my right.

I was sure my heart was beating loud enough for others to hear, but the only real sounds around us were the moaning treetops and that faint awful crying.

Then it happened. The world went dark. So much light bled out of that clear emerald air that I could barely see my own hands. The whispering in the trees above us fell away and the world went deathly still.

Something hard punched me on the wrist, and again on the point of my shoulder. A third tap hit me directly on top of my head. A noise like a roaring crowd rolled over me and the rain began to fall in earnest.

In seconds I was surrounded by a shimmering steel curtain, soaked to the bone. I looked for Bex, couldn't even see the tree trunk beyond the one I was standing under. There was no way I could call out to her without giving our presence away.

I hoped I didn't get turned around in the rain.

I hoped Bex was all right.

I said a short and silent prayer for us all and started moving again.

Forty-Nine

I didn't get lost. It turned out I was closer to the edge of the treeline than I knew. A few dozen shuffling steps and one unseen tree branch trying to take my eye out were all it took.

Once branches quit slashing at my face and the pine needles underfoot gave way to thin soft grass I knew the cabin, garage and smokehouse should be in view by now.

I knew the buildings were less than fifty yards away on the other side of that lawn. In this downpour I could still wander right past them and into the lake.

I had no idea where Bex was. I knew I couldn't wait.

It was only late afternoon. I still couldn't see more than five feet through the shimmering gray curtain around me. Not until the lightning. Strikes were landing among the trees on the far side of the lake: close and getting closer. A sudden flash lit up the world around me, transformed it into flat white planes and crisp black shadows. Thunder rumbled long and hard through my body, vibrating the bones in my chest. By then I was already headed across the field in a low run.

Fifty yards on a paved road is nothing in a car. But a football team can spend two hours of hard effort and never cover that distance even once. I stayed low to the ground and made the best time I could. I ran blind in the rain, slipped and fell twice on the slick grass.

I knew to try to turn the fall into a roll, but it wasn't the sort of thing I practiced, not since I was sixteen, anyway. I managed not to drown or lose my weapon, but that's about it.

Right after my second fall and about halfway across the field, lightning hit the surface of the lake. There was a sudden warm prickling along one side of my body.

I looked up just in time to see a pillar of fire bridge the gap between sky and water. It tore the air around it with a sound that ripped through my body like an axe blow.

I was knocked off my feet again, and the thunder seemed to rumble on forever.

As soon as I could make my legs obey me, I scrambled up, off and running again. I felt like a bug on a plate exposed out in that field.

There was a glow off to my right, a row of faint yellow specters hovering in the distance. I stopped, saw that I was looking at windows, and headed towards them. I was off course and would have run right past the cabin and into the lake.

Twenty feet from the cabin, I still couldn't make out the shape of the building in front of me. The windows hovered suspended in the rain.

Those two glass squares were portals to another world. Behind them, firelight danced on plank walls and heavy rafters.

Just then, all the hair on my body stood up. My skin felt as though it was covered in thousands of biting ants.

I dove for the ground, slid face first through cold mud as a bolt of lightning turned the world inside out.

The flash was blinding. The sound of it was the single loudest noise I had ever heard. The next thing I knew I was swallowing dirt and water and sliding out of control.

***

I landed under the back porch, lying against the rough-cut wooden uprights that supported it. All I could see were strobing yellow spots against a field of purple and black and my ears rang like they had the night I fired three high-velocity hollowpoints indoors in New Orleans. Every muscle in my body seemed to be cramped. My hands scrabbled to my waist for the butt of the pistol, found nothing but wet muddy skin.

As near as I could tell I was still alive and not on fire: the lightning strike must have been a near miss. I kicked my way further up under the boards of the porch, forced myself to wait for sound and vision to return.

Joanne Tolaffson had spent a long and painful time dying. There was no reason to think it would go any easier for the other young girl in there now. But in my current condition, I would only get us both killed, maybe Bex too. Once again, I prayed silently for her safety.

As though in answer, I felt the touch of an icy hand on my arm and nearly jumped out of my skin.

In the weak light from the back windows, I saw Joanne under the porch with me. Her face was a skin-covered skull, points of light still burning in dark shrunken sockets. A few wisps pasted to her scalp were all that remained of the thick spill of blonde hair she had proudly worn over one shoulder in her yearbook photo. The black iron chains lashed to her frail body were heavier than ever-- only thin knobs of bone and scraps of flesh showed through the massive dark coils.

The ghost raised one gnarled finger to what remained of her lips, pointed upward.

Through the slats in the floorboards, a slice of buttery yellow light opened in the wall of the cabin. The light widened until it painted my body in golden stripes. I was alone again: the ghost vanished.

The light also showed the shape of the pistol outlined against the fabric of my jeans.

I lay stone-still as booted footsteps fell across the boards over my head. Each step boomed like a drum around me.

The heavy footfalls thundered their way up and down the length of the porch. Their sound was a slow deep drumbeat against the pelting racket of the rain on the corrugated tin roof. The steps traveled out to the edge of the railing, stopped. Eight long seconds later, they turned and made their booming return.

Directly over my head, the booted footsteps stopped.

I told myself it wasn't possible for anyone else to actually hear my heart hammering in my chest. The rain clattered onto the roof of the porch, eating all other sounds. I could barely hear the scuff and scrape of the boots turning from one side to another, and that was less than four inches above my nose.

I counted five very long seconds in my head before I felt the deep bass boom of those boots making the final few steps back into the cabin.

The back door slammed closed. I was once again in the dark.

I fished the Glock out of my pants. It must have dropped down my waistband and got wedged there when I landed under the porch. The barrel was halfway down the left leg of my jeans, and I had to unbutton and unzip to get it out. It was the most grateful I had ever been that I didn't carry it with a round in the chamber.

The pistol was in better shape than I was. Water beaded on the oiled steel, but being lost down my pants leg had protected it from the mud.

I dropped the clip onto my belly, worked the slide back and forth and dry-fired a couple times. Everything seemed in order, and no sound was louder than the water drumming on the roof of the cabin.

I slapped the clip back in, racked a round in the chamber and eased out from under the protection of the porch.

I was careful with the pistol. It was ready to kill.

Fifty

Icy needles of rain stung my bare skin as I came around the porch and mounted the wooden steps. Small pellets of hail bounced off the lawn among the rain drops, so white they almost glowed. I moved carefully across the rough decking. Water dripped from my body in soft tapping pats. The falling drops left spots in the wood like dark coins.

I stood a second in front of the closed door, getting my heartbeat and breathing under control. There was no turning back, never had been. Another sick cat scream swelled and burst from inside the cabin.

The door knob turned quietly under my palm.

***

Inside, the cabin was warm and dry. Rain and hail gabbled off the roof, deafening. Hard to believe that a few minutes ago, a slammed car door might have given us away.

The cabin was just three rooms, the large main room I was standing in now and two others through the doorways set into the opposite wall. One was a bedroom, the other held a flush toilet and an enormous bathtub: cast-iron and claw-footed.

Both doors were closed. Bright flickering light blazed from under them both.

I shut the front door behind me, stepped into the main room. The furniture was old, comfortable. The chairs and couches were covered with white cloths, the wood surfaces dry and neglected.

Hurricane lamps hung from hooks in the timber rafters, twirling gently, moved by forces I could neither see nor feel. Around the room, on tables and counters, candles burned in saucers and bowls.

I moved through the room, the pistol in front of me in a two-handed shooter's grip.

Beneath the noise of the storm a terrible sound pervaded the house: a fast high-pitched panting that didn't seem like it could possibly come from a human throat. Running through it in a low murmuring counterpoint, a gentle voice speaking indistinct words, soft like a lullaby.

I couldn't tell which room it came from, chose the door on the left.

I stepped up to the door, wrapped my palm around the knob and came through fast and low, just the way I'd been taught so long ago. High targets get hit. I swept the room, ready to kill anything that moved.

The bedroom was empty. The only things in it were a futon with rumpled and soiled cotton sheets and a massive worm-eaten dresser, virtually transformed into an altar by all the candles blazing on top of it. The walls of the room danced and breathed in their light.

The bedroom was a good guess, but the wrong one. I had made a tactical error, a bad one, and lost no time trying to turn it around.

I trained the barrel of the gun on the connecting doorway to the bathroom, threw the door open and shouted, "FREEZE!"

Fifty-One

The tableau that confronted me was the stuff nightmares are made of.

Christine Nudenberger lay spread on the floor of the cabin. Her limbs were held taught by what looked like black iron nails driven through flesh and bone and wood. Her mouth was bloody, her lips pulled far back from teeth and gums and her eyes rolled up in her head until only the whites showed. The skin all over her body was carved with intricate symbols.

Blood had turned the floor beneath her into one large dark stain.

Lisa Torres knelt in front of that stain. She stared at me in silence. Her face was a war between what might be called fear or regret and a terrible hungry fascination with the gathering blood.

The frightened girl was surrounded by a circle of thick black candles whose melting wax gave off a smell like dried blood and burning hair. The floor was covered in scribbled chalk symbols, and beneath her, lengths of iron chain spread away from her body in a perfect X.

I stepped fully into the room. The barrel of the pistol trembled slightly in my hands.

"Shouldn't you be shooting me right now?" said a voice from my right.

Too late, I noticed something important: The bathroom's second door, the one that led into the main room, had been closed. Now it stood open, the room dim beyond it.

I moved straight for it, the Glock trained in front of me. The whimpering mewl rising from the floor behind me was a nightmare soundtrack to that frozen crystal moment.

"Nice try, dead man," came a raspy voice from the bedroom behind me.

The hard-faced blonde from Dark Rites leaned in the doorway, haloed by the candles burning behind her. She still wore the schoolgirl getup and combat boots. I moved to cover her with the gun and she came off the doorway.

I had never seen anyone move so fast in my life. As I spun to face her the space between us closed, collapsed and vanished.

I managed to fire three shots before the pistol tumbled away from me in a blinding moment of pain and I found myself fighting for my life.

I never got a chance to hesitate about fighting a woman. The blonde was the finest martial artist I had ever seen.

She charged into me in a flurry of punches and kicks that left vapor trails in the air. My brass was still twinkling in the air above our heads, the Glock still sailing off into the useless distance. I was doing all I could simply to keep my feet.

I managed to block or deflect the worst shots to the most vital organs, the blows that would have ended it all right then and there. A few real beauties still sailed right past my guard like it wasn't there, lit up the space inside my head in blasts of white light.

I was in trouble.

I kept ducking and moving, bobbing and weaving, trying to escape the stinging punishing blows that seemed to land everywhere at once. Trying to get some space around us. Trying to find some advantage.

My slapping and scuffling defense got me out as far as the main room. I skipped past a large, dark, motionless figure at the edge of my vision. I came up for air in time to see her booted leg sail into my chest.

I wanted space, and she obliged.

By kicking me through a window.

Fifty-Two

I found myself lying in mud and broken glass. Rain fell in my nose and mouth. Hail pelted my skin. I rolled onto my knees. The icy water pummeled the cut and torn flesh of my back. I coughed up a clot of something red that splatted into the mud in front of my chin.

I tried to will my body to stand, to fight. The best I could manage was to raise my head far enough to see the hard-faced blonde saunter around the side of the house.

Of course. She used the door.

I blamed the adrenalin in my system: her forty foot walk seemed to take a year. I had all the time in the world to notice the little things. The way her pigtails gradually flattened with every rain drop that struck them until her pale hair was dark and plastered to her skull. The way the pleats of her skirt swung from side to side with every step. The way the mud clung to the soles of her heavy combat boots.

Fat circles the color of dirty bone appeared on the shoulders of the white blouse she wore, one after the other, overlapping until the whole garment clung transparent to her muscled pink torso.

I had no doubt that I knew now who had hospitalized Hamish.

And I knew, cold and certain, that unless I did something right away, the blonde was going to kill me with her bare hands.

I made a desperate scramble for my feet, instead fell face-first in the mud again. My right hand wasn't doing anything I told it to. Nothing else was obeying too well either.

I spit mud out of my mouth. Saw her standing over me, so close all I could see were the tops of her combat boots.

She grabbed me by the hair, pulled me back up onto my knees.

The blonde bent down, put her face close to mine, moved my jaw from side to side with her thumb. I could see dull red lights shining behind her eyes. A powerful musky smell like hot cloves rose off her skin and curled out of her body on her breath.

"The mighty killer," she said. "What's the matter, don't you like me?"

She held my jaw between thumb and forefinger, combed my hair with her other hand like I was a little boy.

I hoped she would keep doing it, anything to buy some time. I felt a little better, in that I hurt *everywhere*. It was an improvement over that warm distant feeling where I didn't much give a damn what happened.

She got my hair where she wanted it, cupped my face in her palms. Held my eyes with her own. A look both dreamy and cruel transformed her features, and I knew I had to say something to get her talking.

"What do you mean?"

My voice was a harsh croak, a stranger's.

"I thought you *liked* little girls. Maybe I'm too old for you?"

"I don't know what the hell you're talking about."

Life was coming back into my arms, but they still felt terribly weak, unreliable.

"You will" she said, and cupped one palm over my mouth.

I started to struggle, but she held me firmly in her other hand, brought the palm scraping down across my mouth, wiped it free of most of the mud and blood.

She leaned in, kissed me hard and stood back away from me. Suddenly released, I started to reel. She took me by the armpits and hauled me to my feet.

I heard a sharp hiss, stood swaying while the blonde clutched at her side. Even bent over double in pain, she had the presence of mind to stay out of range. Not that I was in much shape to do anything about it.

She made a visible effort to master the pain, stretched herself up to her full height with hardly a wince. She turned her hand out to face me. Blood marbled the pale flesh.

"Faster than I gave you credit for." She shook her head in disbelief. "You're only the second person who's ever shot me. Don't worry, it's just a scratch. Still, you ought to be proud, dead man."

Pain clouded her eyes again. When they cleared it was like a searchlight shining through broken glass.

"Hurts like a son of a bitch, too," she said. "You're going to *pay* for that one."

The hard-faced blonde turned her palm up to the rain, laughed as the fat drops splatted onto her skin. The water carried her blood in long streams down her.

She rolled her shoulders like a boxer and came circling in close.

I was weak as newborn colt on shaking and unsteady legs. She stalked me, pacing from flank to flank like a jungle cat on the hunt.

"So you're the big tough guy the whole family's been talking about."

She punched me in the mouth, a whip-crack that rolled off her shoulder and struck before I even saw it coming.

"Me, I don't see it."

I got my guard up, half-assed. I tried to give the impression of a beaten and broken man whose only hope now is to die fighting. It wasn't hard. I started circling on painful creaking joints. I wasn't going to get much more than one good shot. I had to make it count.

The hard-faced blonde circled, playing with me. She made little feints and darts, laughing like she had a mouth full of razor-blades.

When she felt like it, she snapped off one of those lightning shots that was already on its way back by the time I felt the pain.

She hit like a surgeon. Tight directed shots to my face, shoulders, biceps. She returned again and again to one spot just below my heart, opening up a blossom of pain the size of a rotten cantaloupe. Pain cored its way through my chest until each blow seemed to come out the other side.

Hands or feet, it didn't seem to matter. She struck hard and fast, from unpredictable angles. My eyes were swollen nearly shut, my face pulped. I couldn't tell where my nose ended and cheeks or mouth began.

The only weakness I could see was that she was reluctant to use her right hand. The dirty wet cloth on that flank was completely pink now, and a dark trickle ran down her leg from under the hem of her skirt.

As though able to read my thoughts, the blonde sent her right fist lashing out. A ball of fire exploded between my eyes. I stayed standing. Just.

She gave a wicked little laugh, spun on her toes with a ballerina's grace and cracked the very tips of her fingers across my right hand. Pain flowered up out of the damaged bones. I bit down hard on my back teeth to keep from vomiting.

If I was going to make a move, it had to be now.

I feinted for her injured flank, threw a swift stabbing kick at the ball of her calf and rolled my weight right behind it into a vicious uppercut. The last part of the combination would have been an elbow strike to the head.

Instead, she moved like nothing I'd ever seen. The toe of my shoe skidded off her already-moving leg and then she simply wasn't there.

One graceful booted foot flashed out from behind me and another great rotten flower of pain bloomed and burst behind my thigh.

I heard that razor blade laugh again.

"Nice. I didn't think you had it in you."

Again that dancer's foot lashed out. White light exploded and blood ran into my right eye, but I was on my feet and covering the shots I could see or even sense.

Too many still got through.

We fell into a fast, slapping, rhythmic dance. My right hand was next to useless, so I was pulling back now and circling in that direction, defending with my left. Her own injury no longer seemed to slow her down at all.

She chased me in a fresh flurry of limbs, trying to break through to that unprotected side. It was a cruel game to her, life and death to me.

I noticed the blonde favored a three-shot combination. Every few seconds she would come out of her guard and flail into me with some kind of backhand-forehand-kick.

It hurt like fuck. It also left her open.

I kept my feet, shuffling and moving as best I could. At least the mud that pulled and sucked at my feet slowed her down too, just not enough. My chin was tucked in tight to the hollow of my shoulder, and I did my best to keep my left arm and any hard bony surface between her blows and their targets.

I didn't have to wait long.

Like some night-blooming plant, she seemed to unfold in slow motion. Her right arm sliced through the silver rain toward my bad right side, her left arm trailing behind it. I could feel as much as see her weight rising up to free the left foot for the vicious kick that would follow.

Instead of covering as she expected, I rolled my shoulders and body inside, safe from the main force of the blow. My left fist and all the body weight I could put behind it came up from the ground to the shelf of her jaw and traveled two feet further, past the top of her head.

Wet pigtails whipped rain into my eyes. Her knees buckled. All the weight I had just brought up high, I sent crashing down, the blade of my forearm or the side of my fist seeking head, neck, collarbone.

The blow never touched her. Less than an inch from the side of her neck, she slid her body out of its path so fast she seemed to melt from under my arm. She covered her retreat with a well-aimed blow just below my kneecap.

At least I knew I'd weakened her: My leg stayed attached.

She stopped and stood a safe distance away from me, hands cocked on her hips. Blood ran freely from her nose and mouth onto her breasts. Her teeth when she smiled were small and pink and sharp inside that red ruin.

The rain streaked the bloody handprints she left on her own skin.

"That was cute. I wouldn't have figured you could move like that on your best day. And this," again that raspy, razor laugh, "this is definitely *not* your best day."

She bent over, spit a bloody wad. I wondered if it would mix with the blood I left there.

"Give you credit," she said, "you're not bad."

She looked up at me then, her eyes like a broken doll's. The red lights in their depths seemed to flare.

"But I'm bored now."

She came for me then. Everything I could do wasn't going to be enough. We fell together, in a tumble of limbs.

She went for a chokehold, didn't have the raw strength to pull it off. It was a temporary reprieve only. I got a hand in my mouth, clamped down hard with my teeth and shot clawing fingers back along the length of her arm.

My thumb caught the soft flesh of her eye, and I dug in for all I was worth. I didn't have any illusions about surviving. I just wanted to give the bitch something to remember.

Her leg found the position it wanted. I went facedown in the mud, her knee in my neck. I dug my thumb in harder, curled my fingers tight into the hair above her ear.

My nose and mouth were forced into the mud. Every breath I tried to draw choked me with more of the wet clogging mass.

An unbearable pressure built under my clawing thumb, popped in a warm jellid explosion. I heard a stony rasping roar above me and ground deeper into the socket. I felt my thumbnail scrape on bone and held on tight.

I couldn't breathe.

Liquid warmth ran down my arm and mixed with the rain and my own blood. Small hard fists beat hard at my arm, not hard enough.

Black stars and red explosions burst across my vision. My lungs were on fire.

I bore down harder on the socket.

The black stars went gray at the edges.

I tried to close my fist.

The black crowded everything else out.

Fifty-Three

There was water in my face and I was sputtering. The rain wasn't falling as hard as before, or else I didn't feel it. Somewhere, a deep voice said an unfamiliar name over and over. Everything seemed muted, far away.

There was danger, but I didn't know what that meant or what to do about it. I just wanted to lie there, swallow a little rainwater. I was very thirsty.

I smelled rotten meat, and rough hands hauled at my clothing. Even through the rain, the stench around me was overpowering. It reminded me of a time an old girlfriend with no home training stored a pound of ground beef in the cupboard and forgot about it.

Heavy mud dragged at my feet and knees. Plank steps smacked a short rhythm along thighs and shins. The rain stopped hitting me, became a rattling on the roof of the cabin and I was dumped on the floor. My body offered no resistance as it fell. My head bounced off the pine boards, a distant flare that could hardly be called pain.

I lay on my side. My breath burst bloody bubbles from my nose and one eye was swollen shut. Ragged flaps of skin hung from my face, and my arms and legs felt like scrap iron strung on frail copper wire. My spine was a chain of knots, soaked in kerosene and set on fire.

A distant tinny voice spoke from a thousand feet above.

"Not on the floor, you idiot. Over there."

Hands slick with mud reached for me, grabbed the front of my shirt. I saw the sleeves of a battered black leather jacket and the garbage smell hit stronger than ever without the rain to damp it down. Blood dripped from my mouth and nose onto my chest, onto the hands grabbing me.

I was hauled upright and into the air, dropped onto a cloth-covered couch. A cloud of dust rose around me as I sank into the cushions, and I was able to look down thirty or forty yards of black leather arms at the face of the person carrying me.

Pale waxy skin over a hard-boned skull. Crusted rash along one side of a gaunt tendoned throat. The worst teeth I had ever seen on another human being, and a jailhouse swastika tattooed across a jutting adam's apple.

In the center of the tattoo sat a dimpled entrance wound, about the width of a pencil. Hayley's kitchen knife still stuck out of the side of his thigh at the same jaunty angle Bex had left it.

I coughed blood and mud, found a croaking imitation of my voice.

"Jack. You're looking pretty bad."

There was no flicker in the sightless eyes, no expression in the slack face as he stood up and away from me. Between the zippered lapels of the jacket I was able to see the red ruin of his chest and belly.

Behind the walking corpse, a large dark figure finished stamping out some flames on the floor of the cabin's main room. Somewhere between backing through the doorway and being kicked through the window, I must have knocked over some candles.

The figure turned to me, lighting a cigar as it did. In the flare of the match, the cherub features took on a hellish cast.

"You think Jack looks bad, you haven't seen a mirror. You look like somebody's half-peeled a baseball."

My face must have betrayed me, because he casually pulled a shining nickel-plated automatic from his waistband and gestured with it, almost gently.

"No, don't get up," he said. "I'll come to you."

He grabbed one of the wooden chairs around the room and straddled it facing me. The pistol rested on one meaty forearm, finger resting on the trigger.

"What's the matter, Sam? Cat got your tongue?"

I licked my lips, tasted blood and dirt and said nothing.

"What? Don'tcha got a kind word for your old pal John?"

Fifty-Four

There was no way I was getting out of this alive, not if John had anything to say about it. If I could get my arms to move, I was pretty sure I could get that gun away from him and seriously fuck up his day. No idea what to do about Jack, though. Just about the point I had myself convinced I had nothing to lose by trying, the hard-faced blonde came limping in, one palm pressed hard against her face. The pupil in view was as wide as a saucer and her balance seemed off.

She shot me a one-eyed look that let me know that no matter what I'd just done to her, my odds had just changed drastically. And not for the better. I focused on my breathing, let my body recover as much as it could while it had the chance.

"Why?" was all I could think to ask.

"I was just gonna ask you the same question, buddy. Don't get me wrong, I'm glad you're here. Saves us the trouble of picking you up tonight, but I was kinda under the impression this here was a private party."

Behind him, the blonde's combat boots clumped on the floorboards as she wore a dripping track back and forth across the floor.

"First you show up at the Terminal when *I* heard you were dead and gone, then you don't come into work on a Monday like you usually do. Now, here you are instead. You're just full of surprises. Come on buddy, don't be shy."

His accent always had a trace of the South in it, now thickening by the minute.

"Marcus. His phone caught you on video." My best hope was letting them think I was worse off than I was, if that was possible. I tried to make my voice sound weak and shaky. I didn't have to fake it.

John shook his head, leaned back behind him to address the blonde.

"See Darla? Just like I said, it's always something."

"Fuck are you waiting for? Just do him and we can get back to work."

When she dropped her hand in a chopping gesture it revealed a dark bloody socket.

"Now sugar, you know Sam here's our special guest."

"I don't give a shit. That asshole just about took out my eye."

"Did he hurt you, Dolly? Come on over here, let me see." He reached out, curled his free hand around her waist and pulled her to him. She perched obediently on his knee while he examined her eye, moving his head on his neck this way and that and making small tutting and cooing sounds.

The body of Jack Rose stood beside them, as motionless and silent as the grave.

"It's bad," John finally said. "I won't lie to you, he fucked you up pretty bad, but once we're done here we'll grow you a new one."

"He owes me an eye." Darla's tone was little-girl petulant, whiny. "Two."

"We've got something else for mean old Sam." John kissed her on the chin, tongued the open sores along the line of her jaw. "Tonight, remember?"

She sucked his lower lip between her teeth, nestled in with her head on his shoulder.

"You always were my favorite little brother," she said in that gravelly broken-glass voice of hers.

"Love you too, sis."

John wrapped one proprietary hand around her muddy rump, shot me that satyr's grin like this was one more joke around a couple of beers. Seeing the two side by side like that, the resemblance was clear.

"What was it I said back at Resurrection Joe's? One big incestuous family. Only ours ain't that big. Just me and my sister here left, ain't that right baby?"

From his shoulder, Darla gave me a sly little smile.

No way I'd be able to get out of bed tomorrow morning if I lived that long, but my body was definitely recovering from the sloppy beating and much more thorough choking. A little more would have killed me, and I was sure Darla knew it. I lay where the walking corpse dumped me, looking helpless, racking my brain for a workable plan. I suspected that when the time came, I would have to improvise. What I needed right now was time. Time and for Darla to drop dead of natural causes.

"What the hell is all this, John?"

"Oh, her?" He tossed his head in the direction of the back room, where Denise Nudenberger's quiet sobbing made an eerie counterpoint to the rain drumming on the roof of the cabin. "Gotta freshen up old Jack here's batteries. I don't know if you noticed, but our boy's looking a bit worse for wear."

"He looks like I feel."

"All in good time, buddy. All in good time."

"How'd you do it? Jack, I mean."

"Get me a beer, darlin?" He nuzzled his sister and smacked her on the rump. "We got a while to wait anyway, no sense being thirsty."

Darla limped over to a styrofoam cooler sitting on the floor by the doorway. There was none of the dancer's grace in her walk now. I was glad to see I'd marked her some too. Even injured, she seemed feral, wild and dangerous.

I thought this might be my chance, but John flicked his eyes at the corpse beside him and it leaned down and gripped my arms. The unnatural strength in its hands made movement impossible. The smell was eye-watering. I had more time than I wanted to see the way Jack's slack features were distorted by the force of the bullet wound above his left eyebrow. Even a head shot wasn't going to put this creature down.

When Darla returned, the revenant stood back upright and stared off as though at a distant and puzzling object.

"Old Jack's a good hard worker, but none too bright." John cracked the top on his can of Grain Belt. He took a couple long swallows, wiped his chin with the back of a meaty forearm.

"See, what you gotta do, you take yourself the corpse of an evil man, and old Jack here was certainly that. Then you gotta take a virgin sacrifice, and believe me, they're not as easy to find as you might think. You got the right ritual, and the talent to pull it off, that little girl's spirit animates that evil man, and you got yourself one hell of a hard little worker."

He leaned back and chuckled, seemingly at ease. With the feral blonde on one side, dead Jack Rose on the other and a cocked pistol resting on his thigh, he could afford to be.

"Only thing is, all that damage does take its toll. That first little girl's spirit's getting all worn out. Time for her young friend back there." He took another sip of his beer, puffed on his cigar and put it back in the ashtray at his feet.

Outside, lightning forked again, bridging the gap between sky and earth and turning the room into a strobe-lit tableau. The crashing thunder seemed to shake the whole cabin around me. There was a crash from the back of the cabin.

Darla headed back to check it out, moving stiff and sore and listing as though on the deck of a ship in a heavy chop. I wondered if I had hit her harder than I thought.

John flicked a glance at the heavy gold Rolex on his wrist.

"Can you believe it's this dark and just three o'clock? We got plenty of time. Anything else I can help you with?"

"Marcus."

"*That* shitrag. You ought to be grateful I did you that favor."

The blonde clumped came back in to stand behind John, rubbing absently at his shoulders. Her low growl purred in his ear.

"Just a tree branch hitting the window."

John kissed the rash inside her wrist.

"Old Marcus had a bit of talent so Darla here got up next to him, found out he didn't have the discipline or the control to use it, nothing like your sisters. Big surprise, way he was melting his brains out through his nose. Those apparitions and that stupid wind trick were about the best he could do."

John's face split into a demented grin. An icy foul wind curled and howled through the cabin. Unprotected candles guttered and blew out all around the room. The hurricane lamps swaying overhead threw crazed shadows and hellish lights. The corpse staggered on its feet and every cut on my face, hands and body flared like cigarette burns. John's throaty chuckle echoed through the room like the Devil's Own Laughter. Outside, pellets of hail bounced across the plank deck and in through the open front door.

"What? Surprised I got some mojo of my own, or surprised I know about your sisters? Hell, your Grandma Roark's a fucking legend in our world." He took a slug from the can, his throat working in great swallows. "Hell, buddy, you got so much power yourself, you practically glow in the dark. Whatever block you got keeps you from using a damn bit of it, well, it's like you amp up everyone around you. You ever notice that, or did you just think the whole world's overrun with warlocks and psychics and shit?"

He drained his beer, crumpled the can in one fist. They were both starting to relax: it's impossible to stay on guard forever, especially when nothing keeps happening.

"Anyway, not only was old Marcus not half the warlock he thought he was, turned out he was dumb enough to try to blackmail me on top of it. That dumbass threatened to tell you all about our little plan, so..."

He shrugged, as though that was all there was to it.

I licked drying blood from my lips. They were so swollen it was an effort to move them to speak.

"This little plan of yours. Want to tell me about it?"

"You'll see, come the Dead Hour. Stroke of midnight, I promise you'll see what we've got in store for you."

"What's this all about, John? I thought we were friends."

"That's what you were *supposed* to think, asshole. You've had this coming for way too long. Or did you think you were just going to get away with it?"

I never could lie worth a damn. The blank look on my face was honest.

"For fuck's sake. On the eve of your anniversary, don't try to tell me you haven't got a single clue. You *know* what this is all about."

And all at once I did. There was only one thing it could be, one thing it had ever been. I said the words.

"Lisa Torres."

Fifty-Five

John's eyes took on a dangerous glitter. It made him look more like his sisters than ever.

"I don't get it," I said. "You've had plenty of chances the last few years. Hell, any of the times we came out here ice-fishing you could have just poisoned my coffee. Why now?"

"Couple things. One is that tomorrow makes seven years since you killed my baby sister, and seven's a right powerful number. Long time after you lost that body you're walking around in and your soul still belongs to me, you'll keep on be feeling the pain. Feeling it for a long time to come."

He reached for his beer again, shook the last few drops back and forth in the crumpled can.

"Also, it only seemed polite to wait for Darla here to get out on parole. You know how it is with family." One meaty pink paw ran up and down the length of her thigh as he spoke. "You believe she got five years for stabbing our daddy down in Morgan City? Should've got a damn parade."

The blonde gave me a hard grin. Her remaining eye glinted, feral and wild.

"I stabbed him in the neck with a pair of scissors. It was self-defense, but they made me plead manslaughter."

"You did stab him thirty-two times, Dolly Girl."

"Still, I bet if *I* had me some high-price New Orleans lawyer, I'd have been out the next morning too!" The blonde stalked in close to me, her face like Lisa at her worst.

Even injured, the blonde retained that dangerous speed. One booted foot lashed out in a triple-kick. Flowers of pain blossomed and burst in my chest, face and injured hand before I ever saw her move.

I screamed and pitched forward, folding around my hand. The silent corpse of Jack Rose pulled her away.

"Sorry buddy," John said. "My big sister's what you might call a very direct person. Fact, it was her idea hiring this big boy holding onto her right now, didn't even much as tell me."

"So why'd she kill him?" My right hand had swollen to a throbbing purple glove, but hidden in the shadow of my body the fingers still moved when I asked. And now I had my weight under me.

"Afraid that one's on me. Cheaper than paying them, and besides, can you imagine this junkie scumbag here *not* selling us out the next time he got busted? Back when he was still alive, I mean. Now, I don't even think he noticed killing his own brother."

Another hiccuping cry came from the back room, and Darla craned her head back to see through the doorway.

"Looks like your little project's getting antsy," she said.

"I guess. Well Sam, it's been nice, but we've got hours of work ahead of us yet if I'm going to be ready for you by midnight. I'm sure you understand."

He got to his feet like a man heading back out to shovel snow or chop firewood, tucked the pistol back into his waistband and followed Darla. I thought of the news accounts of Joanna Tolaffson's mutilated body.

Halfway to the back room John stopped, turned and headed back over to the styrofoam ice chest for another beer. He paused in front of me, popped the can and pointed at my damaged hand.

"Sure am glad we got a chance to finish my tattoo on Sunday." He took a first sip, smacked his lips. "I was tempted to leave it til today. Old Jack here'll keep you company til we're ready for you."

The revenant swayed closer. Its rotting arms reached out for me. I knew what I had to do.

That was the moment that out in the garage, John's truck exploded.

Fifty-Six

I made my move. The roar of the blast shook the wood frame of the cabin, struck my chest like a physical blow and staggered John on his feet. Dead Jack Rose fell face first at me, and I felt ripe wet flesh and greasy leather skid along the side of my face as I pitched my shoulder down across his shins.

The corpse tumbled over the back of the couch. I came out of the roll sloppy and off balance, but with exactly what I wanted.

Bex's kitchen knife held tight in my left hand.

I spun hard on one heel, slashed across John's thighs just to give him something to think about. The adrenalin fugue came back to me, as it always has. Time froze, shattered, began to crawl forward again.

It was all happening at once. Some cold distant part of my brain treated the room around me like a math problem and nothing more.

John's hand found the butt of his pistol, fingers wrapping tight even as my knife opened a wide red ribbon across his upper arm.

The skin pulled away. The flesh beneath looked like raw steak. His index finger found the trigger guard.

My next cut sliced deep into the outside of his forearm. Flesh parted. Blood flowed.

Tendons severed.

Without the opposition to balance them, the tendons inside John's forearm spasmed tight. His hand locked in a death grip on the gun.

And his finger pulled the trigger.

***

It was a long and floating moment. The sound of the pistol was like the soft roar of the ocean. The smell of cordite stung the air.

The hard-faced blonde appeared in the doorway, a barb wire whip still clutched in one bony fist.

Dead Lisa Torres howled her rage and pain.

John crumpled at the knees, began to fall.

I moved to my left, trying to slip under Jack Rose's swinging arm.

The blonde was moving fast.

The corpse hit me. I almost got under, but the point of my shoulder didn't make it. Even that glancing blow was like a boom dropping. White-hot pain exploded down my side.

The knife dropped and so did I.

The hard-faced blonde's steel-toed boot hummed past my temple. I moved as fast as I could. Another stomped the floor so close to my face I could taste the leather.

And Bex came charging through the front door and blew the top of Darla's head off.

Fifty-Seven

There was no time to think. The dead man made a sound terrifyingly like Lisa in a rage and came for Bex.

Cold and focused, she shifted targets and fired. There wasn't much blood left in Jack Rose's body, but a cone of sticky dark matter flew away from the back of his skull all the same.

He staggered, came again. Bex took a couple steps backward, braced and fired a third round. Much of the side and top of its head vanished in another dark spray. It was hard to believe this was the first time she'd ever fired a gun.

From the floor, I could see the black leather jacket hanging in tatters from Jack's back, already shredded by bullet holes. With most of his head missing and the corpse still coming after her, it wasn't hard to see which way this was headed. So I did the only thing I could.

I snatched the knife from the floor beside me and slashed across backs of the dead thing's legs.

Hayley and Paul weren't the sort to spend a lot of money on quality kitchenware. The knife they used to chop vegetables and carve roasts was a cheap little thing, lightweight metal that barely qualified as steel set in a shoddy plastic handle. It might have cost five dollars at Rainbow Foods, or just ninety-nine cents at a Dollar Store. But one thing about those cheap knives, they were sharp.

I aimed for the soft flesh behind one knee, felt the blade bite deep. The thing took its next step and the blade wrenched out of my hand, hung on cartilage or bone, caught in the joint.

Jack Rose's body might have been animated by some unearthly power, but it still had to obey the laws of physics to move. The moment its weight landed on that leg, the corpse crashed to the ground like a fallen tree.

I remembered what Tabitha said about the power of symbols and the protection of iron. I went for it with the knife, determined to drive the flimsy blade up into the creature's cold still heart.

Its remaining eye didn't even seem to see me, its opaque dead stare fixed on some unguessable distance as it took me by the shoulders and flung me across the room.

The knife left my fingers and clattered off into the distance.

I struck the frame of the overturned couch hard enough to blur my vision. The dead thing crawled after Bex on its hands, its bloodstained mouth wide open, foul teeth small and sharp.

The .38 barked twice more, filling the small cabin with the roar of cannon. Great hunks of meat tore away from the revenant.

Its rotting hands clawed the pine boards seeking Bex's legs. She did her best to back away and reload an unfamiliar firearm at the same time. Fresh cartridges spilled from shaking fingers, twinkling in the lamplight as they rolled away.

Too late, she saw that she was backed into a corner.

That was when I noticed John lying beside me in the spreading pool of his own blood. His eyes focused on the towering form of Jack Rose and blazed with a choking liquid hate. The ghost of his baby sister squatted beside him, eager and excited.

It was cocked and loaded, but there was no hope of prying the nickel-plated pistol out of John's hand. Instead I grabbed his forearm and pulled his index finger a small distance off the trigger.

Jack Rose's fingertips left a trail of putrid slime down the front of Bex's calf. There was nowhere left to go.

John's eyes locked on mine, burning in hate and triumph. He jerked his arm out of my hands. The pistol barked.

Bex clubbed at the revenant with the butt of her gun.

I didn't let the pain stop me. I wrestled his trigger finger back, he wrestled his arm out of the way at the last second. Two more shots and half a dozen headbutts before I finally got control of John's forearm.

Bex screamed in rage and pain.

I let go of John's finger. The spasming tendon jerked off one last shot.

The man's magic blew out the top of his head.

All the oil lamps in the room exploded on their hooks and the crawling corpse fell to rotting pieces at Bex's feet.

Lisa Torres screamed with the howling storm, her last living relative dead at my hands.

Fifty-Eight

Getting away from the burning wreckage of the cabin was savage. Bex drove like a madwoman, and I felt every bump and rattle on those country roads.

I lay in the back of the SUV, Christine Nudenberger beside me, the two of us heaped under as many blankets and towels as Bex was able to salvage from the cabin once the oil lamps set the place ablaze. The girl dipped in and out of consciousness, crying out and raving softly. She had Bex to thank that she was still alive. No way I'd have been able to pry those black iron nails out of the floorboards.

Bex kept reaching back over the seat to me, touching me, reassuring herself that I really had survived.

When the first deluge separated us, she had missed the lights of the cabin windows and wandered right past the buildings in the heavy rain. Doubling back, the first building she came to was the garage.

She then drenched a rag with barbeque lighter fluid, draped the rag half out of John's gas tank and lit the end of the fuse.

When I asked, she just shrugged and said she saw it in a movie once and figured we might need the diversion. She said it with that self-deprecating manner that is part of her national heritage. As though it really wasn't worth talking about. As though anyone in her position would have done the same thing.

One we got onto the two-lane the ride was less painful. The rented SUV was a smooth ride, and that slice of the sky I could see seemed less dark.

Bex was safe. I let my eyes close.

Fifty-Nine

The clock beside my bed said 3:42 when I woke. I couldn't have said if it was AM or PM, or what day it was. Codeine will do that. I felt the rumpled sheets beside me and knew that I was alone.

I found her on my front porch, rocking softly in the porch swing and staring out into the dark. The night air smelled warm and rich, so full of life the recent memory and distant promise of ice and snow were impossible to believe. I came out, moving slowly with all my stitches, sat down beside her.

"I wasn't tired," she said. Her eyes were fixed on some distant, personal horizon.

"When's the last time you slept?"

She crimped her lips together, but I waited her out.

"I keep seeing it, Sam."

"I know. It as the same for me, after Lisa. It does get better, though. You have to trust me on that one."

She turned to me. Her eyes were wide and wet and shadowed with pain.

I held her then, held her tight and stroked her back until her shoulders stopped shaking and the little fists curled on my chest eased.

When she broke away to wipe her cheeks and nose I rose and took her hand. "Come on inside," I said. "There's something I forgot."

***

I left her on the couch, shuffled away in my painful old man walk. I came back with a bottle of red in one hand, two glasses tucked in the blue plaster club that had become my forearm. Bex held her wine cupped between her palms, glanced repeatedly at it and away, as though afraid of what she saw there.

"It was a hot night in June," I began, "I had been tattooing late at a little place called Poppabilly's in New Orleans. A teenage girl came in looking for a love heart tattoo with a blank banner. Her name was Lisa Torres."

Just as my fathers had for me, I told my story for Bex. First Lisa Torres, then her brother John. As I did, I was surprised to feel burdens lift that I didn't know I carried.

Bex was silent a long time after I finished. Then slowly, haltingly, she began to tell her own story.

For the rest of our time together, the sun came back to her life.

Sixty

Thirty days after she arrived, I stood with Bex in Minneapolis International Airport, just short of the point where it was Passengers Only. Metal detectors, body scanners, random searches, video surveillance and the end of her Big OE. We held each other tight. Her tears soaked the front of my chest.

With all the stitches in my face, the airport cops were probably keeping an extra eye on me. I didn't notice, didn't care.

Bex held my right hand in her own, lightly touched the tips of my fingers where they peeked out from the blue plaster cast.

"Does it hurt?" She wiped at her nose and wouldn't look up at my face.

"The hand itches like crazy, but it'll be fine in a couple months."

I raised her chin to meet her eyes with mine.

"*This* hurts like hell," I said.

She started to speak, began to cry again. I felt the knot rise, hot and thick in my throat again and pulled her back close to me.

We held each other as long as we could.

Then she had to go.

Sixty-One

I dragged my way through the rest of the summer. The legal fallout kept my lawyer busy and tore my savings to shreds. My shop was a chaos of workers and tradesmen spending their way through the insurance payout. There were hours of physical therapy for both me and Hamish. We spent a lot of time together.

One September afternoon, we sat outside his house in Dinkytown, sipping Cokes from the icebox and watching the returning students bring the neighborhood back to life. I had a black rubber ball to squeeze with my right hand, part of my therapy. The sun felt good and warm, but the first crisp taste of autumn was already in the air. All too soon, winter would return.

The girl Christine had lived. Her sworn statement that she and Joanna had been abducted by Marcus Winton and transferred to John Watson aka John Torres along with her assertion that she had never seen me before in her life probably kept me out of jail.

"Classes start next week," Hamish said. "Figure they'll have the place ready?"

"We can only hope."

"New kid's looking good."

I had been teaching Pete as much as I could without actually picking up a machine myself.

"He's talented as hell, going to be a name to watch in a couple years."

Hamish paused to watch a young woman pass us on the sidewalk. Her walk spoke of energy and confidence, the effortless beauty of youth. Her hair bounced on her shoulders, and the sunlight seemed to kiss her skin.

"You ever get the feeling we're getting old?" he said.

"Day they took out all those stitches. I knew I definitely wasn't a kid anymore."

He just nodded, and we were silent for a while, each with our own thoughts.

There were other things, things I could have said, but they weren't the sort of things guys say to each other on crisp sunny days. I kept them to myself, squeezed my rubber ball instead.

Sixty-Two

I pulled another length of strapping tape off the roll, laid it along the top seam of the box. Three shorter strips going across to reinforce it. Finally, the last box was sealed. Nothing left but to wait for the UPS man.

There were four of them, all medium sized to make things easier with Customs. When Bex ran out of her best friend's house the night Jack Rose came to kill, she left behind her luggage and clothing, her new e-reader. They were impounded as evidence, sat in a storage locker waiting for her to claim them from New Zealand, at least until my attorney stepped in to bring a little sense to the matter.

I'd picked up a few other things for her as well, thrown them in there. Two, maybe three weeks from now, she'd be able to open them. Too bad long distance relationships never work.

"Hey boss," Pete said, "wanna come look at this?"

I got up heavily out of the reception chair, made my way over to the tattoo station. Sitting in the chair in front of Pete was a young Hispanic man with a nervous and hopeful look on his face and a bloody ink-smeared arm. I leaned in closer.

It was Pete's first portrait tattoo, done on a friend for free, a showcase for his tattoo portfolio. The two children actually looked better than their photographs. Without being told, Pete had found the subtle changes in the lines of their faces to take away that stiff posed quality the pictures had. Embedded in the skin of their father's arm weren't two children holding still for a camera. They were two little kids full of laughter and spontaneous joy.

"What do you think? Not too bad, eh?"

"They're great," I said. And I meant it.

I couldn't tell who was prouder, the children's father or the tattooist. Their smiles lit up the room.

***

An hour later, the UPS guy had dropped off a fresh supply of tattoo ink, piercing needles and jewelry, but the truck doing pick-ups still hadn't arrived. I was trying unsuccessfully to distract myself with a magazine, massaging my right hand between flipping pages.

For the hundredth time that day, I thought about Bex and the way she had seared her presence into my life like a branding iron. I wondered where she was, what she was doing. I wondered if this pain would fade.

On reflex, I looked to my elbow, still expecting dead Lisa Torres to make one of her cruel and cynical remarks. But the skinny little teenager born in East Texas and died in New Orleans didn't come around so often anymore.

I still saw her from time to time, but always at night, usually on the very edge of sleep. She was much quieter now. I wanted to believe that on that terrible night in June, she finally let go of the anger that had defined her through so much of her life and after her death. I wanted to believe that even in death, people could change.

Sometimes, Bex and I talked about it late at night on Skype. She thought that perhaps some element of Lisa's black rage had been fueled by the hatred her surviving family had for me, their lust for revenge. Or that the dead girl was just grateful they were gone.

against her shivering body, her face contorted in hissing argument with the man beside her.

As we passed, they leaned out to crane down the street, looking for the lights of the bus. I saw Hamish watch my face carefully, then relax at whatever he saw there. A warm easy smile played at the corner of his mouth.

I heard a lot of talk about her after that. She was rumoured to be doing something in movies out in LA, a prostitute in New York, dead of an overdose in Chicago. A couple months after she dropped out of the scene, the talk finally petered out. It was almost like she had never existed.

It didn't matter to me. That one night was the last time I ever saw her, but long before that was the last time I cared.

Sixty-Four

"You got everything you need?"

"I'm the one's supposed to be asking *you* that," Hamish said. "The kid's up to scratch, we're going to be fine."

Hamish looked as uncomfortable as I felt. I hated goodbyes. One of the cruelest things about life is that we have to say them so often.

"How about you?" he said. "That jacket doesn't look warm enough. You going to be warm enough in that jacket?"

"New Zealand's in the Southern Hemisphere. It's summer there right now."

Hamish shook his head, laughing. He put one hand on my shoulder, looked at me with big serious eyes.

"You'll be fine," he said.

I hugged my brother then, and we clapped each other on the back. As I passed through the tube of the body scanner, I looked back and saw Hamish standing in the distance. He leaned heavily on his cane, trying to hide the way the cold weather bit into the titanium pins in his leg.

He raised his arm and waved, then swiveled away and passed back into the snow outside. The drifting flakes swallowed him in seconds and he was gone.

I started walking to my gate.

I had a plane to catch.

END

Thank you for reading my story.

If you enjoyed it, follow me on Facebook

or visit my website at

http://SteveMalley.com

I'd love to see you.

A Special Bonus

*Not one but **two** sample chapters from*

another of my thrillers,

CROSSROAD BLUES

ONE

Kane picked his note and held it, long and wailing. The sound echoed off the stone faces of the buildings around him. Right at the moment the song could take no more, Kane fanned the reeds of his Oskar. The airtight cup of his two hands was broken, and the harmonica responded, transforming the single sustained note into a wild tremolo.

He bent that tremolo down into a chord change and picked up the chorus of *Black Cat Blues.* Nobody much played Jack Terrabonne's songs anymore, but that one was perfect for the night: a tale of bad luck and bad women, with plenty of humor and bounce. Early drinkers and late shoppers responded. A small crowd gathered, and Kane was rewarded with the clink and jingle of coins.

Christchurch was good to Kane. His hostel bed was thirty-five a night, and every one of the four days he'd busked had earned him at least a hundred and fifty. Another week, Kane would have enough for a plane ticket.

Cathedral Square was where the best action was. The square was a constant churning mass of office workers, tourists and partiers, and every one of the city's musicians, jugglers, and magicians knew it. It was the only part of the city where buskers needed a permit, and the cops kept up a heavy and visible presence to protect the tourists from drug dealers, junkie thieves and pickpockets.

Kane kept to Cashel Mall. The competition was more relaxed here, and since the street was closed to vehicle traffic, every shopper and worker passing was on foot. Kane played to the crowd. Lunchtime, he played a lot of Delta blues, working the harmonica through flashy bent notes and chord changes. Evenings and nights, the offices and stores were closed, and the people on the street were moving from bar to bar. For them, Kane played roadhouse blues and swamp boogie.

A fiddle joined in on another Terrabonne favorite: *Backdoor Boogie.* Kane looked past his scarred knuckles on the harmonica. The kid was back. Kane dipped his head in greeting, and across the street, the kid's fiddle dipped a little salute in reply. His bow danced over the strings, and a quick little riff echoed in the cold air.

They took turns with the lead. Two junkies watched the performance from a doorway down the block, hollow-eyed and twitching. Four sleek young drunks stopped to applaud at the end of the song and left without dropping any change.

Kane dumped the contents of his hat into a Ziploc bag and dropped both bag and hat into his backpack. The boy was already playing again, some generic bluegrass tune that could have been any of four different songs. Kane waited until the end and dropped a wrinkled orange five.

"Still here, hey Yank?"

Kane shrugged.

"I would've thought you'd be gone by now." The kid was maybe thirteen or fourteen, with thin wrists and a shy smile.

"Aren't you out kind of late?" Kane said.

"Mum's picking me up later."

"I don't like you being out here alone."

"Relax, mate. It's not like you're in Los Angeles or anything. And besides, I've been doing this for over two years now. You've only been out here a few days."

Down the block, the two junkies looked back at Kane, put their heads together and whispered.

"Can I ask you something," the kid said, "What's America really like?"

"Mighty big, that's for sure."

Kane stuck his hands in his pockets. He'd picked the heavy coat up in a thrift shop two days earlier.

"Ever been to L.A.?"

"No."

"I want to go there, when I'm older and do my Big O.E. I'll get a record contract and buy a mansion."

"Keep practicing. You want to play the big stages, you need to be tight."

"You ever play any big stages?"

Kane pushed his backpack with the side of his foot.

"I reckon this suits me."

"You *reckon*?" The boy's voice slipped from New Zealand's clipped consonants and trilling vowels into an imitation American accent.

"You make me sound too much like John Wayne."

"That right, punk?"

"No, that one's Clint Eastwood."

"Whatever. You playing or what?"

Kane smiled. "One more number before I call it a night?"

"Mate, the punters are just getting started."

"They're all yours."

"Can we do Wayfaring Stranger?"

"Again?"

"This time save your harp for the bridge and take the vocals instead."

They played, soft and soulful. The boy's fingers were crisp and accurate on the strings, his face serious, almost grim. It was plain the kid had classical training, but he had a feel for this music too. The boy took his time, tried to capture the eerie beauty of its chord changes.

The two junkies were gone from the darkened doorway.

The song was one of Kane's favorites. It took him back to when he was a little boy, memories of church choirs and afternoons helping his father in the fields. It took Kane back to being a hungry and unwanted teenager, busking on the streets.

Kane closed his eyes and sang. His voice was deep and mournful. Every word was the truth.

I'm just a poor, wayfaring stranger

Traveling through this world alone

TWO

"Why are you *doing* this to me?"

The girl's face was a puffy tear-streaked mask. A foot and a half above the top of her head, the black shape of Harlan Winters blotted out the moonlight.

"Shut up."

Harlan wrenched the rope. The girl cried out as rough braided nylon tore soft flesh.

Harlan Winters loved Mexico, especially Jack's ranch in the Yucatan. The night air smelled of stagnant water, wet leaves and vegetable decay.

Somewhere in the trees nearby, an animal was decomposing. The odor carried to Harlan on a shift in the breeze. He closed his eyes and tilted his head back. His tongue flickered gently behind his teeth as he tasted that faint scent of death.

"*Please* mister," the girl said. "Pleasepleaseplease, you can let me go. I won't tell anyone. *Please...*"

"I'll let you go, just not yet." Harlan showed his teeth. A blade of moonlight fell across his face. It lit his eyes, bright and silvery.

"You still smell too much like soap."

"Couldn't you at least loosen the ropes?" she said. Her voice was wet and choked. "Please? They *hurt*..."

Harlan hauled on the rope. The girl stumbled behind him, crying. She tried falling down and staying there, but Harlan wrapped one big fist in the girl's hair and dragged.

A lightning-struck cottonwood stood in the center of the clearing. Harlan raised his arm until the girl hung with her heels kicking in the air. He pulled her higher, until her arms passed over and circled the tree's blasted trunk.

Once the girl's feet touched solid ground, Harlan walked away. She struggled and thrashed and screamed.

Like it mattered.

Jack Terrabonne's Mexican ranch was over a thousand acres in the middle of nowhere. The nearest neighbors were none of them closer than an hour's drive. The only answer to the girl's screams was the guttural cough of a jaguar, hunting in the dark.

Harlan threw his head back and roared, exultant. Branches thrashed further and further away as the jaguar beat a hasty retreat.

This little piece of land was beautiful. Scrub oak and cottonwood, turtles and fish and birds, wild cats and poisonous snakes. The jungle was dotted with the rocky wet shafts of sinkholes, gateways to vast caverns of black water under the earth.

Harlan loved Jack's Yucatan ranch.

Mexico was perfect. For an American, especially a rich and famous one like Harlan's boss, this place was paradise. Jack's money went a long way here. So did his pull with the local cops.

And backpackers came here from all over the world. They came to Mexico for the beaches, the drugs, the Mayan ruins, a thousand things. Sometimes, they found what was left of Boogie Jack Terrabonne.

A few of those found Harlan Winters.

Harlan and Jack both loved the same women, though maybe for different reasons. Even when he'd been married to that movie star, Jack had never stopped chasing the hitchhiker girls, the drifters and runaways and trashy women just passing through. As long as Harlan had known him, Jack had a thing for anonymous women at the edges of society.

Harlan's thing was for women nobody'd miss.

This one was small and blue-veined, junkie-lean. Her hair was shot through with streaks of purple and blue, and her face and body were full of winking pieces of metal. She'd come to Jack's bed with a bad attitude, staring at Harlan like he was some kind of circus freak, treating him like the hired help.

Now she wept and thrashed, staked out in the middle of a jungle.

Harlan stepped into the tree line. He circled around the back of the jeep, with its still-pinging engine, its smells of motor oil and hot metal. The keys were in his pocket, jingling around with the bullets from the gun.

He felt good under the trees. Small animals scurried and skittered, night birds called and owls hunted in silence. The moon was bright and full, throwing silver light through the wind-rattled leaves.

The girl struggled against her bonds. No way she was able to reach the knot. She scraped all hell out of the soft flesh inside her arms. Harlan walked up behind her. The smell of her fear carried to him on the night breeze.

Harlan flared his nostrils and growled. The girl jumped and whimpered. Her hair was still wet from Jack's endless showers. Sweat streaked her flanks and slicked her limbs. Mosquitoes clustered on her neck and face, at the backs of her knees and in the tender hollows behind her ankles.

She no longer smelled like soap.

Harlan leaned in. His breath curled warm and rank along the girl's cheek. His lips brushed the fine wisps of hair that floated loose, just behind her ear.

"It's time. You can go."

The girl trembled at the touch of Harlan's fingers on her skin. Three pulls and the knot was loose. One more, and the rope fell at the base of the charred and blasted tree trunk.

The girl fell shaking to her knees, rubbing at her bloody wrists. She looked up at Harlan with big wet eyes, shimmering puddles showing him twin reflections of the moon.

"I promise, I swear, Iswear Iswear *Iswear* I won't tell anybody about this. I--"

Harlan lowered his face to hers and roared.

"RUN!"

She ran.

Harlan watched her white legs scissor in the moonlight. He dug his fingers into the hard dark earth and waited for her to reach the trees. His lips curled away from his teeth in a tight savage smile, and the blood thundered in his wrists and throat.

The girl looked back over her shoulder. The great hulk of Harlan Winters sat crouched at the base of the lightning-struck tree, waiting.

She ran gasping for the safety of the trees. In seconds, her legs were flashes in the shadows under the dark leaves.

Harlan gave chase.

ABOUT THE AUTHOR

Steve Malley is a novelist, comics artist, painter and tattooist. When he's not writing he can usually be found at The Ink Spot, his tattoo studio in Christchurch, New Zealand.

www.ingramcontent.com/pod-product-compliance
Lightning Source LLC
Chambersburg PA
CBHW070306260626
47160CB00003B/741